AN IMPRACTICAL NOTION

"You're going to tell Kingston tomorrow that you'll marry him, but dammit, Felicia, you won't be truly happy . . . Oh, hell," he said in disgust.

"Are you proposing to me, Adam?"

"I'm going to be an architect and a builder, not a titled gentleman like Kingston. Believe me, I have no illusions about what's best for you. You should marry Kingston and have all that he has to offer—it's the logical and practical thing for you to do."

Felicia laughed. "Since when have I ever been practical and logical? Propose to me, Adam."

He picked her up and turned in a circle, twirling her off the floor, kissing her as he put her back down. He kissed her again, softly at first, then thoroughly, until she was breathless.

"If you marry me, the whole world will say it's folly . . ."

Miss Fortune's Folly
Dawn Aldridge Poore

ZEBRA BOOKS
KENSINGTON PUBLISHING CORP.

ZEBRA BOOKS

are published by

Kensington Publishing Corp.
475 Park Avenue South
New York, NY 10016

First printing: September, 1992

Printed in the United States of America

Chapter 1

Gresham Fortune stood by the window, not looking outside at the spring flowers, but instead looking back into the room, looking at his niece carefully finishing a drawing. The fingers of his left hand drummed nervously on the windowpane. He became aware of the noise and stopped, putting his hand in his pocket. He rather envied Felicia as she concentrated on her drawing—it was more difficult for him to stand and wait than it would have been for him to work.

Felicia Fortune put one last stroke very carefully on the drawing and leaned back. "There! Uncle Gresham, is that what you wanted?"

He strode over to the easel, took the drawing in his left hand, and looked at every line critically. "Perfect, my dear, perfect." He tried to place the drawing on the easel, but it slipped a little. Felicia grabbed the corner and helped him. He started to say something but checked himself and, instead, sat down near her. "I don't know what I'd do without you, Felicia," he said, not looking at her.

Felicia laughed and patted his knee. "No need to thank me, Uncle Gresham. Knowing I've helped you is enough. I just wish I could do more—and I will someday." She paused a second, noticing how gray, tired, and tense he looked, much older than his four and forty years. "When will the Earl of Creswicke be here?"

Gresham pulled his watch from his pocket and flipped open the ornate lid with his thumb. "About two more hours, I'd say." He put the watch away. "I hope he likes the plans."

"He will," Felicia said firmly. "After all, the two of you were such good friends as children. I'm sure he'll love your work."

"Dash it, Felicia, I don't want to be *obligated* to the man—I want him to like my work because I'm a damned good architect and builder." He caught himself and smiled at her. "I'm sorry, my dear. I'm just not myself today."

"I agree, and for that reason, I'm going to insist you go upstairs and rest for a while. I'll have Ridley come get you in plenty of time."

"I can't rest, Felicia. I'm too nervous." He stood and paced to the window. "I wonder what Charles looks like now," he said, musing. "I knew him when we were children, long before he ever had any dreams of becoming the Earl of Creswick. The both of us were in love with Molly Cary, and she chose him while I was studying architecture in Italy."

"I'm sorry, Uncle Gresham. I didn't know there was a tragedy in your background." Felicia could have bitten her tongue—both of them glanced at Gresham Fortune's empty right sleeve that was carefully tucked into a side pocket of his coat.

"No tragedy," he said carefully. "Charles was always besotted with Molly and I understand he still is. This house is for her as a present when he brings her back from Italy. She likes to paint and embroider, and has used this small house for years for that purpose. Charles wanted to make it into another Petit Trianon and surprise her with it." He walked over and looked at the drawings. "Fortunately I talked him out of another Petit Trianon and he agreed to this. I hope he likes it. I think the remodeling can be done in a matter of months." He paused and there was a faraway look in his eyes. "It will be so good to be doing something again, and if nothing else, Charles has given me a little part of my life back. He's the only one who'll take a chance on a builder and architect with one arm." There was no bitterness in his voice, only sadness, and Felicia could have cried for him. Gresham looked at her and realized the effect he was having on her. He smiled and walked over to her. "Pay no attention, my dear. I ramble like an old man."

There was a discreet knock on the study door and Ridley poked his head inside. He was cadaverously thin, tall, and had only a few hairs carefully combed across the top of his head. He was also completely devoted to Captain Fortune and his family. Ridley had been with Gresham Fortune since he first went into the Army and still carefully addressed him as Captain Fortune. Gresham Fortune was as devoted to Ridley.

Uncle Gresham had enthralled Felicia and her sister Rosemary with stories of the way he had been injured in battle—a cannonball had blown his arm away. The major in his company had saved his life, at great risk to his own. The major had watched out for Captain

Fortune and cared for him until they located Ridley. At that point, Ridley always took up the story, telling how he had braved the horrors of war trying to get the captain to a ship on the coast. Felicia and Rosemary always sat spellbound through this tale and Ridley had become a hero to them. Second to Uncle Gresham's story, they loved to hear Ridley tell them about the way he had nursed Captain Gresham night and day through all sorts of perils until he could deliver his beloved captain back to his family.

Now Ridley looked at his master's face and frowned slightly. He and Felicia exchanged a quick look.

"I'm trying to get Uncle Gresham upstairs to rest," Felicia said.

Ridley nodded his head. "Captain, that's the thing to do. Yer lookin' a trifle peaked."

"Ridley, Felicia, I really don't . . ." He looked at the two of them and gave up. "All right, but I want to be notified the moment Charles gets here."

"Fine," Ridley said promptly, whipping a small tray from behind his back. On it were the captain's laudanum drops and a glass of water. "Time for these, Captain."

"Not today, Ridley. I intend to be completely alert when Charles is here. Perhaps afterwards."

"But yer hurtin'. I can tell."

Gresham shook his head. "No, Ridley." He took the edge from his words with a smile. "Later, I promise." Still muttering, Ridley placed the tray on the table and hustled the captain toward the stairs, clucking like a mother hen all the while.

Felicia sighed and turned back to her drawing. She so hoped the Earl of Creswicke would commission

Uncle Gresham to do the renovations on his house at the Priory. Since Uncle Gresham had returned without his right arm, this was the first time anyone had asked him about architecture or building. When he had first received the letter from the earl, it seemed as if he had a reason to live again.

Felicia and Rosemary were his family, but their parents were alive and well in London, so Uncle Gresham didn't feel particularly necessary as a substitute parent, although the girls tried their best to show him how much he meant to them. "Perhaps I could talk to the earl before Uncle Gresham does," she muttered to herself.

"No, Miss Fortune," Ridley said, coming into the room to pick up the tray and laudanum drops. "The captain's 'ud want to get this one on his own. It's important to him that way." He walked over and looked at the drawing on the easel and the ones on the desk with a critical eye. "That's good, very good. I think the earl will want this for his wife's house. What's the name?"

Felicia couldn't stop a smile. "Which name—the earl's, his wife's or the house to be renovated?"

Ridley looked offended. "The house, of course. I'm not such a flat that I don't know the earl's name. I've met the man, you know. His sweet lady and his little brat of a boy as well."

"I stand corrected, Ridley." Felicia laughed. "The house is called the Abbott's House and I understand Lady Creswicke has used it for years. Tell me, if you've been there, was the main house once a church? Uncle Gresham said it's called the Priory, so I rather fancied it must have been a church."

9

"Not at all." Ridley preened. He simply loved knowing something no one else did. "It was one of those Catholic things with the men in robes running all around. You know what I mean."

"A monastery."

He thought about that for a minute. "That's right. At least that's what Creswicke's boy told me."

Felicia sat down and motioned Ridley to do the same. "Ridley, if the earl commissions Uncle Gresham to redo the Abbott's House, you and I are going to have to take very good care of him." She noticed Ridley's offended expression. "You already do," she amended hastily, "but I mean we're going to have to shield him from distractions like Rosie and perhaps Creswicke's heir. Both you and Uncle Gresham have referred to him as a brat."

"That he was," Ridley said, remembering. "But that was a long time ago, twenty years or more, afore the captain went off to the war. I suppose the boy 'ud be, say, about six or seven and twenty now. Hardly a brat anymore, but from what I heard in London, a real hell-raiser. Beggin' your pardon, Miss Fortune."

"You know you can be honest with me, Ridley," she said. "If Creswicke's heir *is* that way, we have all the more reason to keep him away from Uncle Gresham."

"No need. I heard the boy's in Italy staying with his mama. She's down there trying to recover from some illness."

"Good. Now I suppose all we need to do is—" She was interrupted by a whirlwind banging open the study door. "Felicia, I'm sorry, I'm *really* sorry!" This was followed by a series of long, racking sobs as Rosemary, filthy and wet, stood before Felicia, her left arm

10

cradled carefully in her other arm and hand. She looked up, her blue eyes huge in her dirty, scratched face. "I think I broke it, Felicia. I didn't mean to, honest." A large tear tracked its way down through the mud on her face.

Felicia found her voice. "Of course you didn't. Rosie, what have you done?" She felt along Rosie's left wrist. She was no doctor, but even she could see the wrist was broken. "Ridley, send for Dr. Norris. Come on, Rosie, I need to clean you up as much as I can until Dr. Norris gets here. What happened?"

"It hurts, Felicia," Rosie whimpered, her dark brown hair falling over her face. There were twigs and bits of leaves still stuck into her wet hair.

An old hand at Rosie's dodges, Felicia repeated her question. "And I want to know the truth," she added.

Rosie bit her lip. Clearly she didn't want to tell. Felicia stared hard at her. "I want to know. Now."

"You know how Roger and James are always saying that girls can't do things and they can." Rosemary paused, and Felicia prompted her. "Yes, Rosie, we all know about those two." Rosie was speaking of the neighbor's two boys, two hellions if there ever were hellions in the world. "Tell me everything—I want to hear it all."

Rosie hesitated. "I know you told me never to climb up into the mill because the floor was rotten, but they dared me and I did it." The words came out all in a rush, almost like one word. Rosie looked up at her and attempted a wavering smile through her tears. "You were right, Felicia, the floor was rotten and I fell into the mill pond."

"Good Lord." Felicia fell back into her chair as her

knees gave away. "You could have drowned, Rosie. Thank goodness the boys were there to pull you out."

"That's just it, Felicia—they didn't help," Rosie said. "They ran away as fast as they could and"—she stopped, sniffling as she remembered her scare—"and I thought I was going to drown and my arm hurt something awful."

"Do you mean you had to get out of the mill pond by yourself?" Felicia was horrified. For a moment she itched to get her hands on the hellions.

"No." Rosie's face took on a strange look. It took Felicia a moment to recognize it as adoration. "Felicia, they had a boy with them who was visiting and he pulled me out. He was wonderful."

Felicia looked sharply at Rosemary. She was growing up, she had turned sixteen on her last birthday, and evidently this strange boy had made much of an impression on her. If he was visiting Roger and James, he was probably much of the same stripe— another incorrigible hellion. Perhaps, she thought, it was time for Rosemary to go to London and stay with Mama and Papa for a while. Mama would see to it that Rosie was introduced into society. Poor Aunt Soledad always let Rosie get by with anything. Felicia paused and shook her head—she had to take care of Rosie right here and now. "Whoever he was, I'm glad he was there," she said, looking at her little sister fondly. "I wouldn't want anything bad to happen to you. This is bad enough." She touched the broken arm gingerly. "Dr. Norris will be here shortly, so let's get you cleaned up. Uncle Gresham is expecting company as well, you know." She put her arms around Rosie and they went upstairs.

Rosie's arm began to swell after a short while, and she sat next to Felicia whimpering while they waited for Dr. Norris. Once Felicia thought she heard a carriage come up, but when she inquired if Dr. Norris had arrived, she was told he had not. She and Rosie sat very still, with Felicia patting her shoulder and rubbing her forehead in an ineffectual attempt to make her feel better. It was well after four o'clock before Dr. Norris got there, rushing into the room explaining that he had been to attend Mrs. Waters who had had complications with her first baby. "Not a pretty sight" was the way he described it and Felicia quickly showed him Rosie's arm to forestall any descriptions. Dr. Norris was particularly fond of graphic descriptions.

Ridley came in to help him set Rosie's arm, and Felicia was afraid they were going to pull it apart, but the bone snapped back into place. Then Dr. Norris left instructions for Rosie to remain completely quiet and he would return in a day or two to check on her. Felicia put Rosie to bed and collapsed into a chair, drained. "Ridley," she said, as he came into the room with some chocolate for Rosie, "I don't know if I have the energy to face the Earl of Creswicke when he gets here."

"Not necessary," Ridley said, placing the chocolate by Rosie's bed. Ridley loved to take care of people. "The earl's done come and done his business and gone on."

"What!" Felicia sat bolt upright. "What do you mean?"

Ridley turned to look at her quizically. "I mean he's been here, told the captain that the building was just what he had in mind, they settled on all the particulars, and he left."

"What do you mean, he left?"

Ridley looked at her as if she had lost her wits. "I mean he got in his carriage and headed off. Said he was going back to the Priory and then he was agoin' to It'ly to stay with his wife for a while. He won't be there while all the building is goin' on." Ridley was enjoying this very much. "Said for the captain just to go ahead and take care of it—the captain even asked him about hiring a bunch of Army veterans to do the work—and Creswicke said for him to do what had to be done. Said his son was on his way back here from It'ly and would keep an eye on things. Creswicke's goin' to meet the boy in Paris and go over things so the boy will know."

Felicia sat back in the chair to absorb this information. "Ridley, are you sure you're telling me the truth?"

Ridley drew himself up and stared down at her. He was obviously offended beyond words. "I *always* tell the truth, except when I don't," he said reproachfully.

Felicia thought about this for a moment, then glanced over at Rosie and motioned to Ridley. "Dr. Norris's medicine is working. Let's go downstairs so Rosie can sleep."

"I need to see to . . ." Ridley started, but Felicia interrupted him. "Ridley," she said firmly, "I rather think you need to tell me everything that went on. And I do mean *everything*, Ridley."

"Of course," Ridley said, standing up tall. "Don't I always."

Felicia didn't answer him, instead leading the way down the stairs and into the study. There she sat Ridley in a chair across from her. She sat down and pinned him with her gaze. "Now, Ridley. I want to hear everything. And I mean every word."

Ridley squirmed. "Just what I told you, but if you want every word—well, the earl came in the room and he said 'Gresham, how good to see you,' and the captain said 'Charles,' and they both spent a minute or so not looking at the captain's arm, and then the earl said 'I'm sorry, Gresham' and hugged him and then the captain said 'Thank you, Charles,' and—"

"Ridley, please. Skip all the amenities and just tell me the important things."

"Well, you said *every* word."

Felicia struggled with her temper. "I *know* what I said, Ridley, but you know what I meant. I meant every *important* word, please, and you don't need to tell me who said what and when."

Ridley shrugged. "Well, as I said, they went through all the hellos and such, then they talked a speck about how things had changed since they was young'uns, then the Captain asked about the countess—'How's Molly?' he said—and the earl allowed as how he was really worried about her."

"Ridley." Felicia was gritting her teeth.

"Well, you said you wanted to hear what was important, and this is important. If it wasn't, the earl would be staying around." Ridley looked affronted.

"Fine, Ridley. Go on, please." Felicia smiled at him.

Ridley scratched his balding head. "Well, let me see. Then the earl says as how he's going to It'ly to stay because he's worried about the countess, and that he wants to have everything ready for her when he brings her back in the late summer." Ridley paused and shook his head. "Although why anyone'd want to keep a sick woman in It'ly in the summertime beats me. The

15

captain and me was there once, and I thought I'd either roast or get carried off by bugs."

"Ridley." Felicia was trying to keep calm.

"Sure enough. Well, then the captain showed the earl all of your drawings and they talked awhile about what needed to be done, then the earl said everything looked fine to him, and he was sure his good friend Gresham Fortune could handle everything to his complete satisfaction. They shook hands on that note, and the earl told the captain that he could have a something, I'm not sure what, but I could have swore he said the captain could have a cart. Don't make sense to me, I tell you."

"*Carte blanche,* no doubt," Felicia supplied.

"By Jove, that must be it." Ridley nodded solemnly. "That's it for sure. Then the captain allowed as how hundreds of good men had been turned out of the Army and had no jobs, and would the earl mind if they was hired, and the earl said that was a splendid idea. He allowed again as how his good friend Gresham could take care of anything." There was a pause.

"That's all?"

"That's the important part."

Felicia closed her eyes and took a deep breath. "Ridley, do you know that someday you're going to send me into apoplexy?"

"I never would do that!" Ridley was alarmed. "Are you feeling poorly?"

Felicia had to laugh. "No, but I'm going to be exhausted simply trying to extract information from you. What was all that fustian about the earl's son?"

Ridley shook his head slowly. "Not fustian. It's really true. The earl said his son—the captain called him Viscount Kingston—would be staying around the Priory. The earl said he'd be seeing the boy in Paris and they'd go over everything. He said he'd be sure to tell the boy and also give the captain a letter that said that the captain was to be in charge of everything, and the boy was to assist the captain in any way possible." Ridley paused. "That's what the man said."

Felicia leaned back in her chair. "Famous, Ridley. If Viscount Kingston is such a lover of pleasure, we may expect he'll be in London most of the time and won't be a bother." With a wave of her hand she dismissed all thoughts of the viscount and turned to other subjects. "Ridley, we've got to make sure everything goes smoothly for Uncle Gresham. He told me a while back that this project would reestablish his name in the architectural world and prove that the loss of his arm wasn't the loss of his abilities." Felicia stared hard at Ridley. "It's up to us, Ridley."

Ridley swallowed hard, his Adam's apple bobbing. "You know you can count on me where the captain's concerned," he said gruffly. "In your absence, I'll do everthing you would—except the drawin' of course."

"What do you mean, Ridley? I expect to be right there, helping Uncle Gresham as I always do."

Ridley's Adam's apple bobbed rapidly. "I collect as how the captain told me that he thought you and Miss Rosemary should go stay with your parents in London. The captain thought as how a construction site might not be a place where—might not be considered quite a suitable . . ." Ridley broke off. "Well, Miss Felicia, it just ain't *done* to have a fetching young girl around those places." He stopped and mopped sweat from his neck.

Felicia thought about it for a moment, then looked at Ridley and smiled. "You're quite right, Ridley. Thank you for bringing it to my attention."

"Then you ain't goin' to ring a peal over me?"

She laughed. "Of course not. You're quite correct—a place like that is certainly no place for Rosemary. With her arm as it is, she'll have to go to London until it heals. That will leave me free to assist Uncle Gresham."

"But Miss Felicia . . ." Ridley was mopping his face now.

"No quibbles, Ridley. Uncle Gresham needs me, and I intend to go with him. I know what you're thinking, and I assure you that Aunt Soledad will be more than delighted to accompany me." She smiled broadly at Ridley and rose. "I'll go talk to Aunt Soledad right now." With that, she went out, closing the door behind her.

Ridley, a look of sheer horror on his face, stared after her for a moment, then closed his eyes and mopped his face again. "Lord help us all," he muttered, shaking his head. "What *will* the captain say to this?" In a short while, he stood and wobbled over to the cabinet in the corner. There he inspected the bottles, selected one that was almost full, and poured himself a liberal glassful of the captain's best whiskey. He held the whiskey up to the light to see the sparkle in it, then closed his eyes and downed it in one long gulp. "Women and buildings," he muttered, eyeing the empty glass. "It'll be a catastrophe, mark my words."

Chapter 2

In spite of her uncle's protests, Felicia had her way. Aunt Soledad agreed to chaperone, so there was really no reason for Felicia not to go, and Gresham Fortune knew that his niece's assistance would be sorely needed. The only problem was Aunt Soledad: neither Gresham Fortune nor Ridley could abide the woman. Poor Aunt Soledad had a problem—she was horribly inept at whatever she tried to do. If she did embroidery, it became a tangle of threads bunching up on the cloth; if she tried sewing, sleeves were put in upside down and hems were carefully stitched on the wrong side; if she tried housekeeping, either nothing was ordered or else carts full of unwanted provisions appeared. In self-defense, the family had officially engaged her as Felicia and Rosemary's chaperone and given her absolutely no duties.

So Aunt Soledad stayed with them, supposedly chaperoning Felicia and Rosemary and seeing to their lessons and deportment. Uncle Gresham and Ridley insisted, however, that Miss Soledad Smith spent most of her time being a thorn in everyone's flesh. "And a damned big thorn," Ridley had been heard to mutter more than once. Felicia disregarded this completely since Aunt Soledad was a short, very thin woman. She wasn't at all frail, more on the wiry side, with frizzy gray hair that was constantly escaping the bun at the back of her head. Aunt Soledad constantly tried caps, but they always seemed to be slipping and falling into her eyes.

With all her faults, she had become a permanent part of their family, and Felicia and Rosemary loved her, primarily because they could talk Aunt Soledad into anything. When this happened, and it did frequently, Aunt Soledad protested vigorously, then gave in to them. She always did the same thing at that point—she sat rocking back and forth in her parlor chair muttering to herself. Every time Uncle Gresham came upon Aunt Soledad sitting and moaning "Oh, dear! oh, dear! oh, dear!," he knew either Rosemary or Felicia was into something that shaded propriety.

Aunt Soledad wasn't really anyone's aunt—she was a cousin of Felicia's mother, a woman who had dozens of cousins. No one knew exactly where on the family tree Aunt Soledad belonged, so everyone simply called her Aunt. It was easier that way.

Things were almost in readiness for the move to a house near the Priory. Uncle Gresham had gone up to London to take Rosemary to stay. Rosemary had not accepted this dictum quietly, and it had taken everyone's persuasive powers to get her to do it. The final persuasion was Uncle Gresham's promise to buy her a horse when he finished work on the Priory. At that point, Rosemary agreed to go, but gave Felicia careful instructions to expedite the project at the Priory so the horse could be purchased well before winter.

Uncle Gresham had written to a friend of his, Major Adam Temple, and asked him to hire the work crews needed. He and Major Temple had been very close when they were in the Army, the major being next in command above Uncle Gresham. Although Adam Temple had been well born—his father was a vicar, and his mother from a good family, the family had not been wealthy, and the man had achieved his rank on his own. Uncle Gresham had often told Felicia that the major was one of the bravest, best men he knew. The major had taken a ball in the ankle and had been forced to return to England. Now he was having a difficult time of it. Adam Temple, too, was a builder but his talents had not yet been acknowledged. Now Uncle Gresham wished to give him that opportunity as well as return a great debt—Major Temple was the man who had helped him when his arm had been shot off. Felicia was glad to know the man would be repaid since Uncle Gresham often said that Major Temple had saved his life.

Major Temple had written that all was ready on his end, and Uncle Gresham had gone to meet him in London to make the final decisions on the work crews. Yes, Felicia thought, as she sat down to work in the study, things were falling into place nicely.

Felicia was putting the finishing touches on some of the lists of materials that were still to be ordered. Uncle Gresham had taken the list of things that could only be ordered in London, and had asked Felicia to double-check the lists of things that would be ordered locally from merchants around the Priory. The earl had requested that as much be purchased there as possible in order to help the merchants.

She wiped ink from her fingers and carefully sanded, then stacked the lists. She would make a fair copy either tonight or tomorrow so Uncle Gresham could have one and she could have one. She thought a moment—perhaps if she had time to make another, there should also be one for Adam Temple. From what Uncle Gresham had said, Major Temple would be second in command on this project.

Ridley knocked discreetly. "Miss Fortune," he said, combining her name with an apologetic cough, "I think you need to see this gentleman."

Felicia glanced down at her ink-stained apron that covered an old, worn gown. "I'm certainly not ready to receive anyone, Ridley," she said. "Ask if he'll come back another day."

Ridley turned to speak to the person in the hall, but was quite effectively shunted aside as a tall man, dressed in the latest of expensive London elegance, walked into the study, quite as if he belonged there.

"Well!" Felicia managed to register her displeasure.

He gave her a cold look. "Madam, I realize my breach of manners, but I need to see Captain Gresham Fortune, and I really don't have any time to spare." His tone was icy.

Felicia stood and matched him tone for tone. "I'm sorry, but Captain Fortune is not at home. Had you written for an appointment, I'm sure he would have arranged it."

The man sat down, his silver-headed cane making a thump as he did so. "Damme," he said, "I need to see him now. It's important."

"I'm Captain Fortune's niece," Felicia said frigidly, "and I'll be glad to give him a message when he returns."

The man looked at her with an expression that clearly showed he believed her incapable of passing on even the simplest of messages. He turned to look at Ridley. "Are you Captain Fortune's man?"

Ridley nodded assent, then glanced at Felicia. She was livid at the man's lack of manners and breeding. "And you, sir," she said, her voice dripping acid. "I don't believe we've met."

He put his hat on the table beside the chair and propped his cane against the chair arm. "Viscount Kingston," he said briefly.

Felicia sat down hard, taking in his appearance as she did. He looked just as she had expected, or almost so. She had expected a puffed-up London dandy; Kingston was dressed in the latest, but with a subdued elegance that didn't have the slightest touch of the dandy. She had expected a rather dissipated, bored young swell; Kingston was quite handsome, dark, and tall. There was only a hint of dissipation in the set of his mouth, a whisper of arrogance that she wondered about. There was also something else: he had a reckless air, a touch of danger about him, a touch that went quite well with Ridley's description of him as a "hell-raiser." All in all, Felicia didn't think she would ever wish to be around him, but right now, Uncle Gresham's fate was in the man's hands.

She smiled and adopted a bland air. "What may we do for you, Viscount Kingston? Uncle Gresham has gone to London to see about some materials and isn't expected back for several days."

He made a face. "Lord, what a mess." He took in Felicia's startled glance. "My apologies. I didn't mean you, Miss, er, Fortune, is that correct?" He paused as Felicia nodded, then smiled briefly at her. "The situation is a mess. I had counted on being able to see Captain Fortune, even though I realize my coming was unannounced." He glanced at Ridley. "I believe Captain Fortune is preparing to start work at the Priory in just a few days."

"That is correct," Felicia said as Ridley glanced at her for help. "I assist my uncle, so if you have questions, I may be able to answer them."

"Really?" He gazed at her coolly, as though he couldn't believe a mere girl could contribute at all. "I suppose he does need someone to help him." There was a pause while Felicia said nothing, but the distracted Kingston didn't notice her silence. In a moment, he continued. "I need to speak to Captain Fortune about the work. I'm not going to be able to be there for a few weeks."

Felicia tried not to smile. "How terrible. However, I'm sure Uncle Gresham will be able to do the work satisfactorily."

"Oh, I'm sure he will. My father simply wanted me to be available if there were any decisions to be made or any changes that needed authorization. He and Captain Fortune made detailed arrangements, but there are always unexpected occurrences." He smiled broadly at her and Felicia was amazed. He had a wonderfully warm and charming smile.

She smiled back, thawing a trifle. "I understand, but I'm sure Uncle Gresham will be able to manage. Will you be gone long?"

He spread his hands and Felicia, realizing her rag-manners, rang for tea and cakes. "I don't know how long I'll be. My sister is in Brussels and has commanded that someone come rescue her darling son from the horrors there. Actually," he mused, with a touch of that warm smile, "I'm probably rescuing my sister from that terror she calls her son." He smiled again. "At any rate, I have to go to Brussels, collect my nephew, and make arrangements for my sister to travel to Italy to be with my mother. It may take some time."

Felicia poured him some tea and handed it to him. "I understand completely," she said soothingly. "I'll be glad to pass on any messages to Uncle Gresham."

"No, no messages, other than the fact I've gone, and I'll return as soon as possible. I wish I could meet the man since my father spoke quite highly of him. Actually"—there was that smile again—"Creswicke felt I might not be needed at all since Captain Fortune is an excellent architect and builder and has my father's complete confidence. If there were any question at all that the project couldn't be completed as my father wished, I wouldn't consider leaving, even to answer a summons from my sister."

"Uncle Gresham is eminently qualified," Felicia said. "I'm sure he'll fulfill every confidence the earl has in him."

The Viscount drained his teacup. "Creswicke does not give his confidence lightly," he said, "so I'm quite sure Captain Gresham will do an excellent job. However, there are, as I said, always unexpected occurrences, so I'll return as soon as possible." He rose and gathered his hat and cane. "Thank you for the tea

25

and your time, Miss Fortune, and I'm sorry I can't stay longer, but I need to be on my way." This time she noticed his smile made the corners of his eyes crinkle slightly.

"I completely understand." She caught herself smiling back at him. Still smiling, she stood, thinking to hurry him on his way. "I'll be glad to pass on your message to Uncle Gresham."

"Good." He smiled at her again, and Felicia noted that his eyes seemed to change from a hard brown to a warm amber when he smiled. It was most peculiar. "Again, my apologies for bursting in on you so unexpectedly, but I'm sure you understand."

"I do." Felicia walked with him to the door and saw him on his way, then returned to the study, turned, and closed the door behind her. She leaned against it until she heard Kingston ride away. To Ridley's consternation, she then threw back her head and whooped.

"Really, Miss Fortune," he began, but stopped as Felicia grabbed his hands and danced around.

"Isn't it wonderful, Ridley? Do you know what this means?"

Ridley skidded to a sudden stop and stepped backward, mopping at his face. "Do I know what what means?"

Felicia pirouetted. "He'll be gone, Ridley. That will make our job so much easier—we'll have no puffed-up London viscount to deal with and Uncle Gresham can work in peace. It'll be wonderful, Ridley, we can count on it!"

Ridley, forever the pessimist, sighed. "If you say so, Miss Fortune, though I ain't one to be beggerin' fate."

"Hush, Ridley, whatever can go wrong now?"

There was, as Felicia remembered the viscount's term, an unexpected occurrence when Uncle Gresham returned with Aunt Soledad and a visitor. Rather than simply conferring in London, Major Adam Temple had come back with Uncle Gresham so they could make detailed plans before moving to the Priory. Aunt Soledad was quite upset. "It simply isn't done, I told Gresham, but the man ignored me. How does it look for a gently born female like myself to be traveling in the company of two such gentlemen. Oh, Felicia, I know my age gives me some protection, but I was worried about my reputation. Thank goodness we didn't meet anyone we knew." Aunt Soledad pulled a tangle of wools from her basket and stuffed it under her coverlet, then put her pillow in the clothespress. "You know how gossiping tongues can destroy even the most innocent." Aunt Soledad sat on the edge of her bed. "Oh, dear! Oh, dear!"

Felicia retrieved the pillow from the clothespress and put it back on the bed, then put the wools into a workbasket. "It will be fine, I'm sure, Aunt. In addition to your connection to Uncle Gresham, I'm sure the ages of Uncle Gresham and Major Temple will also be a deterrent to gossip."

Aunt Soledad's eyes widened. "Oh, not at all, Felicia. The major is a young and most handsome man. Didn't you meet him?"

Felicia shook her head. "Remember, I had gone to the village, and by the time Ridley told me he was here, the major had already been put into the green bedchamber. I suppose I'll meet him later."

Aunt Soledad looked hard at Felicia. "You're what

now, my dear, three and twenty? Just so. Felicia, it's really time you thought about settling down and having your own family. I know you've devoted your time to Gresham, but now . . ."

"Enough, Aunt." Felicia looked at Aunt Soledad, her hair floating around her face, and laughed. "Is this your so subtle way of suggesting I should look upon Major Temple as a possible suitor?"

"He isn't married. I asked." There was a pause, while Aunt Soledad pursed her lips and thought. "I told him about you, Felicia. I said you were an exceptional girl."

Felicia sat down and laughed out loud. "Well, really," said Aunt Soledad, obviously miffed.

"Aunt Soledad, how could you? No wonder the major hid in his chamber as soon as he got here. He probably thinks I'm one of those females who throw themselves at every available male in the vicinity." Felicia stopped laughing and wiped tears from her eyes, but she couldn't stop chuckling. "Really, Aunt, how could you?"

Aunt Soledad sat up primly. "Its for your own good, Felicia."

"You sound like Mama. By the way, how were Mama and Papa? I doubt they were too happy to have Rosie since she's complaining every minute, either about her arm or having to stay in London."

"They won't know she's there," Aunt Soledad answered absently, stating the truth. Neither Felicia nor Rosemary knew their parents very well. Papa was in government and didn't like to be bothered with children, while Mama was caught up in the social whirl and didn't like to be bothered with children. Both girls had spent their lives in the country away from their parents, seeing them only occasionally. Mama had wanted Felicia to come to London for a coming-out season, but Felicia had refused. That had been the year Uncle Gresham had come home with his wound, and she had refused to leave him. Besides, she and Rosie agreed that London lived up to the name Dr. Johnson had given it—it was certainly "a great wen." Neither girl cared for it at all, an attitude that baffled their parents.

"Back to the prospect of Major Temple," Aunt Soledad began. "I really think, Felicia, that . . ."

Felicia interrupted her. "No, absolutely not," she said firmly. "I have no interest in getting married, and I'm sure, if Major Temple is the prize catch you say, he already has one or two eligibles dangling after him."

Aunt Soledad shook her head. "No, I asked about that."

Felicia stopped and stared. "You didn't!"

Aunt Soledad nodded happily and pushed her hair out of her eyes and tucked it behind her ears. "Of course, but you may be assured I asked most delicately, Felicia. How else was I to know? Major Temple has absolutely no idea he gave me such information." She smiled sweetly at Felicia.

Felicia took a deep breath and spoke slowly. "Aunt Soledad, I do not intend to marry anyone, not even a prize like Major Temple."

"Nonsense."

Felicia ignored her and went on as if her aunt hadn't spoken. "Besides, Uncle Gresham needs me."

"Oh, dear. Felicia, Gresham would never stand in the way of your happiness, and furthermore, I *promised* your mother that I'd talk to you about coming to London to meet some eligibles. If you'd take my advice and settle on Major Temple, you wouldn't have to go."

"I won't go anyway," Felicia said, a stubborn set to her mouth. "In the meantime, Aunt Soledad, please remember that I have no interest in Major Temple or anyone else, so please don't press me." She gave her aunt a hug to take the sting out of her words. "I know you must be tired. Why don't you rest awhile and I'll have cook put supper off until later."

Felicia left Aunt Soledad dozing off and went to hunt for Uncle Gresham. He was in the study, going over some of the lists she had carefully made. Felicia stopped in the doorway, staring at him. She hadn't noticed his appearance before because she was around him all the time, and perhaps, too, his trip had made him overly tired, but Uncle Gresham looked bad. His skin was a pale, pasty color, and the lines on his face had deepened in an expression of pain. For the first time since she'd known him, Uncle Gresham looked like a tired, sick, old man.

Putting the thought out of her head, Felicia ran to him and hugged him. "Uncle Gresham! We've missed you so."

He smiled at her and made an effort to erase the weariness from his expression. "I've missed being here." He glanced down at the list he was holding. "You've done an excellent job with these lists, Felicia. I'll have Adam make a copy for himself."

"Adam? Oh, you mean Major Temple. Don't worry, Uncle Gresham, I've already made copies for him of everything necessary. Here." She pulled a sheaf of papers from a long box. "These are his."

He smiled broadly at her. "Whatever would I do without you, Felicia? I hope you realize I opposed your moving to the Priory with me only because I thought you might not like it. I'm really quite glad you're going to be there."

"I wouldn't leave you, Uncle Gresham," she said simply. "Would you like some tea?" She reached for the bell.

He shook his head. "No, Ridley has insisted that I rest until supper, so I suppose I shall have to. I just wanted to come in and make sure everything was ready for me to discuss with Adam tonight."

"Yes, it is, and furthermore, you can have a good nap. Aunt Soledad was so tired that I told cook to delay supper for an hour."

Uncle Gresham smiled at her and rose, giving her a quick kiss on her forehead. "Capable, as always, Felicia." He started for the door before Felicia remembered that she had a message to deliver.

"Oh, Uncle Gresham, I almost forgot! While you were gone, Viscount Kingston came by. He was on his way to Brussels."

Uncle Gresham frowned. "Viscount Kingston?" He ran his fingers over his tired eyes. "Viscount Kingston?"

She nodded and looked at him anxiously. "The Earl of Creswicke's son—the one Ridley described so graphically."

"Ridley describes most people graphically, especially people who disturb him, and as I recall, when we visited there years ago, the boy tormented him mercilessly. I can hardly think of that little hellion as a viscount." He chuckled at the thought.

"Well, Uncle Gresham," Felicia answered dryly, "the boy looks to be around six and twenty now, but I really can't say how much he's changed. He stopped by to tell you that he'll be gone for a while. He had to go to Brussels to get his nephew and make arrangements for his sister to go to Italy. He didn't know when he'd be back."

Uncle Gresham frowned. "Am I to wait until he returns to begin or did he say?"

Felicia thought about the conversation. "He didn't come right out and say anything about that, but I assume—no, I *know* you're to begin, since he said Creswicke had every confidence in you and that he, the viscount that is, was only going to be there to advise you on what he called unexpected occurrences." She paused and looked at him anxiously again. "I believe Ridley told me that the earl was going to tell Kingston that you were to be completely in charge."

Uncle Gresham breathed a sigh of relief. "So he did. I have almost forgotten that in all the bother about making sure everything was going just right. If Charles said he would do it, then he did." He smiled at her. "When you mentioned the boy, I was rather worried about having to deal with him. Young men usually don't understand building—they think everything should be done in the space of a few days at most." He rubbed at his eyes again and looked exhausted. "I believe I will surrender to you and Ridley and go rest. Until tonight, my dear," he said, forcing a weary smile as he closed the door behind him.

Felicia frowned and paced the floor, worrying. Uncle Gresham's condition concerned her. She would have to take extra care of him. With a sigh, she sat down to write Rosemary a letter since Rosie had sworn she would decline if she didn't hear from someone every week. She had gotten as far as describing the visit from Kingston when she heard someone at the door. She looked up sharply as a man walked into the study.

She caught her breath. At first glance, he didn't seem that handsome, but there was something about his bearing that suggested authority. On second glance, she was struck by his face and expression. He reminded her of a statue of a Greek god she had once seen, proud without being arrogant, handsome without being pretty. Or, she thought to herself with a smile, were Greek gods all blond? This one had brown hair, not a nondescript brown, but a rich, glossy brown that was cut fairly short. His eyes were blue, not a commonplace blue, but a dark blue. Aegean blue? she wondered.

He smiled briefly at her. "I'm sorry to interrupt," he said, "but I didn't realize anyone was in here. I was looking for Captain Fortune." He walked into the study, and from long habit with Uncle Gresham's infirmity, Felicia forced herself to concentrate on the man's face rather than on his very noticeable injury. The man walked with a very pronounced limp that must have been terrible for him to live with, she thought inadvertently. She could see it was painful for him, and must be that way most of the time. As he came closer, she could see the lines of fatigue and pain around his mouth, almost like those she had seen on Uncle Gresham's face.

"Captain Fortune is resting after his trip," she said, coming around from behind the desk. "I'm his niece. Could I help you?"

"Miss Felicia Fortune? I thought as much," he said

with a smile. "Your uncle has been singing your praises." He glanced at the chair behind him. "Do you mind if I sit down, Miss Fortune?" He sat and very carefully stretched out his injured leg. "There, much better." He smiled again. "I'm Adam Temple."

It hadn't been necessary to tell her, she had known, but she smiled and sat down across from him. "I'm delighted to meet you, Major Temple. Would you like some tea? Since Aunt Soledad and Uncle Gresham were so tired, I've asked cook to put off supper."

"Tea would be nice, thank you." He waited until she rang for tea and then continued. "Your uncle has told me that you know all the details of the project at the Priory. As you know, I'll be partially in charge of the project—the work crews are my responsibility—and I wanted to get a better idea of the materials and so on so I could plan a work schedule. May I see the lists?"

Felicia handed him the wooden box. "I've made copies for you of every list. I thought that way you, Uncle Gresham, and myself could keep track of things. If you will, check things off when you get them, so we can follow expenses."

He looked at her admiringly. "You're certainly organized, Miss Fortune. Your uncle told me that you'd take the project in hand, but I didn't believe him until now." He smiled and riffled through the papers. "Thank you for doing this. It will certainly make my work easier."

Felicia, to her surprise, found herself blushing and tongue-tied. She was saved from having to comment by the arrival of the tea tray. As he looked through her copies, she took the opportunity to look at him from under her lashes as she poured him some tea. He didn't

34

look at all as she had imagined. She had expected him to be older, somewhere around Uncle Gresham's age, and to be very tall and thin, something of a cross between Uncle Gresham and Ridley. In fact, Adam Temple looked to be about eight or nine and twenty, and wasn't as tall as she had thought he would be, although he was taller than most. He was dressed well, although not at all extravagantly. His right boot had a metal brace built into it, and the right leg seemed to be shorter than the other and slightly twisted. To her mortification, he glanced up from the papers and caught her looking at his leg.

"I took a ball through the ankle shortly after Captain Fortune received his accident. It's never really healed well." His voice was carefully controlled.

"I'm sorry. I didn't mean to notice it."

To her surprise, he laughed aloud. "It's rather like Gresham's arm—it's damned difficult to ignore something that pronounced. Don't apologize, Miss Fortune, I'm quite accustomed to questions."

Felicia felt her face flame. "Major Temple, I assure you that I don't plan to ask questions. I've spent enough time answering busybodies who asked about Uncle Gresham."

His eyebrows, and very finely shaped ones they were, she noted, raised slightly. "Then I apologize, Miss Fortune. I've simply found that the best way to treat my, ah, infirmity, is to mention it first and then forget about it." There was a pause. "Of course, as you've probably noticed with Captain Fortune, there are times when it can't be forgotten," he said softly, rubbing his knee. "I'm afraid I tend to be more than irascible during rainy weather."

35

"I'll remember that and, on those days, arrange to be elsewhere," she said with a laugh. "More tea?"

The door opened and Aunt Soledad came in, "Felicia, I simply couldn't rest . . ." she began, then caught sight of Major Temple. She glanced from one to the other and her eyes widened. *"Oh, dear!"*

Chapter 3

Major Temple stayed only two days. Felicia wondered if he had possibly shortened his visit somewhat to avoid Aunt Soledad. Despite her continually mentioning to Felicia that she needed to marry and here was her golden opportunity, Aunt Soledad had decided that there existed a great possibility for scandal every time the Major and Felicia said more than good morning, and refused to leave Felicia's side. As a result, Felicia was forced to leave the major and Uncle Gresham to talk alone. It was simply too much trouble to try to talk around Aunt Soledad's comments about the weather and to keep picking up her embroidery. As soon as the major left to return to London, Felicia made Uncle Gresham have a long talk with Aunt Soledad—it was either give her an ultimatum or leave her at home since Felicia wouldn't be able to work at all at the Priory if Aunt Soledad continued her chaperonage. Afterward, Aunt Soledad came to Felicia's room as she was packing.

"I was merely trying to protect you, Felicia. After all,

every girl must have a spotless reputation, and it takes only the merest breath of scandal to ruin someone. It's for your own good, you know." She sat and looked so despondent that Felicia was overcome with guilt.

"I understand, Aunt Soledad." Felicia hugged her. "It's just that I have no designs whatever on Major Temple or anyone else. However, since Major Temple will be in and out discussing the plans and materials of the building once we're at the building site, I need to be free to talk to him."

"This simply isn't proper. You shouldn't be doing these things for Gresham. No good will come of it, Felicia. I can see it right now." She was trying to wear caps again and this one fell over one ear. She shoved it back, the edge skirting the top of her head.

"Nonsense. In the first place, no one's going to know anything about it, and in the second place, I'm really not that interested in what the gossips say." Felicia picked up two gowns. "Should I take these, Aunt Soledad, or do you think the yellow is too bright?"

"Don't try to fadge me, Felicia, I know your tricks. You're trying to change the subject. Well, I want you to know that I promised Gresham that I wouldn't be in the way at the Priory, and I wouldn't try to restrain you." She stood and her cap fell down over her right eye as her hair floated over her left ear. "I promised, but I don't have to like it."

"Aunt Soledad," Felicia said, coming over to her aunt, straightening her cap, and tucking in her hair, "have you ever known me to do anything improper?"

"No." There was a pause while Aunt Soledad glared at her. "But there's always a first time and that Major Temple has a way with the ladies. Just look at how

38

pleasant he's been to me."

Felicia tried to suppress a laugh with a cough, and wound up getting strangled.

"I know you agree with me, Felicia," Aunt Soledad continued, pounding her on the back, "but you're like Gresham—simply too stubborn to admit it. Well, I won't say anything, Felicia, but let me tell you I can feel it in my bones, and you know my bones are never wrong—no good is going to come of this!" With that she marched away dramatically, her cap falling again, onto her nose this time, covering both her eyes. She walked right into the door. "Oh, dear!"

Felicia put her arm around Aunt Soledad's shoulders. "Here." She removed the cap and put it on the bed. "I promise I won't do anything I shouldn't, Aunt. Now, come help me pack. You always know what I should wear." Surprisingly, that was true. Aunt Soledad had an unerring eye for color, and was always able to select things that went with Felicia's vivid coloring—coloring that was so unfashionable in London, but had been inherited from a Spanish grandmother who had been an acclaimed beauty in two countries. That grandmother had been the original Felicia—Felicia Ines Soledad Rodriguez—a dark-haired, brown-eyed beauty who had captured the heart of Felicia's grandfather when he was an envoy to Spain. From the portrait in the hall, Felicia looked very much like her. Rosemary, on the other hand, looked very English, like all the Fortunes. She was pale, freckled, with brown hair that was very much like Aunt Soledad's—it frizzed and floated all around her head. No one ever thought the two were sisters.

At last, all the packing was done, all the trunks had

been sent ahead, and all was in readiness. Even Aunt Soledad's dire predictions weren't able to dampen Felicia's sense of adventure as they departed for a house that Major Temple had engaged for them. He had written that the house was perfect—small enough for Felicia, Aunt Soledad, Uncle Gresham, Ridley, and a bare-bones staff. It was also almost on the grounds of the Priory, and the landlord insisted that it had once been part of the monastery, although, Captain Temple wrote, he doubted that was true since the house appeared to be much newer. Also, the house was quite near his lodgings, and was well furnished and elegant. It had, he wrote, been christened with the strange name of Marston's Misericorde, although the neighborhood had shortened that to simply "the Misery" and everyone called it by that name.

"Isn't this exciting, Aunt Soledad. To think we'll be living in a house that's known as 'the Misery.' Can you imagine that?" Felicia asked, sitting in the swaying carriage as they traveled on their way. She had pulled the letter from her reticule and was reading it again for perhaps the twentieth time.

"There has to be a story behind that name. Probably a great tragedy." Aunt Soledad pursed her lips and looked dismally out the carriage windows at the passing scenery and the damp, gray day. Aunt Soledad was sitting squarely in the middle of the seat, bolt upright, hanging on to the straps on either side. "Misery. It's fitting, Felicia, and I still tell you to mark my words: no good is going to come of this."

Felicia laughed and put the letter away. "Don't be in the dismals, Aunt Soledad. Major Temple said the house was associated with the monastery in some way.

A misericorde is the place where the monks gathered to eat and rejoice after fasting. A refectory, I believe. Perhaps the owner or builder wanted to imply that this house was a place for feasting and rejoicing."

"Misery," Aunt Soledad said flatly. "I'm telling you, Felicia, I feel it in my bones."

Other than Aunt Soledad's dire predictions, the move was easy as moves go. Aunt Soledad and Felicia had been in charge of the packing and had, to their surprise, remembered to take everything necessary. They were delighted with the house Major Temple had taken for them—it was small but delightfully proportioned, three stories tall, and made of mellow brick. Even better, it was in short walking distance of the Priory and the Abbot's House.

Major Temple was at the Misery almost every evening for the first few days. He, Uncle Gresham, and Felicia went over list after list, drawing after drawing, schedule after schedule. Felicia hadn't realized how much paperwork and planning went into building. Major Temple and Uncle Gresham were exactly alike in two respects—they both had a passion for building and everything had to be absolutely perfect.

They had been there for a week before Felicia felt she had enough extra time to explore the surroundings. She had dressed in her walking dress and walking shoes and was just putting some papers on Uncle Gresham's table when Major Temple walked in.

He glanced appreciatively at her striped dress. He was dressed in his usual working garb: black boots, a clean shirt that was rapidly getting dusty, a hastily tied cravat, a blue coat, and buff breeches. The Major, Felicia had noticed, paid little attention to his appearance other than to make sure he was spotlessly clean at the beginning of every day and that everything was mended.

"Do you need something?" she asked with an answering smile. "I thought I'd take time to explore the country for an hour or so. I haven't been outdoors since we got here."

"Part of that is my fault," he said, handing her some tradesmen's bills. "I've been working so hard trying to take the burden off Captain Fortune that I'm afraid I've shifted some things to you that you shouldn't be doing."

"That, Major Temple," she said with a laugh, "is exactly what I want you to do." She glanced at the bills. "Is this all you need today?" She looked up to see him studying her and felt a blush creep up her cheeks. "Do you have time for a cup of tea?"

He shook his head. "No, I don't care for any tea, but I could spare the time to tramp around the country with you for an hour or so and show you some points of interest if you wish. I don't mean to invite myself, and if you'd rather go alone . . ." He let his words trail off.

"I'm delighted you invited yourself, Major Temple. I would have asked you, but I didn't realize you had any spare time."

He took a deep breath and Felicia was surprised to see the fatigue around his eyes. The man was tired. "I don't really," he said. "Captain Fortune is supervising right now, so I probably should go back."

Felicia came around the table and put her hand on his arm. "Absolutely not, Major. Uncle Gresham, if I know him at all, is having the time of his life ordering everyone around. Why don't you show me around the grounds of the Priory and the Abbot's House, then we'll come back here for luncheon."

"I really don't know . . ." He paused.

"I insist. Walking always makes me ravenous, and I hate to eat alone. Although," she added. "I never have the opportunity because Aunt Soledad is always at my elbow, swearing the house is going to fall in, ghosts are going to materialize, or the end of the world is at hand."

He laughed, a full, rich laugh that lit up his face. "You've persuaded me, Miss Fortune. A walk, then luncheon it is." He glanced down at his leg encased in his special boot with the metal brace. "There's one thing . . ."

"I'm in no hurry at all, Major. Shall we go?"

They went slowly down the path that led to the Priory while Felicia chatted inconsequentially about the spring flowers. In truth, the country around the Priory was beautiful. Felicia almost envied Viscount Kingston his estate, but then, he probably never looked at the scenery.

At the top of a small hill, Major Temple stopped. "This is off the beaten path, but I think it well worth your while if you wish to view the Priory from a vantage point I've found." He paused awkwardly, then said gruffly, "I certainly wouldn't do anything to offend your aunt."

Felicia laughed aloud. "Major Temple, any male who happens to be breathing is an offense to Aunt Soledad. I assure you that she'll never know we haven't been in full sight of an entire company of nuns." She looked around. "Here? I can't see very much."

"No, this way." Major Temple led her to a clearing to

the right of the path, a place on the top of a knoll where she could see all the grounds at one glance. The sight almost took her breath away. The Priory was nestled into a little cleared hollow and was surrounded by cleared lands that faded into woodlands on the higher hills. "It's beautiful," she said, looking at the buildings.

Adam Temple looked over the terrain. "Yes, from a builder's point of view, the site is perfect, and the buildings seem to fit right in. I'm glad Captain Fortune talked Creswicke into keeping the spirit of the Priory in the remodeling of the Abbott's House. You knew he wanted a replica of the Petit Trianon, didn't you?"

"That wouldn't have suited this place at all, would it?"

Adam shook his head. "No, but what Captain Fortune plans will shine like a jewel in this setting."

Felicia glanced at him, surprised. She hadn't realized the Major had such an artistic streak. "What's that?" She changed the subject, pointing to a crumbling tower.

"That's part of the original monastery. Most of it was leveled, and then the house built over the foundation. They left that part, but it's not used for anything except to give a little gothic atmosphere to the place."

Felicia laughed. "Aunt Soledad would feel right at home."

Major Temple laughed with her then pointed to a small place to the right of the main house. "There's the Abbott's House, of course, and that house further back, just at the edge of the woods, is the Dower House. The stables are all over this way." He pointed to the left. "Over here, you can see the kitchen and herb gardens, dovecotes, chicken houses, and so on—all the things you need to run a huge house and estate."

"Could we go down from here to the Abbott's House?" Felicia looked doubtfully at the steepness of the knoll. "I'd like to walk on down and surprise Uncle Gresham if we can. He's been talking and talking about the Abbott's House and the remodeling, but I haven't really seen it myself."

"Of course. I think he'd be delighted for you to visit." He gave her his hand and then Felicia could have flogged herself for making him go down the slope. He didn't say anything, but she could see from the expression on his face that his leg was hurting him a great deal.

"Major Temple," she began.

He smiled at her, although the smile didn't reach through the pain in his eyes. "Adam, if you don't mind. I've been meaning to mention it. After all, we'll be working fairly closely for several weeks, and I think Major Temple is too formal."

"All right, but only if you feel free to call me Felicia."

He chuckled. "I'll do that, but do you think you could have a word with your Aunt Soledad about it? She'll be horrified."

"I see you've come to know her." Felicia started to laugh, but then caught her breath and watched his expression as they skidded down a steep spot. They were at the bottom of one hill now, but there was another, smaller hill they still had to descend. "Adam, do you mind if I rest a moment?" In truth, she could have walked another hour, but he needed to stop and stretch his leg. She knew he wasn't the kind of man who would admit that he had to stop. "I haven't done much walking lately, and I do need a moment to rest."

"Over here in the shade," he said, leading her to a little hillock that was in deep shade. They sat down on the side of it and Felicia noticed a door just barely visible. It looked as if it had once been covered with sod. "Major—Adam, what is that? Are we sitting on a cellar or something?"

To her dismay, he got up to explore. After a moment, her curiosity got the better of her, and she went after him. Adam pulled what remained of the sod away and then checked the heavy, wooden door. It wasn't locked and he opened it partially, then looked inside, bending over to step into the darkness. "You can't come in," he said in a muffled voice. "There's only a tunnel running back this way." He was gone for several minutes as Felicia peered in after him. She could see nothing except darkness. Once she saw a flare of light as he struck a flint, but that lasted only a moment.

Shortly he wiggled out, hunched over in the small doorway, and shut the door back, replacing the sod across the bottom. His trip through the low tunnel had left dirt on his clothes and he brushed in-effectually at his coat and breeches. He had dirt on his hair and Felicia had to resist shaking it off.

"I think," he said with a smile as he sat back down and extended his leg, "we've stumbled onto the ice house. I struck a flint, but I could see for only an instant. I couldn't see the ice, but it was cold enough in there and there was sawdust mounded over everything. It's usually used for packing and insulation. There's a deep, good-sized pit that's been dug in there. There's also a block and tackle hanging from a beam, so that would be how they'd get the blocks of ice in and out."

Felicia made a face. "An ice house. How prosaic. I just knew we'd stumbled on a mass grave of deviates, heretics, or something of the sort so I could tell Aunt Soledad a horror story." She laughed. "Is there much ice in there? We had a cold winter."

"It looks about two-thirds full—what I could see of it anyway." He glanced down toward the Abbott's House. "Are you ready to walk down and see how the work's progressing? If we're fortunate, we might talk Captain Fortune into stopping long enough to eat with us. He's working much too hard."

Felicia didn't need any more prodding and got up to walk beside him. "I know Uncle Gresham's working too hard. I've tried to tell him to pace himself, but he seems to think everything needed to be completed yesterday."

Adam glanced at her. "I know he needs to slow down, but I understand his feelings. It's as though he—and I—have to do this job perfectly. Both of us were architects before we went to war, and now, whether because of our injuries or whatever, it's as though we have to . . ." He paused, searching for the right word. "We have to *validate* ourselves by doing a perfect job." He turned and smiled at her. "Please excuse me. I don't wish to appear as though the war made a difference. I was glad to go."

"It made a difference, though, Adam. There's no denying that."

He glanced down at the brace on his boot. He was tired now and his limp was pronounced. "That it did."

Felicia could have bitten her tongue. "I didn't mean in that way. Both you and Uncle Gresham have come

47

home physically different, but I meant the war changed you mentally." It was her turn to stop and try to find the words. "Because of what he saw in the war, I know that Uncle Gresham seems to be more conscious of how short time really is. Maybe both of you push yourselves too hard because of what you went through." That wasn't what she had really wanted to say and she knew it, but she didn't know how else to express it. Adam, however, seemed to know what she meant. "I think you're right," he said as they caught sight of Gresham Fortune climbing a ladder, teetering dangerously. "However . . ."

"Adam, he's going to fall!" Felicia grabbed Adam's arm, her eyes wide with alarm. He put his hand over hers. "He's fine—it looks worse than it is. Covington's holding the ladder for him." Felicia let her breath out in a long sigh as she looked where Adam was pointing and did indeed see a burly man holding on to the ladder.

Felicia was amazed at the amount of work that had been done in such a short time. She had gotten only the barest glimpse of the Abbott's House from the carriage window as they had driven past on their arrival, but now the facade had been removed, the roof removed, and parts of the inside gutted. Adam noted her look. "Taking it all down was the easy part," he said with a laugh. "The hard part is putting it all back together."

They got to the house at the same time that Captain Fortune descended the ladder. He smiled at them, but Felicia was astounded to note that, in the bright daylight, he looked worse than usual. He was pale, almost white, from exertion, and was breathing heavily. He was a sick man, anyone could see that. Still, he smiled broadly at them.

"Don't tell me you've come to take all the fun away," he said to Adam. "I haven't enjoyed anything so much in years."

Adam Temple shook his head. "Felicia wanted to see how things were going. It's one thing to see it on paper, but another entirely to see the actual building." He glanced over the building, not noticing Gresham Fortune's lifted eyebrows when he used Felicia's first name so casually. "Everything looks good, doesn't it?" Adam said, satisfaction in his voice. "I knew these men would do an excellent job."

"And they have." Gresham Fortune led the way to a pile of cut rocks and sat down, motioning for them to sit beside him. "I have news of a sort: I got a letter from Viscount Kingston telling me he'll be here in a few days. Evidently his trip to Brussels didn't take him as long as he thought it would." He stopped and looked around with a slight frown. "I don't think he can complain, unless he doesn't know anything about building."

"I'd say that's a good possibility," Adam said dryly. "Perhaps we can get the roof back on the house before he gets here. It'll look better then."

"Exactly what I thought." Uncle Gresham began outlining the work for the next two weeks as Adam listened intently, putting in his own suggestions as they occurred to him. In the meantime, Felicia let her mind wander. Her attention was caught by the men working—they worked almost as if they were a theater troupe that had rehearsed working together. Each man did his part and it all came together. She mentioned this to Adam and Uncle Gresham when the two of them had finished scribbling notes on bits of wood.

Adam laughed at her observation, a laugh with a

touch of pride in it. "That's the way they're supposed to work. Most of these men were with Captain Fortune or me in the Army and didn't have any way to make a living when they were mustered out. When Captain Fortune and I told them what we wanted, it was like our regiments all over again. Every single one of them fell in as if he were born to it."

"Good men," Uncle Gresham added. "And every one of them loyal through and through. I think they'd do anything either one of us asked of them."

"Right now, I'm going to ask the two of you to come back with me and have luncheon," Felicia said. "Now, Uncle Gresham, I want no arguments—Major Temple has already agreed."

Uncle Gresham smiled at her, and Felicia noted again how tired he looked. "I can't, Felicia, my dear. I'd love to, and I promise I will as soon as possible, but I planned to meet with some of the workmen today at the inn. I'll eat there."

There was no persuading him, so Major Temple and Felicia started their walk back toward the Misery. "I'm worried about Uncle Gresham," she said, biting her lower lip as she thought about the way her uncle looked. "Ridley and I both feel he's pushing himself too hard."

Adam Temple glanced at her. "I suppose I should say he isn't, but I agree with you. I've tried to talk to him, I even tried to get Ridley to call in the captain's physician, but the captain insists he's fine. As I told you before, I understand why he's pushing himself, but I wish he wouldn't."

"I understand, or I try to, at any rate," she said, trying to control her anger. "Couldn't you take more of

50

the supervision, or let me do more, or even hire someone else to come in and do something?" Felicia looked around for something to vent her anger on and saw nothing except the major. "It's just a house, and everything seems to be going so well. I don't see why Uncle Gresham has to be there every second."

They were at the front gate of the Misery. Adam Temple paused a moment and leaned against the gatepost. His leg must be bothering him again, Felicia thought, but before she could say anything, he took her arm. "Let's sit here for a moment, shall we?" He led her to a bench under a large tree that shaded the front of the house and sat down, stretching his leg out in front of him. As he spoke, Felicia noted that he rubbed his knee. "Let's finish the conversation we began before we got to the Abbott's House," he said with a smile.

"I understand all of that, Adam," Felicia said miserably. "It's just that I'm afraid for Uncle Gresham."

"I know you are," he answered, looking at her, his smile reaching his eyes. "We all are, but I'm sure as well that your uncle has emphasized to you that this building can reestablish his career as an architect and builder. For some men, there are things more important than merely existing, and perhaps you haven't really thought through what this means to Captain Fortune. I know because I'm much the same way." He paused and looked at her. "I'm not saying this to garner sympathy, but I want you to know how it feels."

"Are you implying I've been inconsiderate of Uncle Gresham?"

"Heavens, no!" he said hastily. "If anything, probably just the opposite. I imagine you've smothered him with consideration. Please, Felicia, just hear me out."

Felicia started to say something else, then closed her mouth. "All right."

He nodded at her. "Before we were in the Army, we had futures, things that we planned to do and we all in some fashion had our lives planned out. Gresham and I were, of course, planning to be architects, turning every village into a Palladian showplace." He tried to keep a tinge of bitterness out of his voice, but wasn't successful. "Then we went to war for God and country because we thought it was the right thing to do, and I suppose it was. In the Army, we still had a goal, we had men we were responsible for, and we had something to reach for. Then, for Gresham and for me, the war ended abruptly when we were wounded; for the men in our commands, it ended when they came home and had no jobs, broken families, and no money." He looked at her and his eyes were searching hers. "This is an opportunity for us—for all of us. The men we've hired are men who haven't had any jobs, or if they had jobs, it was the worst sort of hard, brutish work. Now, because of Captain Fortune, we've all got a possibility, because if we pull this off in the way it should be, there'll be more buildings, more work for us and these men. Also, and certainly not the least consideration, Gresham Fortune's name will be recognized as one of the great architects of our time." He broke his somber mood with a smile and touched her hand. "That's the end of my sermon. I hope I've explained why this is so crucial to your uncle."

She smiled back. "You have, although I hope you realize that having Uncle Gresham is more important to me than anything. He's been more of a parent to Rosie and me than my parents have."

"I understand that, but you know that being the kind of man he is, Captain Fortune is going to want to do as much as he can. We can only make things as easy as possible for him. I'll try to be a buffer between him and the viscount. Maybe that will help. On this end"—he paused and glanced at her with a smile—"perhaps you and Ridley can tie him down. That's the only thing that will stop him."

"I think you're right," she said with a laugh as they stood and started up the walk. "I also think I see Aunt Soledad peering out the windows. Perhaps you should walk on the other side of the yard. She's going to think this highly improper."

They glanced up to see the curtains whisked quickly back into place, and in a moment, the front door was opened by Aunt Soledad. She looked at the two of them, walking along, at least three feet apart, but *unchaperoned*. "Oh, dear. *Oh, dear!*"

Chapter 4

Since Viscount Kingston was expected the next week, Uncle Gresham wanted to have the roof replaced and as much done to the exterior of the house as possible. To this end, he pushed himself and the men to the limit. No matter what Adam or Felicia or Ridley said to him, he shrugged it off, telling them he would rest as soon as everything was ready for the viscount. On Friday evening, he ate a hasty meal of soup, and welcomed Adam Temple into the study so they could discuss some small changes in the plans. Uncle Gresham reached for some papers that Felicia was handing him. Suddenly he made a choking sound, beat his chest with his fist as though to dislodge something, and turned first, chalky white, then a bluish color. Right before Felicia and Adam's horrified eyes, Uncle Gresham collapsed.

Felicia screamed for Ridley, who came running with Uncle Gresham's medicine in his hand. They pried open the captain's blue lips and poured it down him, but it did no good this time. Adam suggested Ridley go for the nearest physician, but Ridley refused to leave his master. He and Adam carried the captain up to his chambers and put him to bed. Felicia and Ridley hovered over the still form while Adam went for old Dr. Quigley. He found the doctor in his favorite place, sitting at a table at the Monk's Inn. Dr. Quigley had been sitting there drinking for longer than he should have been, and was thoroughly soused. Adam dragged him to the back and shoved his head under the pump. That didn't help a great deal, but at least the doctor was able to speak coherently by then. Adam realized the man wouldn't be able to hurry to the Misery on foot, so, remembering the captain's blue color and the need for haste, he rented a carriage from the landlord and took Quigley to the Misery. Quigley entertained them with a selection of tavern songs as Adam drove.

At the house, Quigley looked to his patient, sang a sea ditty as he felt the captain's chest, and winked at Aunt Soledad.

"I think we need to send for another physician," Adam told Felicia, a worried frown on his face. "I know Gresham had been to see Quigley and told me that Quigley was a good doctor when he wasn't in his cups, but right now the captain needs someone else."

"Someone sober, you mean? I quite agree. Uncle Gresham told me the same, but this man is completely incompetent."

Dr. Quigley finished his examination, winked again at Aunt Soledad, then came over to Ridley, Felicia, and Adam. "There isn't anything you can do except make him comfortable," he said bluntly, his words clear as a bell, although he reeked of whiskey. "Ridley, increase his laudanum drops."

"Really, Dr. Quigley," Felicia began, but Ridley interrupted her. "Do you think that's all we can do?" Ridley asked, very pale.

Quigley nodded. "I examined the captain a fortnight ago, and told him this was on the way. He knew it, I knew it, and if the truth be told, I suppose you knew it. There are miraculous recoveries, I suppose, and he may rally, but sooner or later, he's going to die." He glanced at Felicia. "Sorry, miss, but I'm a plain-spoken man. I told the captain he'd probably go sooner."

Ridley nodded. "The Captain and me talked about it."

"Ridley, whatever are you talking about?" Felicia asked.

"Wait a minute, Ridley," Adam said, taking Felicia's arm. "Aunt Soledad, perhaps you and Felicia should come downstairs with me while Dr. Quigley and Ridley give the captain his medicine."

Ridley gave him an approving look. "Good idea, Major." He nodded his head and Felicia found herself being propelled outside the room. Ridley shut the door behind them before she had time to protest.

"Just stop this for a minute," Felicia snapped, turning back toward the door, but Aunt Soledad stood in her way. "Felicia," she said, pushing her wispy hair behind her ears, "let's go downstairs and have some tea." Aunt Soledad's voice was firm and so was the pressure of her hand on Felicia's arm. Felicia was so surprised that she walked along beside her, looking back over her shoulder at the closed door.

Downstairs, they sat down and Aunt Soledad brought in tea. In just a few minutes, Ridley and Dr. Quigley came down. Felicia could have sworn that Ridley had been crying. Aunt Soledad offered Dr. Quigley some tea and he accepted, sitting down and making small talk. He appeared completely sober.

"Do you want me to stay longer?" Dr. Quigley asked, looking at Ridley and Adam. "I'll be glad to if you need me."

"I think not," Felicia snapped. She had determined to send someone back home to try to bring Dr. Norris to the Misery.

"Fine." Dr. Quigley was not at all offended. "Call me if you need me." He put his cup down and stood.

"I don't think Miss Fortune quite understands the situation," Adam said, "and I really do think it advisable that you stay if you possibly can. Captain Fortune may need you in the night."

Dr. Quigley looked around at the group and they all nodded in agreement except Felicia. "I think we should send for Dr. Norris," Felicia said. "After all, he's treated Uncle Gresham for years."

"Felicia, I understand your distress, but it would take days to fetch Dr. Norris," Aunt Soledad said, "providing he was even willing to come. He has dozens of other patients and wouldn't want to leave them for any length of time."

Felicia was near tears. "Uncle Gresham would want it, I know. Dr. Norris has always been able to make him feel better."

"Not this time, he wouldn't," Ridley said grimly. "And the captain knowed it. He told me so. Told me to get Quigley here if he needed anyone. He said he had confidence in him."

"Thank you, and my thanks to the captain," Dr. Quigley said, taking more tea from Aunt Soledad. "It's my professional opinion that we've done all we can do."

"I suppose you're right, although I hate to admit it," Ridley said, shaking his head slowly. "In all my years with him, I ain't never seen the captain in this kind of shape before, and I've seen him plenty bad."

Adam, Aunt Soledad, and Ridley exchanged glances, glances which Felicia intercepted. "I refuse to believe this!" Felicia snapped. "Uncle Gresham has never been one to give up, and you know it! Rest is all he needs. That, and a good doctor." She glared at Dr. Quigley. "We all know how hard Uncle Gresham's been pushing himself. He's just tired, that's all."

Adam made a face and bit his lower lip, worrying what to say. "I think it's worse than that, Felicia. I've seen men in combat like this. I think . . ." He paused, trying to find just the right words to say what he needed to say.

"What the major's sayin', Miss Felicia, is that the captain's just worn out." Ridley looked stricken.

"That's what I'm saying, Ridley. If he rests . . ."

Adam put his hand on her arm. "Felicia, he's dying." He said it as gently as he knew how.

She pulled away from him. "That's a lie! You're just trying to . . . I don't know what you're trying to do! Leave me alone!" She ran out of the room and up the stairs, stopping before she got to Uncle Gresham's room to wipe her tears. She forced herself to smile as

58

she opened the door. Aunt Soledad caught up with her as she stepped into the room. "Felicia, don't make this worse," she said, patting her on the arm. "Gresham would be the first one to tell you to face up to it. The major's right, you know."

"He's not," Felicia whispered fiercely. Before she could stop herself, she started to cry.

"Oh dear," Aunt Soledad said, hurrying out into the hall. She returned with Adam in tow. He put an arm around Felicia and helped her out of the room. She was still crying. Adam held her and she cried into his shoulder while he patted her on the back and made soothing noises.

Finally Adam and Aunt Soledad got her back downstairs where Ridley and Dr. Quigley were sitting. Dr. Quigley reached into his bag and poured some powder into a glass of water, then handed it to Adam. "Here, Felicia, drink this," Adam said, putting the glass to her lips.

She shoved it away. "No, that'll put me to sleep, won't it?" She looked at Quigley, who nodded yes. "If anything's going to happen to Uncle Gresham, I want to be here and be alert." She took a deep breath and forced herself to be calm. "I'm all right now, I promise."

She sat down beside Aunt Soledad while Ridley and Dr. Quigley went back upstairs to sit with Uncle Gresham. Adam sat downstairs with them, the only sound the quiet hiss of the small fire he had built to knock away the night chill, and the chime of the clock as it struck the long hours.

It was in the early hours of the morning when Dr.

Quigley came downstairs and picked up his coat. Felicia looked at him and tried to speak, but no words came. "To my surprise, Captain Fortune seems to have rallied somewhat," Quigley said. "He's sitting up in bed and has decided I'd be better off in my own bed as well. He's sent me home." He chuckled. "These Army types are all the same—couldn't kill them with a stick and a snake." He glanced at Felicia's shocked face. "Begging your pardon, Miss Fortune. That was a compliment on the captain's endurance. Is there someone who can take me home? If not, I'll walk."

Felicia jumped to her feet, overjoyed at hearing that Uncle Gresham was better. "I wouldn't hear of your walking at this time of night, Dr. Quigley." She rang for a footman. "John will take you home in the carriage Major Temple got at the inn."

He nodded. "Mind, I'm not saying that my original diagnosis was incorrect," he said. "I still think the captain could go at any time. He's a tough campaigner, but he's a mighty sick man. You send for me at any hour, Miss Fortune. Even if it's before morning," he added significantly.

Ridley appeared in the doorway and addressed Felicia. "Captain Fortune would like to see you. He's also asked for Major Temple if he's still here."

"I'm here," Adam said, standing stiffly on his leg. He had been sitting with it propped on a footstool, but Felicia could see from his careful expression that it was causing him a great deal of pain. "Felicia," he said, turning to her, "go on up. Tell Captain Fortune that I'll be up in a moment."

Felicia nodded to him and rushed toward the stairs,

noting that Adam was taking time to talk to Dr. Quigley and see him to the carriage. Felicia thought to herself that she would apologize for her comments and thank Dr. Quigley profusely, but later. Right now she had to see Uncle Gresham.

Ridley was in the process of propping Uncle Gresham into a sitting position. Felicia stopped and looked at them. She had expected Uncle Gresham to look like always, but instead he looked terrible. He was pale and gasping for breath as beads of sweat popped out on his forehead with the strain of sitting upright. Felicia closed her eyes for a moment and took a deep breath as the realization hit her that Uncle Gresham's rally had given them false hope—he was indeed dying.

Ridley plumped the pillows behind him. "Took all of his strength to lull Quigley," he said, "and now he's wore out again."

"We could leave," Felicia began, but Uncle Gresham stopped her, motioning her toward him. "Felicia, my dear," Uncle Gresham said, trying to smile as he reached out to her. "Come closer. I want to talk to you." He coughed and a spasm of pain crossed his face. "Where's Adam?"

"I'm right here." The voice came from the doorway and was carefully even. Felicia imagined that Adam Temple was as shocked as she was. She didn't look back at him, but heard him come across the floor, his foot dragging on the polished wood. He came over by the bedside and stood beside Felicia.

"I needed to talk to you two," Uncle Gresham said, speaking with an effort. "I know what I'm going to say will sound like the ravings of a lunatic old man, but I ask you to please hear me out." They nodded and he continued. "You know what the Abbott's House means to me. I had hoped to finish it, but it doesn't look as if I will." There was the ghost of a smile. Felicia started to protest this, but realized there was no need. Uncle Gresham went on. "I want it finished in my name. Do you know what I'm asking?"

Adam nodded. Felicia touched Uncle Gresham's hand. "It will be. Adam and I will see to that."

"I know you will." Gresham Fortune's voice seemed to become stronger. "I'm asking you to finish it as though I were still here and still doing the work." He glanced at Adam. "I know this is hardly fair to you, but it means a great deal to me."

"To me as well," Adam answered him. "And to the men we've hired. Someone else would probably bring in his own crews and these men would all be out of work again."

"What do you mean? What are you saying?" Felicia asked, looking from one to the other. The two men seemed to be in agreement.

"Let me explain it," Adam said to Uncle Gresham, trying to help the Captain save his strength. He turned to Felicia. "Captain Fortune is in charge of everything on this project. If he—if he isn't here, then Viscount Kingston will feel he has to call in someone else to be in charge. That person will develop his own plans, his own revisions to the house, and will hire his own crews of men. Everything we've done or put together will be undone."

"Uncle Gresham could supervise from his bed," Felicia said wildly, looking from one to the other. "You and I could carry messages and instructions . . ."

"No, Felicia, my dear," Uncle Gresham said, "I'm through. I sent Quigley away because I wanted to discuss this with you and Adam. I'm going to die now, but no one must know it until the Abbott's House is finished. Do you promise me this?"

"I promise," Adam said, followed by Felicia's shaky voice, "Uncle Gresham . . . I promise."

Uncle Gresham closed his eyes and sighed. "Good. Thank you both. I know what I've asked of you seems impossible, but I know the two of you can do it. Felicia, if it can be done, I would like to be buried in Devon next to my mother. If it can't be done, that's all right. I long ago accepted the possibility that my remains might be placed anywhere."

"I'll see to it, Uncle Gresham," Felicia said. Her voice was sturdier as she tried to accept the inevitable.

"Thank you. However, the most important thing is finishing the Abbott's House. Adam, do what you have to do, and Felicia, promise me you'll help him. Both of you know all about the plans and what's needed. Watch out for Viscount Kingston. Remember he's coming in a few days, so you'll have to come up with a plausible story for my absence." He smiled crookedly and reached for Felicia's hand. "I leave everything to the two of you and die with the comfort that you will do everything you can to carry out my wishes." He paused and coughed, a long, rattling kind of cough. "Felicia," he said, gasping, "I thank you and Rosie for your love. The two of you have made all the difference in life for me. You know you have my love, and give my love to Rosie." He smiled sweetly at her and closed his eyes.

There was a rattle deep in his throat as Adam turned her away from the bed.

Felicia put her hand over her mouth and pressed hard to keep from screaming. From far away she heard Adam's voice saying, "It's over, Felicia. Always remember he died with a smile on his face."

Then everything went black.

Chapter 5

When Felicia woke up, she was downstairs on the sofa, Aunt Soledad hovering over her head, while Ridley was waving hartshorn and vinegar under her nose. "There—her eyelids are fluttering," Aunt Soledad said. "Oh dear."

"Sit her up and let her drink this," Adam said, helping Ridley prop her upright. He held a glass to her lips, but Felicia shook her head. "No, I don't want anything," she said.

"Take it," Adam said, an authoritative tone to his voice. "It won't put you to sleep. It's just brandy, and I think you could use it."

Felicia took the glass from him and drank it in gulps. It burned going down her throat and she coughed, shaking her head. Adam took the empty glass from her. "I'm sorry not to coddle you," he said, "but it'll be daylight soon, and we need to make some plans."

"Plans?"

Adam and Ridley exchanged glances. "Yes," Adam

said briefly. "We need to decide exactly what we're going to do, how we're going to do it, and what kind of story we're going to tell. Finally, we need to do something with the body."

"Oh dear, oh dear," Aunt Soledad said, dabbing at her eyes with a handkerchief.

"The body. Uncle Gresham." Felicia remembered the scene at Uncle Gresham'a bedside. "What do you mean—what are we going to do with the body?"

"Well, we certainly can't leave it upstairs in the bedroom. Not in the summer heat anyway," Adam snapped.

Felicia flinched. "Must you be so . . . so uncouth?"

"I'm sorry," he said, not sounding sorry at all. He ran his fingers through his hair, and Felicia noted the lines of fatigue on his face. "I'm not insensitive, but we don't have time for all the little courtesies that grease the wheels of society. We have to decide right now what we're going to do and then we've got to start doing it. Kingston will be here before we know it."

"Still . . ." Felicia began, but Ridley stopped her. "Major Temple is right, Miss Fortune. The captain would want it this way, he surely would."

With a sigh, Felicia leaned back and closed her eyes for a moment. Then she opened them and looked at Adam. "What do you suggest? It's going to be difficult to pretend that Uncle Gresham's alive."

"That it is." He sat down beside her and rubbed his knee with his fingers. "We can fob off everyone for a few days by telling them the captain's sick. We might even get a few more days out of telling that he's gone to Devon to see his doctor." He grimaced as he moved to make his leg more comfortable, and Felicia noted the heavy lines of pain and fatigue around his mouth. "The hell of it is that it's going to take more than a few days to finish the Abbott's House, and we're going to have Kingston to deal with besides. He's the one I'm worried about—I don't know how we're going to deal with him. He'll be asking questions."

"He's never met him, has he?" Aunt Soledad said, "Or at least I don't recall him ever meeting him, although he may have sometime or the other."

"What? He? Who?" they all asked, almost in a chorus.

"Viscount Kingston, I mean," Aunt Soledad said with a frown. "I don't think Gresham has ever met him, or would it be that the viscount had never met Gresham?" She looked around at all of them. "That is, Kingston wouldn't have any idea what Gresham looked like."

"They met a long time ago." Ridley said with a frown. "The boy was maybe five or six years old. Do you think he'd remember what the captain looked like?"

Adam frowned as he thought about it. "If there's a chance at all, it's slim," he finally said. "It may be our best hope. What do you think?" He looked at Felicia.

"I don't think he'd remember, if he was that young when he saw Uncle Gresham." She looked at Adam and Ridley sharply. "But what are the two of you proposing—an imposter? That would never work."

"I wasn't thinking of an imposter, but that's a possibility. At this point, anything's a possibility," Adam said.

"It could work," Ridley offered, "but it might not."

"Probably not," Adam said shortly, glancing at the clock. "It's four o'clock in the morning now, and we need to do something with the captain's body. Do we bury it in the garden or something? Whatever we do, we're going to have to do in a hurry. After daylight, there's a risk of being seen."

Felicia stood and put her hands on her hips, then glared down at Adam. "Absolutely not. I will not allow anyone to bury Uncle Gresham anywhere except in Devon next to his mother—my grandmother. I promised him."

"Fine," Adam said mildly, pouring himself a glass of brandy, glancing over at Ridley, then pouring one for him. "If you don't want to bury the body, just tell me what to do with it. If we take it to Devon now, word will get out. We've got to hide it somewhere until we finish the Abbott's House."

Felicia paced the floor while Adam and Ridley sipped their brandy. There was no place, no solution. Finally Adam spoke. "Felicia, I know you don't want to discuss this, but that body is going to decompose. If it were winter, we could possibly pack it in snow or something, but right now—"

"I know! Adam, I know!" Felicia interrupted him, snapping her fingers. "The ice house! Do you remember when we found the cave or cellar or whatever you call it? We could put Uncle Gresham in there and he'd be . . . he'd be fine until we finish the house. It's perfect. No one would possibly find him there."

"Unless someone went in after some ice." Adam's voice was dry.

"That's a chance we'll have to take," Felicia said. "Can you come up with a better place?"

Adam stood. "No, I can't, and I think it will do until we can come up with a better plan. Ridley, do you think the two of us can carry Captain Fortune to the ice house? It's dug into the hill looking down over the Priory, just this side of the Abbott's House."

"I'm going with you," Felicia said. Adam looked at her expression and shrugged his shoulders. "All right. Perhaps you can watch for us. We'll be lucky to get him there before daylight."

It was difficult for Ridley and Adam to carry Uncle Gresham's carefully bundled body up the hill toward the ice house. Ridley wasn't too strong at best, and Adam was in excruciating pain from his leg. He didn't say anything, but Felicia could see from the expression on his face and the pain in his eyes that the man was in agony. Once or twice he stumbled and grunted in pain. It seemed to take forever to cover the walk that had seemed so short before.

At the top of the hill, they put their bundle down while Felicia peered out over the grassy hill, shielding her lantern so it couldn't be seen from the main house.

"It's all clear," she whispered to Adam as he came up to stand beside her.

"I think we should go down and open the door so we can take the Captain right inside. If we wait around, someone may see us. Give me the lantern." He took the lantern from her fingers and the two of them went down to the cellar door. As before, Adam removed the sod at the bottom, opened the door, and Adam went into the tunnel, lantern in front of him. He was back out in a few minutes.

"What did you do with the lantern?" Felicia asked as he got to his feet.

"I left it in there to light us. There's enough light for us to get down to the platform over the pit, but it's dark as pitch in there. There's a block and tackle with an attached basket for moving large chunks of ice, so we'll attach the body and hide it at the back side. You stay here." He went back toward Ridley, dragging his foot. In a moment, the two of them returned, carrying Uncle Gresham's body between them. Adam bent over and went in first, then Ridley pushed the body in, dropped to his knees, and followed it.

Felicia waited a few minutes, listening to the muffled sounds they made. She heard Adam cursing fluently and then heard a muffled answer from Ridley. The sky to the east was streaking with pink and she decided to go inside and see what they were doing. She dropped to her knees and entered the tunnel. It was dark, darker than the night had been, and smelled of damp earth. She kept her eyes on the light at the end where Adam had placed the lantern. At the end of the tunnel, there was another door, a thin one that swung easily on its hinges, and beyond that, a large pit dug into the ground. Ice covered with sawdust was stacked carefully inside. There was a ladder going down into the pit, a block and tackle built out into the middle for hoisting ice up to her level. She looked down to see Ridley and Adam hiding Uncle Gresham under the bottom layer of ice and sawdust. They had used the large basket attached to the block and tackle to lower the body and it swung over them, casting a shadow like a hangman's noose in the lantern light. Felicia suppressed a shudder. For a second, she wondered if what they were doing was illegal and concluded that it probably was.

The men finished covering the body and made their way around to the ladder. Ridley came up first and held the ladder steady as Adam came up. He grunted in pain every time he had to put his full weight on his bad leg. As he scrambled from the ladder onto the dirt at the top, Felicia reached out and put her hand on his arm. "I'm sorry, Adam," she said. It was inadequate, but it was all she could think of to say.

"It's all right," he said gruffly. "I'll survive." He reached behind him and unhooked the lantern. "We'd better get out of here. Ridley and I will come back tonight and make sure we've covered our tracks. I don't think anyone will be around here before then." He held the lantern so it lit the tunnel and motioned Felicia forward. "Let's go. Some of the farmers will be getting up and out with the sun and I don't want them to find us anywhere near here."

Felicia dropped to her knees and crawled out of the tunnel while Adam came behind her, holding the lantern as high as he could. Felicia glanced down at the damp earth between her fingers and was suddenly worried about her dress. She hadn't thought of it as she crawled inside, other things had been on her mind. Now, she felt a stab of guilt in thinking of such a mundane thing while Uncle Gresham lay hidden behind the ice. Still, she thought wistfully, reaching the end where the early daylight seemed to spotlight the dark stains on the front of the dress, this dress would never be the same. Ridley and Adam emerged from the

71

tunnel, and she heard them close the heavy door behind them.

Adam followed her gaze down toward the dark, damp stains on her dress. He blew out the lantern and glanced at her as he went to the top of the hill to see if anyone was around. "You'll probably have to burn that dress as soon as you get home, Felicia," he said, not smiling. "Let's get away from here."

They hurried up the hill, Adam limping badly and trying not to groan in pain. Felicia tried to stop, but he hurried her on, not pausing until they had reached the cover of the woods. Back at the Misery, Adam paused at the door. "I'll tell the men that Captain Fortune is ill and won't be in today. Tonight we'll sit down and decide what to do." He stopped suddenly and ran his fingers through his hair. "Tonight. Good God, I had completely forgotten!"

"Forgotten what?"

Adam bit his lip in annoyance. "I promised my nephew that he could come stay a few days with me. He'd been staying with some friends from his school, then went home and was thoroughly bored. I promised he could come help me for a while, and I'm to go fetch him here tonight."

"How could you do such a ninnyhammer thing?" Felicia made a face.

Adam glared at her. "Ninnyhammer? May I remind you, Miss Fortune, that I didn't plan on this sudden occurrence. Actually, I thought the time spent with me might do Cavendish a world of good." He made a face. "Perhaps I can get rid of him in a day or two. He is, unfortunately, uncommonly curious."

"Just what we need," Felicia said with a sigh, then

realized how she must sound. "I'm sorry, Adam. I didn't mean to be churlish. I'm just tired, and any obstacle above and beyond what we already have on us just seems too much."

"That's all right." He turned with a sigh. "I'm afriad we're going to run into much more than Cavandish," he said. "I'll stop by this afternoon and we can talk for a few minutes." He paused and ran his fingers through his hair. "Felicia, if we carry this off, it'll be a miracle." On that happy note, he turned and walked off, the picture of dejection.

Felicia went inside. Aunt Soledad was sitting there, sewing her black dress. Felicia went over and took it from her. "No, Aunt Soledad, we can't appear to be in mourning," she said firmly.

"It isn't right, you know," Aunt Soledad said, pursing her lips. "Going into mourning is the least we can do for Gresham."

"I know, Aunt, but remember what we promised him. We owe him that first. Everything must appear as usual."

"Well, I can do it, I suppose," Aunt Soledad said, standing, "but I certainly don't like it."

"Does anyone?" Felicia asked as she wearily started for the stairs. She had to get this dress off and burned before anyone saw her. Maybe Adam was right—if they managed to pull this off, it would be a miracle.

After breakfast, Felicia felt better. She and Ridley resisted the impulse to grieve and instead gave themselves up to devising first one plan, then another. Nothing seemed to be foolproof.

In midafternoon Adam came back to the house. Clearly he hadn't slept at all. "Have you eaten anything?" Aunt Soledad asked, hovering over him.

Adam was surprised. "No, I haven't," he said with something that resembled a smile. "Perhaps that's what's wrong with me."

Aunt Soledad hurried off to the kitchen to see about food while Ridley and Felicia sat with Adam around the round table in the study. "I realize that the more people who know about this, the more our chances of being discovered," he said without preamble, "but I felt it was necessary that some of the men be informed."

"Adam, why?" Felicia felt the blood drain from her face. "You know they'll tell."

He shook his head. "I don't think so, Felicia. As I told you before, they all realize that they owe their jobs to Gresham Fortune. I gathered some of the men—the ones who had served with either Gresham or me in the Army—and told them about it. I stressed that if anyone, especially Viscount Kingston, knew Captain Fortune was dead, there would be a new architect and builder engaged and our men would be out of work. I think, with times the way they are, that's enough to ensure secrecy. The men all agreed with me that secrecy was essential, and they're willing to play any part we ask of them."

Felicia bit her lower lip as she worried about it. "I wish you hadn't needed to tell them."

"I wish so too, Felicia, but I felt I had no choice. They all knew Gresham and knew he was around the project constantly. There would have been questions. This way, the men are part of this . . . this deception."

"You make it sound so illegal," she accused. "We're not criminals."

"Beggin' your pardon, Miss Fortune," Ridley said

74

slowly, "but I'm thinkin' we might be. Criminals, that is. Don't you think so, Major?"

Adam took a deep breath. "I think we probably are, Ridley. The important thing is for us not to get caught. Now, I've got to leave tonight to get Cavendish, but I'll be back later. He's with my parents over in Glenley Close, and that's not too far." He paused and smiled at Aunt Soledad, who bustled in with a tray full of food.

"Your family is that close?" Felicia was surprised. She was even more surprised when Aunt Soledad sat down between Ridley and Adam. "Of course, Felicia," Aunt Soledad said. "Don't you recall that Major Temple's father is the vicar in Glenley Close? From my inquiries, I understand that he's a fine man, or so I hear." She didn't see both Felicia and Adam look at her in amazement.

"Felicia tells me that everything must appear as normal." Aunt Soledad turned to Adam and continued, "And I want you to know I'm prepared to do my part. Oh dear." She sagged as she ran out of courage. "It's this house, you know," she confided in a whisper. "I told Felicia no good would come of it, but I'm prepared to do my best."

Adam stifled a grin behind his teacup. "Thank you," he said gravely. "If we work together, I think we can fulfill Captain Fortune's request."

"I'm not so sure," Felicia said slowly, drawing a letter from her pocket. "This came this afternoon from Viscount Kingston. He'll be here early next week. It's definite."

To her surprise, Adam seemed relieved as he glanced over the letter and tossed it in the middle of the table. "Good, that gives us several days to think of something and have a plan in place. Tomorrow we can decide what to do next. That's our first problem."

"That's only *one* of our problems," Felicia snapped. "Adam, do you realize we could go to jail for this?"

"I thought we were agreed on that," he said mildly, buttering a piece of bread. "It's a distinct possibility."

They looked up at a muffled sound to discover Aunt Soledad staring at them with round eyes. "Oh dear, oh dear, oh dear," she moaned, rocking from side to side. "Newgate! Australia! Oh dear, *oh dear!*"

Chapter 6

Felicia didn't see Adam until the next day when he stopped by with some lists of purchases for her to check off against the tradesmen's bills. He had Cavendish with him. Whatever Felicia had expected the boy to be, Cavendish wasn't it. First, she had thought he was a small child—Cavendish was, she guessed, around seventeen or eighteen. Second, she had thought he would look something like an urchin—in fact, Cavendish was going to be the handsomest male she had ever seen. Unless Felicia missed her guess, in about five or six years or even sooner, Cavendish Temple would break every heart in London. Third, from Adam's description, she had thought his nephew would be an uncouth, unmannered boor—Cavendish was quiet and well mannered as he sat and talked with Aunt Soledad. Felicia mentioned as much to Adam.

"Don't let him fool you," Adam said with a knowing glance at his nephew. "I threatened him with decapitation if he made one step out of line. He's really on his best behavior."

"I think you probably overexaggerate the case," Felicia said, taking the lists from him. "Let's go in the study so we can examine these bills." She gave him a significant glance.

He pulled his watch from his pocket and flipped open the cover. "I suppose I can spend an extra few minutes. I left Connaught in charge and he knows what he's doing." He grimaced slightly. "I suppose he's really second in charge now."

Once inside the study, Felicia sent for Ridley. As soon as he came in, they all sat down at the round table. Felicia spoke without preamble. "We've told the servants that Uncle Gresham is sick and doesn't want to see anyone except the family."

"And me," Ridley said defensively.

"Well, of course, Ridley. I think of you as family." To Felicia's complete amazement, Ridley started to sniffle and had to reach for his handkerchief. "Ridley," Felicia said softly, "have you been worried about what will happen to you?"

Ridley sniffled again, blew into his handkerchief, and nodded.

"Don't worry about anything," she said, patting his hand. "I helped Uncle Gresham write down the terms of his will, and he left you well provided for. And besides, even though Uncle Gresham provided for you, Rosie and I want you to stay on with us." She smiled at him. "I certainly can't imagine life without you around."

Ridley patted his cadaverous face and replaced his handkerchief. "We're family," he said in wonderment. "Well, well. You're the only family I've got, you know."

Felicia smiled at him. "Now, as family, we've got to decide what we're going to do. I don't think we've the time right now to plan ahead very much, but what about now?"

"I agree, we're not going to be able to plan ahead very much," Adam observed, running his fingers through his hair. "I think a great deal of our planning is going to simply be reacting to whatever situation occurs."

"True, Major," Ridley said, nodding. "That's what an army on its feet does, as the captain was wont to say."

Felicia got back to the subject. "Are we going to say for right now that Uncle Gresham is sick? We've been careful to say that only Ridley can care for him and take his meals in and so on." She looked at Ridley. "By the way, Ridley, what did you do with the breakfast Mrs. Sprague sent up?"

"It was only barley water and some toast. I waited until up in the morning, then took it outside and threw it away."

"Good." Adam nodded, thinking. "We can do this for a while, anyway. Perhaps we should plan on Captain Fortune having to take a short trip to London about the time Viscount Kingston arrives."

"Or maybe a trip to Devon to see his own doctor?" Felicia suggested.

Adam considered this. "I rather think London. We don't want Kingston to think Captain Fortune is too ill. If Kingston thinks that, he may want to see Captain Fortune with his own eyes and find out how sick he is. Kingston might even want to replace him, which would

79

defeat what we're trying to do."

Felicia took a deep breath. "This could get complicated. All right, London it is." She looked at Ridley. "You'll have to go to London then as if you're with Uncle Gresham or someone might be suspicious." She put her hands over her face for a moment, then turned to Adam. "I'm beginning to see how complicated this is going to be. How do people ever manage to be thieves and highwaymen? I had no idea a life of crime had so many entanglements."

Adam laughed, the first time in days that Felicia had seen a real smile on his face. "You should be in my shoes: the son of a vicar doing all this dissembling. With every word, I'm sure I've taken another step on the road to purgatory."

"I'd forgotten your father was a vicar," Felicia said, straightening the papers into a neat stack.

"Yes, a cousin of Creswicke's," Adam said negligently, then rose, changing the subject. "I'm going back to the Abbott's House. I won't be by any more than necessary until Cavendish leaves. I wouldn't put it past him to go climbing up the side of the house to see if Captain Fortune is really ill."

"I doubt that," Felicia said, rising and walking with him to the door. "Adam, I'm beginning to feel better about this. I think we can do it, I really do."

To her surprise, he turned in the doorway and touched her hand. "I hope so," he said, but his voice wasn't convincing.

By the first of the next week, Felicia felt Adam had been wrong. The men had kept their secret about Uncle Gresham. Dr. Quigley had asked Adam about the captain and been told he was on the mend. The doctor had raised an eyebrow, muttered a few words about the power of miracles, and proceeded to drink another pint of ale that Adam had provided. Most importantly, Connaught and Adam were working like fiends, so the work was ahead of schedule. Even Aunt Soledad was almost normal, other than wandering around mumbling to herself most of the time. That was just Aunt Soledad, however. It's going to work, Felicia thought to herself with a smile.

No sooner had she done exactly like Aunt Soledad and said this aloud to herself than Ridley knocked on the door. He was, if possible, paler than usual. "He's here," he gasped, shutting the door behind him and leaning against it for support.

"Who? Adam? Show him in, Ridley. I need to talk to him about the plasterers."

Ridley shook his head until the hairs across the top flew around his ears. "No, not the major. I mean *he's* here—Viscount Kingston."

Felicia sat down with a thud and felt all the blood drain from her face. "No! Ridley, he's early. He wasn't supposed to be here for days. What will we do?" She stopped and took a deep breath. "We can do this, Ridley. Send someone to warn Adam and you go into the hall and make a scene over Uncle Gresham's barley water or calf's-foot jelly or some such. Send Kingston in here and"—Felicia paused, biting her lower lip as she thought—"Ridley, whatever you do, don't leave him alone with Aunt Soledad."

Ridley's eyes widened and he started to sweat. "That's where he is, Miss Felicia. She's in the drawing room pouring tea down him." He pulled out his handkerchief and mopped at his neck. "I didn't even know the man was here until I walked by the drawing room and saw them sitting in there. I had been to the kitchen trying to pry some tea and biscuits out of Mrs. Sprague and came back by the drawing room door. I tell you, Miss Felicia, I almost dropped everything right there in the hall when I saw that." His eyes got even wider. "You don't suppose she's told anything?"

"With Aunt Soledad, who knows?" Felicia said, dashing around the table, patting her hair in place. "I wish I had on my striped dress." She paused at the door. "Hurry, Ridley. I'll go in and see what they're talking about and try to fob the man off. You send word to Adam that he's here and then you make some kind of scene in the hallway in front of the drawing room door." She stared hard at Ridley—he seemed to be frozen to the door. Felicia finally reached over and shook him hard by the shoulder. "Ridley! This is our first real test—don't fail now!"

Ridley drew himself up to parade stance and Felicia thought he was going to salute her. Instead he opened the door regally and motioned her out. "Don't worry about me, Miss Felicia," he said.

Felicia ran down the hall and only managed to slow down before she reached the drawing room door. She stopped, took a deep breath, and slowly walked into the room. "Viscount Kingston! What a pleasant surprise! Uncle Gresham told me you had written that you'd be here, but I didn't know when." She held out her hand and Kingston stood to take it.

"Yes," he said, a social smile on his face, "I collected

82

my nephew and brought him back to the Priory. It didn't take as long as I had thought it would."

Felicia sat down across from him and he sat, politely refusing an offer of more cakes from Aunt Soledad. "Lord Kingston plans to be here for a while," Aunt Soledad said, rolling her eyes almost up into the lace of her cap.

"Wonderful," Felicia said, smiling with the broadest smile she could muster. "How was your trip?"

Kingston launched into an amusing description of his misadventures with his nephew, the honorable Simon Lucius Cary Charles Knightsbridge. It seemed Simon was five years old and the despair of his mother and assorted governesses and tutors. According to Kingston, the only way he had been able to bring him across the channel had been to lash him to the masts. Felicia didn't believe a word of it, but it made a charming story. She could see how Lord Kingston had made his reputation in London.

Just when Kingston was telling them about discovering Simon dressed in his best shirt, pretending to be the ship's captain, there was a noise outside the door. In true theatrical fashion, Ridley was loudly talking to Mrs. Sprague, the cook, about Captain Fortune's lunch.

"He's a sick man," Ridley roared, "and he demands the best of care. How do you expect him to get well if you keep sending up such unpalatable dishes?"

Cook, an enormous local woman who seldom hurried, got flustered, or got angry, mumbled a reply. Ridley realized immediately that the listeners in the drawing room couldn't hear her.

"What's that you say? I'm telling you that Captain Fortune sent me down right this minute to get him some soup. He said to me not five—no, not three—minutes ago, 'Ridley, tell Mrs. Sprague that I need hot soup.' Madam, we must do as he asks and get the man back on his feet as soon as possible."

To Felicia's horror, the cook, who had never been known to utter a cross word, chose this moment to yell and made a rude suggestion to Ridley about what he could—and should—do to improve himself and furthermore stated that she was doing the best she could, and if they wanted her to, she would just quit.

"I think, Miss Fortune," Kingston said, trying to keep from laughing, "that you should try to resolve this domestic crisis before you find yourself cooking supper tonight."

Felicia, her face flaming, jumped up. "You're quite right," she said, dashing out into the hall. Behind her, she could hear Aunt Soledad muttering, "Oh dear, oh dear."

Out in the hall, Felicia dragged both cook and Ridley back to the kitchen. Ridley had to sit down and mop at his face with a thoroughly bedraggled handkerchief. "Lor, Mrs. Sprague," he said to cook as soon as he could speak, "I certainly didn't mean for you to fly off like that. I just wanted—"

Felicia interrupted him before he said something he shouldn't. "Mrs. Sprague, what Ridley is saying is that we're all quite upset about Uncle Gresham's illness. I want you to know that we appreciate what you've been doing, and most of all, Uncle Gresham thanks you. I'm sure those soups and restorative jellies you've been making have done wonders for him."

"True," Ridley managed, still paler than usual. "The captain's taste is just off."

"What does that mean?" Mrs. Sprague asked, still not mollified.

"It simply means that Uncle Gresham can't fully appreciate your efforts, Mrs. Sprague," Felicia said with a warning look at Ridley. "Right now he can't taste very much." Felicia almost choked on this, thinking how true it was. "However, I'm sure things will change in the future."

"I hope so," Mrs. Sprague said, giving Ridley a venomous look. "And I'd like to say that I don't appreciate *some* people in my kichen nosing around."

"I didn't," Ridley said in a squeak. "The captain merely wanted some hot soup and some barley water."

"Right here." Mrs. Sprague slammed down a pitcher. "Just let me know what the man wants and I'll fix it." She looked at Felicia. *"He's* a good man, he is, not like some I could name."

Ridley stood up. "Now see here . . ."

Felicia grabbed his elbow and propelled him toward the door. "Thank you for your efforts, Mrs. Sprague." She shoved Ridley out into the hall. "Ridley, did you sent word to Adam?" she whispered.

"Yes. I'm telling you, Miss Felicia, that woman needs taking in hand."

Felicia could not by any stretch of imagination see Ridley or anyone else taking someone the size of Mrs. Sprague in hand, but right now, there was no time to argue. "Yes, Ridley, I agree, but not now. Now you go upstairs as though you're seeing to Uncle Gresham. I've got to get back to the drawing room." She clapped her hand to her head. "Good Heavens, Ridley, we've left Kingston in there again with Aunt Soledad."

"A bad move," Ridley said sepulchrally. Felicia didn't waste time agreeing with him. Instead, she passed by him and sped down the hall, turning the corner into the room too quickly. Kingston had gotten up and was ready to leave. Felicia ran right into him and knocked him into the tea tray. There was a tremendous crash as the teapot and teacups went flying all over.

"Oh dear, oh dear," Aunt Soledad said, wiping cream cake from her face. With a sinking heart, Felicia noted that the impeccable Kingston had collapsed into a chair, tea on his cravat and thick cream dripping from his knees onto his highly polished boots.

Felicia stared in horror at him, and was speechless for a moment. Aunt Soledad finally broke the silence. "Oh dear, oh dear *Lord!*" Felicia glanced at her, unsure whether Aunt Soledad was calling on the diety for assistance, or commiserating with Lord Kingston. Aunt Soledad was still frozen to her seat, staring at the bits of cream cake as though she had never seen them before, repeating "oh dear Lord!" Aunt Soledad had to be calling on the diety, Felicia decided, and He seemed to have momentarily deserted the Fortunes.

Felicia ran to Kingston and removed some pieces of the teapot from his lap as she called for a maid. Kingston glared at her, almost shaking with the effort of keeping his temper. As soon as Kingston had regained his feet, he looked down at his clothes and managed a weak smile. He was gracious about the accident, but Felicia could see that he was not accustomed to being knocked about. Although polite and still smiling, he declined her and Aunt Soledad's offer to have his clothing cleaned, and took his leave of them as soon as possible. He did note that he had planned to go straight to the Abbott's House but now thought he would go to the Priory and change clothes.

"A very wise choice," Aunt Soledad said, nodding so vigorously that her cap fell across her face. "After all, Gresham isn't available." She stopped suddenly as Felicia stomped on her foot. "What I mean is . . . I think that . . . oh dear."

"What Aunt Soledad means," Felicia said with what she hoped was her most charming smile, "is that Uncle Gresham should be better and out in a day or so. I'm sure Major Temple can show you around the Abbott's House until you can talk to Uncle Gresham."

"Major Temple? Yes, I believe my father mentioned him."

"A connection of yours, I believe," Felicia said, trying to hurry him toward the door before Aunt Soledad said anything else.

"Connection?" Kingston stopped in the doorway and Felicia noted that there was still a small rivulet of cream slowly inching its way down his boots and onto the floor. She hoped he didn't notice it. Kingston was still speaking, and she forced herself to pay attention to him. ". . . no Temples that I know of. Of course, there are always distant relatives, but no, I don't believe I can place him."

Felicia frowned. "I'm sure of it. He said his father was a cousin of Creswicke's. His father's the vicar in . . ." She couldn't remember where.

"Glenley Close," Aunt Soledad supplied.

Kingston lifted his eyebrows. "Oh, *those* Temples. Yes, I had forgotten. My father helped secure Mr. Temple's post, I believe, but I hadn't heard very much about the family since that time." He glanced down at his boots. "I'm going back to the Priory to change, then I want to see how the work on the Abbott's House is going. Do you believe—what was his rank—Major Temple would be able to tell me about the renovations?'

"I'm sure of it," Felicia said. "Uncle Gresham puts the utmost confidence in Major Temple."

"Not too much, I hope," Kingston said. "After all, Captain Fortune *is* the architect, and he should be the one supervising."

Felicia was stung. "I assure you that he is." Behind her, she could hear Aunt Soledad muttering, so she stepped farther out onto the porch. "Uncle Gresham knows every inch of that building, Lord Kingston, and I can promise you that Major Temple does as well."

Kingston smiled at her. "I accept your word on that, Miss Fortune. Please tell your uncle that I'm looking forward to having a long talk with him as soon as he's well. Since we're in the midst of this building, I hope that's quite soon."

"I think he'll be up and about in a day or so," Felicia said, pulling the door closed behind her as Aunt Soledad began making inarticulate noises. "Uncle Gresham's much stronger than he appears."

"I have yet to meet him, but I'm looking forward to it." Lord Kingston put on his hat, adjusted his gloves, and swung his cane. "I also hope, Miss Fortune," he said with a charming smile at her, "that you and I can further our acquaintance while I'm here. It's devilishly dull out here in the country, and beautiful company such as you would be most welcome." With that, he went off down the walk, his cane hanging decoratively at his side, leaving Felicia standing agape. She went inside quickly and shut the door behind her, leaning against it. "Good heavens," she muttered.

"Does he know?" Aunt Soledad whispered, sidling up to her. "Felicia, he knows, I just feel it in my bones."

"Hush, he doesn't know anything." Felicia looked around. "You know how the servants listen. Let's go in here." She pulled Aunt Soledad into the drawing room, but there was a maid in there, busily cleaning up the floor and sofa. She looked up in surprise at Felicia, but couldn't speak since she had all the cream bun crumbs in her mouth. Felicia nodded at her and propelled Aunt Soledad out of the room. "Let's find Ridley, and find out what he thinks about Kingston's visit. Then I'm going over to talk to Adam."

"You can't do that! What would people say?" Aunt Soledad was aghast.

Felicia paused on the stairs. "Aunt Soledad, desperate times call for desperate measures. You can go with me if you want to, but I simply *must* talk to Adam. Kingston's going over there as soon as he changes his clothes."

"Oh." Aunt Soledad thought a moment. "I understand now. You did that on purpose then—ruined Kingston's clothes, I mean so you'd have time to discuss things with Major Temple. What a *brilliant* idea, Felicia! I would never have thought of it."

Felicia started to deny it, but saw there was no point since Aunt Soledad was firmly convinced. Instead, she motioned for Aunt Soledad to come into the small breakfast parlor where Ridley was sitting staring at an almost empty bottle of sherry.

"I hope, Ridley," Felicia remarked, sitting down across from him, "that you haven't been losing yourself in the bottle."

"It's a temptation, but no," Ridley answered with a sigh. "One small glass only, and it's only sherry." He got right to the point. "What did you think?"

"I think the viscount's very dashing," Aunt Soledad said, adjusting her cap. "Very much up on all the London gossip, I'd say." She looked around at them. "He even knew about cousin Martha eloping to Gretna Green with Wrixley's second son."

Felicia closed her eyes briefly. "Ridley, *I* think the viscount's intelligent enough to find us out if he even suspects anything. I'm going over to the Abbott's House to tell Adam that Kingston's been here and what we think. It won't hurt to forewarn him that Kingston will visit him sometime this afternoon." She gave Ridley a significant glance. "Kingston wants to meet Uncle Gresham and talk with him."

"And that means . . ." Ridley said sepulchrally.

"That means we have to come up with Uncle Gresham," Felicia said shortly.

"My dear, the day has been too much for you." Aunt Soledad put her hand on Felicia's arm. "Gresham's dead. You know that. We certainly can't raise the dead."

Felicia nodded, looked at Ridley, then laughed

hysterically while Aunt Soledad looked at her in puzzlement. "Do you know something I don't, Felicia?" Aunt Soledad asked in an injured tone as soon as Felicia stopped laughing. "I've certainly never seen anyone raised from the dead, although I wouldn't deny that it could happen. To someone besides Lazarus and Jesus, I mean. After all, in this age of electricity and magnetism, anything is possible." Aunt Soledad looked at Felicia sternly. "My dear, I do believe you need a glass of water."

Felicia shook her head and accepted the sherry Ridley handed her. She ignored Aunt Soledad's shocked "oh dear" and downed it in one gulp. "Now," she said, taking a deep breath, "back to the problem at hand. What I had in mind, Aunt Soledad, was producing another Uncle Gresham—an imposter."

"An imposter? Felicia, have you lost your mind? Where in the world are you going to find a one-armed impostor who looks, walks, and talks like Gresham Fortune? The man had presence, you know." Aunt Soledad was so agitated she took off her cap and wadded it up into a ball.

"Oh God, the arm. I had forgotten about that," Felicia said. "Ridley, I'm afraid Aunt Soledad is right."

"It appears that way." Ridley sat in silence for a moment as he mulled the problem over. Then he poured himself another glass of sherry, almost emptying the bottle. He glanced at what was left, about a half a glassful, and put the bottle aside. "Now what?"

"I've got to talk to Adam," Felicia said, getting up. "Right now." She paused at the door and looked back at the pair still sitting. "Aunt Soledad, are you going with me? You don't have to if you don't want to. Ridley, you'd better lock yourself in Uncle Gresham's room in case someone gets curious and tries to get in there. We can't be too careful."

"It's this house, you know," Aunt Soledad said, toying with Felicia's glass. "We're doomed. Doomed." She poured the rest of the sherry into the glass and downed it in one long swallow. "Oh dear!" she gasped, choking.

"Now stop that, Aunt Soledad," Felicia said, coming over to stand beside her. "If you begin thinking that way, we are doomed. I, for one, intend to go down fighting. Do you want to go with me to the Abbott's House? Adam might have a solution."

"On the other hand, he might not," Ridley said.

Felicia had had enough. "Stop it, both of you. Surely the four of us put together can outwit Kingston long enough to finish the house. Adam thinks it will be completed in a matter of a few weeks. We can manage a charade until then. From this moment on, I don't want to hear any more of this nay-saying. Think positively."

Aunt Soledad looked dismally at the dregs in the sherry bottle. "Positively. Be positive." She looked up. "Felicia, I'm positive we're going to jail."

"I give up." Felicia turned for the door. "You're going to talk us into Newgate. I'm going to see Adam."

"Wait until I get my shawl." Aunt Soledad looked for her cap.

"Aunt Soledad, your cap's in your hand, and your shawl's in the breakfast room. Hurry." Felicia pinned Ridley with a glance. "Go lock youself in Uncle Gresham's room, Ridley. I wouldn't put it past

Kingston to bribe a servant to try to get in there and assess Uncle Gresham's condition."

Ridley's head jerked up and his eyes widened. "I hadn't thought of that." He brushed past Felicia. "I just hope he doesn't try to send Mrs. Sprague up there. Just so I'll know it's you, knock on the door when you get back—three short knocks." With that, he ran up the stairs.

"A *short* knock? Ridley, what in heaven's name is a short knock?" Felicia didn't receive any answer, and as Aunt Soledad had her cap on somewhat and her shawl on correctly, they left for the Abbott's House.

Chapter 7

The Abbott's House was organized chaos, Felicia thought, as she stood for a moment watching the men work. She found she enjoyed this kind of atmosphere, even if Aunt Soledad didn't think it proper. She liked the smell of the wood freshly sawed; the sound of the hammers, saws, and chisels; the touch of the plaster and paper. She found she even liked the distinctly male conversations that always went on. She also liked, although she would never admit it to Aunt Soledad for fear of shocking her, the male smell of the men as they worked and sweated. That thought shocked even her.

The day was hot, and some of the men had taken off their shirts. "Turn your head," Aunt Soledad hissed as they drew near the house. "I knew we shouldn't have come here. This is not for young eyes to see."

"Just older eyes?" Felicia asked mischievously as Aunt Soledad fought down a blush.

"Don't be impertinent, Felicia," Aunt Soledad said. "Oh dear. Don't look that way. Look over here."

Felicia obediently turned away and looked in the

direction Aunt Soledad indicated. At that moment, Adam came through the door right in front of her, almost running into her. His shirt was untied and open down the front, he had sweated until it was damp all over and clinging to his body wetly. Felicia looked from his bare chest right up into his eyes and speech left her. She was only dimly aware of Aunt Soledad. "Oh dear, oh dear, Major Temple. Nothing would do Felicia except to come find you. This is *most* improper."

"I quite agree," Adam said, looking down at Felicia. She felt her cheeks blaze, and forced herself to look right into his eyes. That didn't work either, and then she had to force herself to stop staring at his face. When she lowered her eyes, she found herself staring at his bare chest instead. She tried to catch her breath, and there was this . . . this . . . this *masculine* smell. It was all too much. She closed her eyes. "Adam," she said, eyes still closed, "we have a slight problem we need to discuss."

He clasped both of her arms. "Has the heat overcome you?" He frowned as he looked at her.

It was as good an excuse as any, she thought. "Yes," she said faintly. "Could we find some shade where we could talk for a few moments?"

Adam let her go, glanced down, and without embarrassment, retied his shirt. "Connaught," he yelled, "take over for a few minutes. I'll be back." He took Felicia's arm. "Out this door. There's a nice little grotto with a pool back here. I think Lady Creswicke used it for a place to sit in the summer. It's nice and cool." He led the way out the back, picking up his coat from a pile of lumber as they walked.

"You don't have to put on a coat as hot as it is," Felicia said. She was beginning to feel normal.

"Ah, but think of the consequences. We must observe the proprieties, mustn't we?" he said, with a wink at Aunt Soledad.

"I'm glad someone thinks so," Aunt Soledad sniffed. *"Some people* never worry about their reputations."

Adam laughed and led the way to two small, ornate benches placed on either side of a small pool. It was a beautiful spot, full of blooming flowers, the sound of splashing water, and best of all, it was nice and cool. Felicia and Aunt Soledad sank to one bench gratefully as Adam sat down across from them.

"Now, do I understand there's a problem?"

Felicia made herself concentrate. She had been wondering why she hadn't noticed how very *masculine* Adam was, but she forced herself to think about their problem. "It's Kingston," she said shortly. "He came by and wanted to see Uncle Gresham."

"So he's here now." He paused a moment, licking his lips. "I thought we had decided that Captain Fortune was going to be ill for a while, in London for a while, and then we'd figure out what else to do." Adam glanced at her sharply. "Were you able to take care of Kingston? Allay any questions, I mean."

Felicia nodded. "For the time being, at any rate. Adam, he's no London dandy with a noodle for a brain. If we're not careful . . ." She let her words trail off.

"We can do it, Felicia. Keep telling yourself that. After all, he's the one who has to find Gresham Fortune. We can keep saying he's around, just unavailable."

"He wants to *see* Uncle Gresham," Felicia wailed.

"So would I if I were in his boots," Adam said. "After all, if you're paying a man to do a job and do it correctly, you'd want to talk to him."

"Ridley and I thought about an imposter. Someone who could appear to be Uncle Gresham, but I had forgotten about the arm. Kingston would know that Uncle Gresham had only one arm. Where in the world could we find someone with the . . . the savoir faire to carry off a conversation with Kingston and also had a missing right arm?"

"We'd have to find an actor to carry it off." Adam let out a long breath. "I don't know of any one-armed actors. Hell, I don't know any actors, period. Excuse me, I wasn't thinking about my language." He nodded in the direction of Aunt Soledad.

"Think nothing of it, Major." Aunt Soledad looked at Felicia. "Desperate times call for desperate measures. And words," she added, nodding her head vigorously.

"Kingston's coming here today," Felicia told him. "Just as soon as he cleans up."

"Cleans up what?"

Felicia was forced to tell him about Kingston's accident with the teapot and tray. Aunt Soledad offered the information that it had been a brilliant idea of Felicia's to delay Kingston. Adam merely shook his head, and Felicia realized he was trying not to laugh aloud. "Go on and laugh," she said icily. "You weren't there, trying to cope."

Instead of apologizing as she had thought he would do, he laughed. He threw his head back and laughed, then stopped and laughed some more. "I hardly thought it that funny," Felicia snapped. "In fact, it was

97

rather mortifying."

"I daresay." Adam had laughed so hard he had to wipe his eyes. "I wish I had seen it." He became serious. "I can handle Kingston coming here today. I want you to go back home, though, If he sees you here, he might think it rather strange, although we could tell him you were carrying messages from Captain Fortune." He paused. "I'd still feel better if he didn't see you here."

"Most judicious," Aunt Soledad agreed.

Felicia stood up. "All right, but will you come to the Misery tonight so we can talk about this? We're going to have to do something, Adam, and I don't know what."

"I'll give it thought today and be over tonight."

"Come for supper," Felicia said impulsively. "We can all talk together afterwards."

"I'll have to bring Cavendish with me."

Felicia thought a moment. "Would he amuse himself while we talked?"

Adam grimaced. "Probably. He'd probably rearrange the floor plan of the house, drive the servants insane, and who knows what else, but I'm sure he'd be amused."

"Another Rosemary," Felicia said with a laugh as she and Aunt Soledad looked at each other in agreement. "I think it has something to do with the years between fifteen and twenty."

Adam took her arm to escort her back up the path. "But, of course, we were never like that." He smiled. "If my father hadn't been a man of God, I shudder to think what might have been."

Aunt Soledad rearranged her cap and stepped firmly between them. "I'm sure God will straighten out

Rosemary and Cavendish in His own good time. Major Temple, may we expect the two of you for supper then?"

Adam nodded as Felicia and Aunt Soledad headed back for the Misery. Felicia risked a glance over her shoulder and saw him stripping his coat back off, only this time, the shirt followed it. He was, she noted with interest, quite tanned above the waist. And quite muscular.

"Felicia." It was a command from Aunt Soledad. Obediently Felicia turned away and walked around the bend in the path.

Supper was a surprisingly subdued affair. Felicia thought Adam might have been doing Cavendish an injustice since the boy sat quietly, had perfect manners, and spoke only when spoken to. Adam didn't talk very much; Ridley absented himself with the excuse, delivered in a rather loud voice, that he was going to take a tray up the captain. It was left to Aunt Soledad to entertain them, and she spent the time discussing her school days in Bath. As soon as was possible, Felicia caught Adam's eye. "I think we need to go over the accounts, if you have time," she said, mentally congratulating herself on how accomplished she was becoming at subterfuge and prevarication.

"Of course." He turned to Cavendish. "As I told you, I need to see to this. Can you entertain yourself for a while? Quietly?"

Aunt Soledad smiled before Cavendish could speak. "I'll be glad to entertain the dear boy. Tell me, Cavendish, do you play cards at all? I haven't had an entertaining game of cards in a while."

Cavendish glanced in desperation at Adam but got

no help from that quarter. "I'm not a good card player," he said, a note of panic in his voice. "Chess, perhaps?"

"Chess?" Aunt Soledad was blank. "If not cards, then perhaps music. Do you sing or play?"

"Let's play cards," Cavendish said. He sounded resigned to his fate.

Felicia led the way into the study. "I think you're too hard on the boy, Adam. He's a pattern card of manners."

"I threatened him." Adam grinned. "No, you may be right. He has been behaving lately. He's growing up, I suppose, and I think there may be some interest in a girl somewhere. He's skirted around the edge of a few questions on how to deal with the fairer sex."

Felicia laughed. "And no doubt you gave him the benefit of your vast experience."

He smiled at her, and Felicia caught her breath. He was very close to her and smelled of soap. She had a quick image of the way he had looked standing in the afternoon sun, bronzed and sweaty. She licked her lips and moved away, sitting down at the table as far away from him as she could get. "I asked Ridley to join us," she said. "He should be here in a minute or two."

"Good." Adam sat down across from her and ran his fingers through his hair. "Maybe Ridley will have some suggestions."

"Did Kingston come by to see you this afternoon?"

Adam nodded. "He looked everything over carefully and asked some questions. The man's no fool, Felicia. You told me he was no London dandy, and you're right. He sees everything and asks about everything." There was a short pause. "This whole scheme is so bizarre that I have to keep reminding myself that I made a promise to Gresham Fortune. If it weren't for that . . ."

Felicia nodded. "But we have to keep it, Adam. We all promised."

Ridley came in and shut the door carefully behind him. He took a key out of his pocket and showed it to Felicia. "I've taken to locking the captain's room," he announced, sitting on one side of the table between Felicia and Adam. "I understand we have a problem by the name of Kingston."

Adam laughed aloud. "What an understatement, Ridley. I'd say you're right." He told him in a few words about Kingston's tour of the Abbott's House during the afternoon, and about his assessment of Kingston's character.

"He's goin' to be a hard 'un to fool, he is," Ridley said pessimistically. "We was thinking about an imposter."

"So I heard." Adam smiled. "I'm told that all we have to do is come up with a one-armed actor who knows enough about building to discuss it intelligently and has enough polish to talk to someone like Kingston." He laughed. "That should be easy enough."

"I thought of Bill Bentley since he's got only one arm, but he's definitely Newgate bait," Ridley said. "Anyone else you know with one arm?"

Adam thought for a moment. "No one except Cartwright but—let's see: no, he lost his left arm—and MacDonald." He stopped and he and Ridley looked at each other. "MacDonald," Adam said, snapping his fingers. "That's it."

"Right you are, Major. I don't know why I didn't think of it myself. William MacDonald—the Great

Scot." Ridley smiled in satisfaction. "I think you've hit on it."

"Who," asked Felicia peevishly, "is William MacDonald, and why do you think he's the answer to our problems?"

Adam glanced at her. "He isn't the answer, but he's as close as we're going to get. Tell her about William, Ridley. You know him better than I do."

"Is he an actor, or at least someone who's familiar with the ton enough to talk to Kingston?" Felicia asked.

Ridley's face reddened and he looked at Adam. "Not exactly an actor, Miss Felicia," Ridley said, reaching for his handkerchief, "but he could talk to Kingston and convince him, I'm sure. That Scot's got a silver tongue." He paused. "Major, you tell her what you know about MacDonald, and I'll add the details."

Adam put his elbows on the table. "I might as well be blunt, Felicia. William MacDonald did serve in the Navy for a while—not as a patriot or anything so glamorous, he was impressed. He lost his right arm in the Navy. Before he went to sea, he worked in London, and did quite well. He was "—Adam couldn't resist a smile as he spoke to her—" a swindler and a thief."

Felicia put her hands over her face. "Oh, my goodness. Are you two out of your minds, thinking we can get a swindler and a crook in here to impersonate Uncle Gresham. What would Uncle Gresham say?"

Ridley stared hard at her. "He'd take one look at William and say 'If that's what you've got to do, Billy, then do it.' Captain Fortune was a practical man."

"But a *thief*," Felicia protested. "You know this MacDonald will take one look at Kingston and decide he could make more money there. It won't take a day until Kingston knows all about our—um—our secret."

"What do you think, Ridley?" Adam asked, raising an eyebrow. "Do you think the Great Scot would betray us?"

"The Great Scot?" Felicia looked puzzled. "You called him that name before. What does that mean?"

"That's what everyone called MacDonald," Adam explained with a laugh. "He came down from Edinburgh to London years ago, did a magic act and juggled at fairs and such to get started until he learned how to pick pockets. Then he discovered he had a talent for bilking London swells out of their money. I understand he was quite good at it until he got drunk one night and woke up aboard a ship bound for our latest altercation with Jefferson, John Paul Jones, and the former colonies."

"Did he lose his arm in battle?"

"He'll probably tell you he did, but no, there was nothing so dramatic. I think a loaded barrel fell on him, and the surgeon had to amputate his arm. Of course, it was difficult for him to come back and take up his trade. A one-armed man is rather easy to remember and find."

"And he certainly couldn't go back to juggling either," Ridley added solemnly. "You know, Major, I think he'll do right nicely. He always could walk right up to those swells and strike up a conversation. You'd have thought he was to the manor born."

"I don't like it at all," Felicia said. "I still think we're taking a chance."

"Felicia," Adam said patiently, "we've been taking a chance since the minute we walked out of here with

Captain Fortune's body. Frankly, I don't think we have a choice." He looked at Ridley. "Could you go to London to get MacDonald? Last I heard, he was living down by the docks somewhere. It might take some time to find him."

Ridley nodded. "I can ferret him out, Major. Don't worry."

"Oh, fine." Felicia was exasperated. "And what do we do in the meantime? Ridley won't be here, Uncle Gresham's supposed to be in his room sick, and Kingston will be asking question after question."

"That's no more of a problem than it's been," Adam said, motioning for Ridley to hand him a bottle from the sideboard behind him. Ridley poured both of them a glass. "Only ratafia for you, Felicia," Adam said with a grin as he drank the port. "About Kingston: we'll simply have to tell him that Captain Fortune has gone to London to see about something—paint or plasterers or a mural artist or some such—and that he plans to stay a few days and visit his doctor as well. I think it'll fly." He gestured toward Ridley. "His loyal man, of course, had to go with him. After all, you can't have a man get out of his sickbed and go straight to London, even if he does plan to see a doctor." He paused. "I don't think Kingston can do anything about it."

"He could go to London," Felicia said.

Adam reached over and took her hand. "Felicia, quit borrowing trouble—God knows we've got enough already. Yes, Kingston could go to London, he could alert the Bow Street Runners, he could engage another builder, he could go to Rome to see his parents, he could do any one of a dozen things. If he did go, and chances are he won't, by the time he got there and asked

104

a few questions, Ridley would have had time to locate MacDonald and be back here." He smiled at her and looked into her eyes. She lost her train of thought and had to remind herself to listen to him. "Let's take this one step at a time, Felicia," he was saying. "This is just like a plan in battle: you do everything you can to cover emergencies, then you pray a lot, trust to luck, and do the best you can."

Felicia stopped thinking about his eyes and laughed shakily. He was still covering her hand with his. "I had no idea. I always thought battles were won by daring and courage."

Adam let go of her hand and sat back in his chair, accepting another glass of port from Ridley. "Hardly. Daring and courage have their places, but a great deal of winning any battle is slogging through the mud and still being able to keep the powder dry." He laughed and glanced at Ridley.

"True, Major Temple." Ridley nodded vigorously. He and Adam began planning the trip to London while Felicia sat and watched them. They talked about places and people Felicia had never heard of, the demimonde and the stews that lined the back streets of London. Evidently MacDonald could walk on either side of the street. The two of them decided that sooner was better—Ridley would leave as soon as possible in the morning. They were stopped by a commotion outside, and it took Felicia a moment to place it as the sound of a carriage drawing up to the front of the Misery.

"Kingston?" she asked warily. "Should he find us here like this?"

Adam glanced around. "I don't see why not. After all, I've merely come to consult with Captain Fortune

105

about what I should do tomorrow. However, Ridley has decided Captain Fortune is quite tired, has given him some laudanum drops, and the captain has gone back to bed. He is, therefore, quite unavailable."

"I'm going to get all these tales mixed up," Felicia muttered, standing up. "By the way," she asked, looking at Adam before she went out to greet their guest, "how did you become such an accomplished liar?"

"Practice," he said with a grin. "Haven't you heard all those old stories about the way vicars' sons always turn out?" Felicia made a face at him and went into the hall to greet Kingston.

Except it wasn't Kingston. The door burst open and Felicia was enveloped in a bear hug. "Felicia, I've missed you so, and everyone went away, so I came here to keep you company." Rosemary stepped backward. "Look, my arm's all better." She flexed her arm to show Felicia. "I've even brought a present for Uncle Gresham. Where is he?" Aunt Soledad came tearing out of the drawing room, her cards still in her hand. "Rosemary, whatever are you doing here?" she demanded, "and who brought you? Surely you didn't come by yourself! Rosemary, you didn't! Tell me you didn't!" Aunt Soledad looked faint.

"Now Aunt Soledad, don't take on . . ." Rosemary stopped speaking abruptly and looked over Aunt Soledad's shoulder to where someone else was standing in the drawing room door. "Cavendish!" she gasped. "I didn't know."

Adam and Felicia looked at each other, then at Rosemary, who was standing quite in shock staring at an equally astonished Cavendish, who was standing staring at her while his cards dropped from his fingers one by one. "Rose . . . Miss Fortune," he finally said, and bowed slightly from the waist, very formally.

"I take it that you two have met," Felicia said dryly.

A guilty flush spread over Rosemary's face. "We met in the spring. Do you remember that I told you a friend saved me when I fell into the pond and broke my arm. It was Cavendish."

"You two were in the pond together?" It was too much for Aunt Soledad. She turned to Felicia, gasping. "My vinaigrette, and quickly!" She staggered back into the drawing room and fell across the sofa. "And to think your parents trusted me to chaperone you!" she moaned. "Rosemary, how could you?"

"Well, one of them dared me, and I wasn't going to let that pass." She looked at Cavendish with what appeared to Felicia to be adoration. "Cavendish promised not to tell, so no one knows except us." She looked at Cavendish. "You didn't, did you? Tell, I mean."

He drew himself up. "Of course not." He was greatly offended. "A gentlemen doesn't do that." He and Rosemary stared at each other.

"Good God," Adam muttered behind Felicia's shoulder. "Are we going to be cursed with a raging case of calf love here in addition to everything else? Let me get Cavendish out of here." He bent down to mutter in her ear. "Don't tell Rosemary yet. Let her think Ridley and Captain Fortune have gone to London." He moved away and stood by Cavendish, suggesting they should leave to let the family catch up on news. Cavendish was reluctant to leave, but Adam was firm. At the door he turned to speak to Felicia. "I think we may need to discuss some things tomorrow," he murmured. "I'll leave Connaught in charge around noon and come here. Will that be all right?"

"Anytime." Felicia was trying to be businesslike to counteract the curious stare on Rosie's face. Clearly she thought there was something between Felicia and Adam. Rosie was a born romantic.

Felicia closed the door behind Cavendish and Adam with a sigh of relief. Then she pinned Rosie with a stare. "All right, Rosie, let's hear it. Where are Mama and Papa and how did you get here?"

Rosie put her hand to her head. "Can't all this wait until tomorrow, Felicia? It's been a difficult journey and I'm really fatigued. I'd like to go to bed."

Felicia's voice was grim. "You're going to bed, and when you get up tomorrow, you're going right back to London. I'd wager that Mama and Papa don't even know you're here."

Rosie's face flamed. She started to say something, then decided to go for the truth. "No, but you know they don't care at all. Mama thinks I'm in Brussels with Papa, and Papa thinks I'm in Paris with Mama. You know how they never think about either one of us. When they both left, I got the carriage out and came here." She came over and put her arms around Felicia. "After all, I'm safer here with you than alone in London, you know that."

"Unfortunately, I can't argue that point. I don't want you in London alone." Felicia held her at an arm's length. "I have to know one thing, though. I know you seemed shocked to see Cavendish, but I want the truth, Rosie. Did you know Cavendish was here?"

Rosie shook her head. "No, I swear it, Felicia. I knew

108

he lived somewhere around here—Glenley Close, I think he said, but I had no idea he was here. I was as surprised as he was." She looked hard at Felicia. "You do believe me, don't you?"

Felicia hugged her hard. "You may be a rapscallion sometimes, Rosie, but you're always truthful when I demand the truth. Even Aunt Soledad will agree that you're right—you're far better off here than alone in London. Anything could happen there."

"Then I can stay?" Rosie danced around Felicia. "I'll be good, I promise, Felicia. I'll even do whatever Aunt Soledad tells me to." She stopped and looked forlorn, her hand on her stomach. "Felicia, could I have something to eat? I gave the coachman all my money to buy grain for the horses and something for himself, and I haven't had anything to eat since I left London. Except this." She produced a crumbly loaf of bread. "I swiped it from the kitchen before I left."

Felicia shook her head. "Rosie, ladies do not swipe things. Come on, Mrs. Sprague always leaves plenty in the kitchen." After checking on Aunt Soledad and making sure her vinaigrette had restored her completely, Felicia led Rosie to the kitchen, Rosie talking incessantly. Felicia sat down across the table from Rosie as she ate. Rosie had been truthful about her hunger—she ate ravenously.

After Rosie had eaten, she glanced at Felicia, then stopped and looked hard at her. "What's the matter, Felicia? You look worried and tired." She stopped as a thought hit her. "It isn't Uncle Gresham, is it? He isn't worse, is he?"

"No, he's not worse." Felicia couldn't look straight at Rosie and she fervently wished she had Adam here to tell Rosie about Uncle Gresham. Adam had said not to tell her, but if she was going to stay, she had to know. Still, Felicia thought, looking at Rosie's worried face across from her, there would be time enough tomorrow to tell her. It was going to be hard enough any time.

She forced a bright smile. "Let's go to bed, Rose, my love," she said. "You're tired and so am I. Tomorrow we can have a long talk. You can tell me all about London and Mama and Papa, and I'll tell you what's been happening here."

At the time, it sounded so easy.

Chapter 8

Felicia was awakened just at daybreak the next morning by the sound of someone yelling downstairs. Groggily, she decided she must have been dreaming and curled up under the quilts again. She was still sleepy since she hadn't been able to fall asleep until late. Most of the night she had been trying to think about their predicament, but her mind kept wandering to the image of Adam Temple standing in front of her with his shirt untied. It had been most disturbing.

It wasn't a dream—the noise continued, becoming even louder if possible. She decided to put her head under the pillow and wait for the noise to stop, but then curiosity got the best of her—she had to discover what was going on. Muttering to herself about the indecency of having to get up at such an early hour, she got up and dressed hurriedly in an old dress that was easy to hook, then shoved her hair back and caught it with combs. She glanced in the mirror and decided she looked altogether terrible, but it couldn't be helped. As soon as she discovered the source of the noise, she was going to come right back and crawl into her warm bed.

It was Mrs. Sprague and Ridley. It was difficult to hear who was louder as they were both yelling at the top of their lungs. Mrs. Sprague seemed to be at odds with Ridley, who was insisting on his breakfast *right now* as well as a hamper packed for him to take with him to London. As Felicia came into the kitchen, Ridley was finishing up with his clinching sentence. "After all, it's not really for me, it's for Captain Fortune. A sick man has to have sustenance."

"A sick man don't need all that food," Mrs. Sprague siad, banging a spoon against the table for emphasis. "Meat's too heavy for his condition. What he needs is some soup, maybe some calf's-foot jelly, or some milk toast."

Ridley grimaced at the thought. "I must insist, Mrs. Sprague, that you pack some ham, bread, or whatever else is around."

Mrs. Sprague was looking mutinous when Felicia stepped in. "Thank you for your concern about Uncle Gresham, Mrs. Sprague. You're right, he doesn't need any heavy foods. He's going to have to be moved to London to see his doctor and Ridley is going with him. Could you please pack something soothing for Uncle Gresham and also some ham, bread, and cheese for Ridley. I doubt if Uncle Gresham will want to stop and eat in a public inn." She pushed Ridley firmly out the kitchen door. "As for right now, we'll eat in the breakfast room as usual, Mrs. Sprague, and could you have something ready soon? Ridley needs to be on his way."

"And Captain Fortune? I suppose he needs to be on his way as well?" Mrs. Sprague was not placated.

112

"Of course," Felicia said hastily, shoving Ridley in front of her while she tried to get her hair out of her eyes. One of her combs had slipped. I am, she thought as she tucked her hair into place, going to be just like Aunt Soledad. It was a scary thought.

Felicia shut the breakfast parlor door behind them. The room was small and they were able to talk quietly, watching for Mrs. Sprague to appear with breakfast. Felicia glanced at the small clock on the shelf above the sideboard. It was six o'clock in the morning.

"Ridley," she said with a sigh, "couldn't you have waited?"

"You and Major Temple allowed as how I should start right away," he said in an injured tone. "I was just doin' my duty."

"All right, Ridley. Since Rosemary brought the carriage and coachman from London, it's only logical that you take that back. You can stay at the London house if no one sees you."

Ridley shook his head. "The major and I talked about that. I need to fade into the crowd. If I stay at the London house, everyone will think it strange that I'm alone. Word might get back to Kingston, and here we are telling that Captain Fortune and I are in London together." He dropped his voice to a whisper. "No, I'm goin' to stay with some Army men down by the docks. They won't say a word, and besides, they can help me find MacDonald."

Felicia bit her lower lip as she thought. "Ridley, what are you going to say to MacDonald if you find him?"

"Not if, when."

"All right, when you find him. What are you going to offer him? I was thinking about that last night, and I

113

don't have any money. A man like MacDonald would demand payment."

Ridley nodded. "Major Temple and I talked about the very same thing and we decided to see if MacDonald would take the job on speculation, as it were."

"Speculation?"

"That's right. Major Temple pointed out as MacDonald's used to collecting his money at the end of his schemes, so this might appeal to him. We're going to tell him the truth of it up front—we decided that would be the best way—then he could decide if he wanted in. When Creswicke pays you and Major Temple for finishing the Abbott's House, we'll send MacDonald a cut."

"I still don't like it, Ridley." She stopped as Mrs. Sprague came in with breakfast. "I have the hamper packed as *you* requested, Miss Fortune," Mrs. Sprague said, ignoring Ridley.

Felicia gave Mrs. Sprague the best smile she could muster at that time of the morning. "Thank you, Mrs. Sprague, you're a marvel. I simply don't know what we would do without you. I thank you and I'm sure Uncle Gresham would too if he were here. That is, if he were in this room," she added hastily.

"Thank you," Mrs. Sprague said icily, almost pinning Ridley to the wall with her gaze. "It's nice to know *some people* have manners enough to thank a body." With that, she lumbered off to the kitchen, pulling the door shut behind her.

"Ridley, whatever did you say to that woman before I got there? I just know she's going to quit before we leave, and neither Aunt Soledad or I can cook at all."

She shook her head as Ridley offered her some muffins. "No, thank you, it's too early for me to eat."

Ridley proceeded to pack away an enormous amount of food for such a thin man. About halfway through breakfast , the good smells of Mrs. Sprague's food overcame Felicia's resistance, and she took a muffin and was spreading it with marmalade when there was a furtive knock at the window of the breakfast room. Turning, she saw Adam at the window, motioning for her to go to the front and open the door for him.

"Is anything wrong?" she asked breathlessly as she opened the door. "What's happened?"

Adam peered around to see if anyone had seen him, and followed Felicia into the breakfast room. "Kingston found Dr. Quigley at the inn last night, well into his cups, I think, and proceeded to question him about Captain Fortune's health. Quigley, from what I gathered, told Kingston it was a miracle that Captain Fortune had lived. He—Quigley, that is—also said that he thought Captain Fortune could die any minute." Adam gratefully accepted a cup of coffee and gulped it.

"Who told you this?" Felicia demanded. "Perhaps someone's just trying to scare us."

Adam shook his head. "Connaught heard it. He was sitting at the next table in the common room and heard everything. He came directly to me around midnight, woke me up, and told me. Connaught's a reliable man and I'd swear by his honesty."

"So would I," Ridley said morosely. "What now?"

Adam sat and pulled his chair so they could whisper. "I've thought about this all night and that's why I came over before you left. We need to have the servants see

115

Captain Fortune get in that carriage."

Felicia gave him a disgusted look. "Adam, have you lost your mind? How can we get Uncle Gresham out of the ice house at this time of the morning without being seen? Besides, we can't send a *corpse* to London."

"We're not going to, Felicia. I'm going to get into that carriage, supported by you and Ridley, of course, so no one else can get close. I'm going to be covered up so no one can see my face."

"It'll never work, Adam."

"It beats the alternative, Felicia," he said shortly. "One thing I learned in the Army is that often people will believe something they only *think* is true. Even if no one sees my face, if you tell them I'm Gresham Fortune, and they believe it to be true, they'll tell Kingston they've seen Captain Fortune, and even though he was sick, he was alive and kicking."

"Worth a try," Ridley said. "Did anyone see you come in?"

Adam shook his head. "No, I was careful. I can get into the carriage, change my clothes, and get out on the road where those thick woods are right before Glenley Close. No one will ever know that Gresham Fortune isn't on his way to London."

The clock chimed six o'clock. "Let's do it," Ridley said. "I'd say the sooner the better. I've explained to Miss Fortune the arrangements I'm to make with MacDonald."

Adam stood. "I'll need to go upstairs and put on some of the captain's clothes. I'll pack mine into a bag and change in the carriage." He looked at Ridley. "You will, of course, help me down the stairs and into the carriage. At the bottom of the steps, Felicia," he turned to include her, "you take my other arm so no one can get close. Try to have as many servants at the front as you can and be sure to keep calling me Uncle Gresham."

"Don't worry about me. You'd better hurry."

Felicia opened the door and checked the hall, then motioned for Adam and Ridley to hurry up the stairs. She sat watching the hall and the door for what seemed like an eternity, then heard Ridley at the top of the steps. "Ready," he whispered.

Glancing around at the empty hall, Felicia went back into the breakfast parlor and gathered up all the metal teapots and utensils she could, added a teacup or two, and a teapot, putting it all on a tray. She scurried to the hall carrying the tray and heaved it with all her might onto the floor, being careful to leave a pathway to the door. The teapot bounced off the wall, onto a table, and then onto the floor with a most satisfying clatter, while the teacups broke and scattered. It was a crashing mess. As she had thought they would, every servant in the house came running, led by Mrs. Sprague, surprisingly fast on her feet.

"I was taking Uncle Gresham up some more tea," she explained as everyone looked in horror at the mess. At that point, Ridley and "Uncle Gresham" came down the stairs, Ridley supporting "Uncle Gresham" and telling him to take care with the steps. Adam was bundled up in Uncle Gresham's clothes, including a hat, muffler, greatcoat, and gloves. It was impossible to see his face, except for a bit of his cheekbones and eyes. Ridley had his arm around Adam on one side; Felicia ran up the stairs and got on the other side. "Uncle Gresham," she asked anxiously, "are you all right?"

There was a nod and an inarticulate sound, then an unexpected complication from Mrs. Sprague. "Since your tea is all over the floor, Captain Fortune, I expect you'll be wanting some fresh toast and tea," she said, hands on hips as she watched them descend.

"That won't be necessary," Ridley said, trying to get between Mrs. Sprague's line of sight and Adam. "I took the captain up some toast and coffee earlier." He glanced at Felicia. "Very thoughtful of you, Mrs. Sprague, but unnecessary."

"Yes, thank you, Mrs. Sprague. Now, Uncle Gresham," Felicia said to Adam, "don't fall." Felicia tightened her grip on Adam's arm. "Watch out, Uncle Gresham, we're on the last step. Now, lean on me." To her amazement, Adam leaned heavily on her shoulder, almost throwing her off balance. She could have sworn she heard him chuckle as they went three abreast out the front door.

"Uncle Gresham! Uncle Gresham, wait a minute. I haven't been able to see you." To Felicia's horror, Rosemary came running out of the house, arms open, ready to hug Uncle Gresham. Rosie had evidently heard the commotion in the hall and gotten up, dressed as hastily as Felicia had, and come running downstairs. "Uncle Gresham, I've missed you dreadfully," she cried, running up to them. Neither Ridley or Felicia gave an inch, although Adam turned to see who was behind him calling out for Uncle Gresham. Rosie got close enough to see, and stopped dead in her tracks, amazement on her face. "Felicia, what . . . ?"

Felicia let go of Adam and grabbed Rosemary, holding her so that Rosie's face was on her shoulder and she could whisper in her ear. "Don't say a word," she whispered fiercely, "just pretend that this is Uncle Gresham. Do it, Rosie, everything depends on it." Aloud she spoke for the benefit of the servants who were standing in the doorway, gawking at them. "Oh, my pet," she said, louder than necessary, "I should have warned you before. I know it's a shock, Rosie, but Uncle Gresham's been sick. It's all right for you to give him a hug, but gently."

Trooper that she was, Rosie didn't hesitate. She went up and gave Adam a hug and a kiss on the cheek. "I hope you feel better, Uncle Gresham," she said, really doing it up brown, "and don't you worry about a thing. Felicia and I will take care of everything."

"Exactly what I feared," Adam muttered before turning back to the coach.

Felicia stepped between them. "That's enough, Rosie," she muttered. "This isn't Drury Lane. Let's get him out of here. Ridley, come on!" she hissed in a whisper.

Ridley and Felicia moved him toward the carriage door. "Here we are, Captain Fortune, here's the carriage." Ridley's voice was too loud and he was beginning to sweat. Felicia hoped he didn't reach for his handkerchief right here.

The carriage wasn't quite ready, and the coachman ran over to open the door. Felicia and Ridley stood there impatiently, and Felicia glanced down the road. "Good God in heaven," she whispered urgently. "Get in that carriage and get out of here. There's Kingston coming down the road. He's out riding early."

Ridley wasted no time. He and Felicia shoved Adam into the carriage; Ridley grabbed the hamper and shoved it in beside him. Adam pulled on Felicia's arm and she leaned into the carriage. "Try to stall him if you can, Felicia," he said, his voice muffled by the greatcoat. "I dón't want him following the carriage. He might stop us and try to talk to Captain Fortune. Keep him here just as long as you can." He paused, looking at the doubt on her face. "You can do it, Felicia. Do what you have to do."

Ridley glanced out the window at the figure of Kingston drawing closer. "Let's leave, man," he yelled to the coachman. "I need to get the captain to London, and don't have time to waste."

The carriage rolled out not two minutes before Kingston rode up, the picture of a country squire on a prancing black horse. "Good morning, Miss Fortune," he said, watching the carriage go out of sight around a curve in the road. "Your company is certainly leaving early this morning."

Felicia laughed shakily, hoping he didn't notice that her knees were so weak she was about to fall down. "Oh, that wasn't company. My sister Rosemary came down from London." She gestured toward Rosemary, who was standing there looking puzzled. "We were just sending the carriage back." She walked over to stand beside Kingston and smiled up at him. "Won't you come in and have some tea since we're all up so early? Or have you already had breakfast? If not, we have plenty and we'd love for you to join us."

He hesitated, glanced toward the upstairs windows, and smiled back at her. "I'd like that very much, Miss Fortune." Felicia had to stifle a sigh of relief.

Rosie was still standing in the path, her eyes round with questions. "John," Felicia called to a servant, "take Lord Kingston's horse around back." She smiled at Kingston again and strolled over to Rosemary, still smiling. "Don't say a thing," she muttered through her smile. "I'll explain everything later, but whatever you do, don't talk about Uncle Gresham." She turned again to Kingston and gave him her broadest smile, nudging Rosie as she did. Rosie obligingly smiled.

They walked into the breakfast parlor, Felicia chattering all the while about the weather and whatever else she could think of. As they passed the hall mirror, she glanced into it, noting how very fine Kingston looked in his dark riding clothes and his snowy linen. She also noted with dismay how terrible she looked. Her old dress was wrinkled and her hair was again falling down from its combs and flying around her face. She was hardly, she thought as she went into the breakfast once again, the picture of a femme fatale who could lure Kingston into staying put for an hour or more until Adam was well away.

The formal introductions were made and Rosie sat down, still looking puzzled. Mrs. Sprague was in her element. She almost dashed to the kitchen when she found she was to prepare breakfast for Lord Kingston. Since Mrs. Sprague informed them it would be a few minutes until she could have everything in readiness, Felicia racked her brain for topics to discuss so she could fill the time with small talk.

Kingston, however, had his own topic ready and wasted no time in bringing it up. "How is Captain Fortune this morning?" he asked immediately.

"Oh, much improved," Felicia said hastily, kicking Rosie under the table. "His powers of recovery are quite remarkable."

"So I've heard," Kingston said, accepting a cup of

coffee. "I do need—"

"How was London?" Felicia interrupted, hoping Aunt Soledad would forgive her for this breach of manners. "As you know, Rosemary has just come down, but I haven't been there for ages, and Rosie hasn't had time to tell me all the gossip."

Kingston raised an eyebrow. "London's always the same. The people change from time to time, but the city stays the same."

Felicia laughed. "The niece of a builder knows better than that, Lord Kingston. The city changes almost as much as the latest fashions in society. Uncle Gresham usually keeps me posted on new and renovated buildings—it's something of a passion with him." She smiled at Kingston with what she hoped was a fetching smile, and one of her combs slipped out and fell into her lap. She snatched it up and stuck it back in her hair, hoping for the best. "I was rather," she continued as Kingston tried to stifle a smile, "asking about the people in society in London. I seldom see any of them, and since Mama and Papa are always off to other places, I seldom hear about them either."

"There was another scandal about Byron," Rosie offered. "Mama said I was too young to hear about it, but Masie Bolingstone told me all about it. Do you want to hear about that?"

"No!" Felicia looked at Rosie in despair as Kingston tried to keep from laughing. "Rosemary, that is hardly conversation for the table," she said sternly.

Kingston gave up and broke into laughter. "No, hardly proper conversation, but a devil of a good story," Kingston said, still laughing. His laughter was infectious and Felicia found herself giggling along with

Rosie. "However, I do agree that we probably shouldn't be discussing it here."

Felicia was groping for another subject when Rosie came to the rescue. "What are you doing here, Lord Kingston, when you could be in London? I should think you'd be involved in all the social doings in town."

"Social affairs pale after a while," he said, sipping his coffee. "I enjoy getting away to the country often, although this isn't a pleasure trip. I've come to see your Uncle Gresham." He put his cup down and looked at Felicia. "That reminds me, Miss Fortune . . ."

The door leading to the kitchen opened and a servant came in with breakfast. Felicia was giddy with relief, and almost slumped in her chair. Every bone in her body felt like jelly, and if she hadn't been sitting down, she was quite sure she would be puddled on the floor. "Breakfast, at last!" Rosie said, "I'm simply _ravished!_"

Felicia put both hands over her face while Kingston shook with suppressed laughter. Finally he could stand it no longer and laughed aloud. Felicia looked at him, giggled once, then joined him in laughing as Rosemary looked in puzzlement from one to the other.

"I think you mean 'famished,' Rosie," Felicia said when she finally stopped laughing. "Believe me, there's a distinct difference."

"Oh, well," Rosie said, not embarrassed at all, "no matter. Tell me, Lord Kingston, I know the food at Almack's is atrocious, but what do you think of the ham and ices at Vauxhall?" Rosie filled her plate with eggs, bacon, and muffins. It was rather more than a well-bred young lady should eat, especially in front of a gentleman. "Mama allowed me to go there not long ago as a treat when my arm healed, and I loved the ices. They were delicious."

"My chef at the Priory is excellent with ices," Kingston said, eating a hearty breakfast himself. "Why don't the two of you come over and I'll have him prepare an assortment?"

"Oh no, that would be too much trouble," Felicia said hastily, thinking of the ice house.

Kingston shook his head. "Not at all, Miss Fortune. We have a large ice house and keep it well filled with ice. Actually, we always have more than we need because it keeps so well. I'll send the servants to get ice, and tell my chef to prepare some for us. He makes a superb currant ice."

"Oh, Felicia, doesn't that sound wonderful?" Rosie asked. "I should like that very much."

Kingston looked questioningly at Felicia, who knew when she was defeated. "That would be most kind of you to have us over." Her face felt rigid—all she could think of was someone going into the ice house and discovering a frozen Uncle Gresham. She would have to find Adam as soon as possible. Surely he would know what to do.

"Miss Fortune? Do you think so, Miss Fortune?" She heard Kingston ask her the question and had no idea what it was. "Certainly," she answered, wondering what it was she thought.

Rosie looked at her in surprise. "I didn't know you thought so, Felicia. I was expecting an argument."

"Think what?" She caught herself and felt herself blush. "I'm sorry, I was thinking of something else."

"Currant ice, perhaps?" Rosemary asked, "Or blackberry? Is that what was on your mind, Felicia?"

"Yes, I was thinking about ice." She turned to Kingston and groped for a topic. There didn't seem to be anything to talk about that didn't somehow lead back to Uncle Gresham or the ice house.

"How is your nephew?" she asked in desperation, signaling for the servant to refill Kingston's coffee cup. "Has he settled in at the Priory?"

Kingston smiled. "Simon never settles in anywhere—he simply commandeers a place, which is what he's done. I don't have to watch him very much, however, since his tutor came with him." He smiled. "Simon's not really bad. He's just a little boy who likes to explore and get into everything, and my sister doesn't understand that. She thinks he should have the manners and deportment of an adult."

"Many people think that of younger individuals," Rosemary said archly, giving Felicia a glance. "Some people go so far as to think younger individuals are feather-brained."

"Many younger individuals *are* feather-brained," Felicia answered back, returning her glance. Kingston gave each of them an amused glance. "You two sound remarkably like my sister and me," he said with a chuckle. "I think families are much alike."

They were kept from pursuing this observation by the entrance of Adam Temple. He was limping heavily and had a bad scratch on his cheek. He stood in the doorway as the servant announced him. "I'm sorry to bother you, Miss Fortune, but I needed to pick up my instructions from Captain Fortune. He told me he would leave them on the study table."

Aunt Soledad came bustling up behind Adam. "The noise in this house this morning—I simply couldn't

125

sleep." She stepped up and joined Adam in the doorway. "Major Temple, I certainly didn't mean that you weren't welcome or—" She caught sight of Kingston and stammered a welcome. "How nice to see you this morning! Oh, dear! Major Temple, do join us for breakfast."

"I'm sorry, but I need to get on to the Abbott's House and get the men to work now that Captain Fortune's gone."

Aunt Soledad paled visibly and stared from Adam to Lord Kingston. "You've told him that Gresham's gone?" she asked faintly.

Felicia jumped up. "No, we didn't mention that Uncle Gresham had gone to London this morning, did we?" She turned brightly to Kingston and smiled at him. Aunt Soledad was swaying in the doorway. "Adam," Felicia said, rolling her eyes toward Aunt Soledad, "I'm sure you have a few moments. Why don't you help Aunt Soledad to her chair, and I'll send for fresh coffee." She rang before he could protest.

Adam helped Aunt Soledad sit down and sat himself, right across the table from Kingston, who was regarding him with a long, cool gaze. "You didn't mention, Miss Fortune," Kingston said, his eyes never leaving Adam, "that your uncle had gone to London. I had hoped to talk to him today."

"My goodness, Lord Kingston, I really didn't think of it. Yes, Uncle Gresham went back to London with the carriage. He needed to talk to someone in London—plasterers, did he say, Major Temple?" Felicia stopped, realizing she was talking too fast.

"I believe that's right," Adam said, taking a cup of coffee.

"He's gone to London?" Aunt Soledad croaked, sloshing coffee all over her plate as she tried to drink it. Felicia hoped Kingston didn't notice that her hands were shaking. "How did you manage *that?*"

Felicia spoke quickly. "He was feeling much better. You know how strong Uncle Gresham really is." Felicia smiled at Kingston. "He felt so much better that he thought he and Ridley could make the trip. I believe he's going to consult with his doctor while he's there."

"That should be helpful," Adam said, finishing his coffee. "Thank you for the coffee, Miss Fortune, but I really need to get my instructions and go on. The men will be ready to begin." He got up, nodding to Kingston.

Felicia was torn. She didn't feel she could leave Aunt Soledad and Rosemary to the mercies of someone like Kingston, who could ask questions they wouldn't even know they were answering, yet she needed to talk to Adam and discover just why he was so insistent on talking to her. Still, after Adam had mentioned Uncle Gresham's instructions, there was really no choice. She got up and went to the door with Adam. Glancing over her shoulder as she went out, she noted that Kingston was sitting there in his black coat and snowy cravat discussing the weather yet another time, but now with Aunt Soledad. Felicia closed her eyes in despair: Kingston reminded her of a bird of prey, ready to pounce.

Chapter 9

Felicia closed the breakfast room door behind her and turned to speak to Adam. To her horror, he was a ghostly white and had sagged against the wall. With an effort he stood upright and walked beside her to the study, his lips firmly compressed and his injured leg dragging badly. "What . . . ?" Felicia began, but realized the hall was no place for talking. She waited until they were in the study and had shut the door firmly behind them. Adam sat down in a chair and stretched out his bad leg. He couldn't suppress a groan.

"Adam, what happened?" She ran to him, and sat down across from him. "What did you do to your leg and how did your face get such a scratch?"

He took a deep breath and tried a shaky smile. "Everything happened at once. I looked out the carriage window and saw Kingston get off his horse. I presumed all was clear, and decided it would look good if I could come strolling into the Misery and allay any suspicion Kingston might have. Ridley and I talked about it, and neither of us wanted to have the coachman stop because then we would have to let him in on our secret."

"That's ridiculous. He'll know when they get to London and there's no one in the carriage except Ridley."

"Ridley's going to provide for that one. He's going to send the coachman on a short errand as soon as they arrive, then say that he and Captain Fortune have already installed themselves in rooms. It should work. Everyone will think Captain Fortune's at the inn."

Felicia frowned. "Then if the coachman didn't stop, how did you get out of the carriage? Surely you didn't . . . ?"

He grinned wickedly. "Yes, I did. I changed into my clothes and jumped out. I didn't want to wait too long, because I knew I'd have to walk back to the Misery while Kingston was still here." He leaned forward and massaged his leg. "The only thing I didn't count on was the coachman deciding to hurry in an attempt to get Ridley and Captain Fortune to London. He sprung the horses just before I opened the door and began to jump. I jumped out right over a bank and rolled down into a thicket."

Felicia reached over and put her hand on his. "Thank you, Adam. I want you to know that I appreciate what you're doing for Uncle Gresham, for me. This isn't really your problem, yet you've involved yourself without a question." She looked into his eyes and he smiled at her. Felicia felt dizzy as Adam leaned closer to her. "Felicia," he murmured.

There was a knock at the door. Felicia jumped up and looked around. "Who could that be?"

"Probably Kingston," Adam said. "Hand me that

bunch of papers there—no matter what they are."

"Come in," Felicia said, shoving the papers into Adam's hands and sitting down behind the desk, well away from Adam.

It was Kingston. He smiled as he came in, and Felicia again had the strange sensation that he was a bird of prey, ready to swoop down on her. He must know how guilty she was. Worse, she felt she probably *looked* guilty.

However, instead of swooping, Kingston sat down in the chair near Adam and smiled at the two of them. "I'm sorry to interrupt you, but since you were here, Major, I thought I might walk over to the Abbott's House with you and see what you plan to do today. I'm quite distressed that I didn't have the opportunity to talk to Captain Fortune."

Kingston glanced at Felicia as he spoke and she felt forced to say something. "It was a spur-of-the-moment thing, Lord Kingston. Uncle Gresham didn't really plan to go to London today. However, since we needed to send the carriage back, it seemed a good idea for him to go now since he did have to go to London for a few days anyway."

"Oh, he's leaving the carriage? Then how is he returning?"

Felicia gulped. "Oh, he's bringing the carriage back. My cousin had to have it right away—for his . . . wedding. Yes, it was truly urgent. That's why Uncle Gresham couldn't wait." Felicia felt she needed Ridley's handkerchief.

Adam drew Kingston's attention. "I'd be delighted for you to come with me this morning. I'd planned to walk over, but it may take some time. My leg is bothering me this morning."

Kingston glanced down at his outstretched leg, the brace in his boot clearly visible. "A war wound?"

Adam nodded and offered no explanation. "Would you like to walk with me, or had you rather ride over later?" He stood and folded the papers Felicia had given him, putting them in his pocket.

"I'll just walk with you. I've already had my ride this morning." Kingston turned to Felicia. "Thank you for your hospitality, Miss Fortune, and please give my farewells to your aunt and sister. Don't forget that I'm expecting you this evening."

"This evening?"

"Yes, I thought we had agreed that you and your sister were coming over to the Priory this evening."

Felicia remembered, and worse, remembered that she hadn't told Adam about Kingston sending someone up to the ice house. "Oh yes, for the ices." He *had* to know, so she decided to be brazen. "Major Temple, Rosemary happened to mention that she loved ices, so Lord Kingston has invited us over for some."

Kingston lifted an eyebrow. "Would you like to join us, Temple? My chef is particularly adept at making them."

Before Adam could answer, Felicia started again. "Yes, he sends someone right up to his very own ice house to get the ice. He said he was sending someone up there today." She tried to catch Adam's eye, but he seemed disinterested.

"I appreciate the offer, but I think I'll have to decline," Adam said, opening the door. "I'll probably be working late at the Abbott's House, then I want to talk to Connaught about tomorrow's work.

Thank you anyway."

"Maybe some other time," Kingston said as they went out into the hall. Felicia could see that each step was costing Adam dearly, but she didn't know what to do to make it easier for him. Once outside, the groom brought Kingston's black around for him to lead, and the two men set off walking—Kingston moving athletically and gracefully, Adam leaning slightly to one side as he tried to compensate for his dragging foot.

Felicia watched them until they were out of sight and then went back inside. "I don't think I'm going to live through this," she said to herself as she closed the door behind her and leaned against it wearily.

"I'd say you aren't," Rosemary said peevishly, coming down the hall toward her. "I'm going to kill you myself if you don't tell me what's going on. Where's Uncle Gresham?"

"Ssshhh." Felicia looked around, but saw no one except Aunt Soledad, still sitting at the breakfast table in a state of shock, her hands over her eyes. "Rosie, get Aunt Soledad and we'll talk, but we can't say anything here. Come to the study."

Inside the study, Felicia checked the windows and doors, going so far as to open the door again to make sure no one was listening. Then she turned to Rosemary and put her arms around her sister. There was no easy way. "Rosie, we both know Uncle Gresham was sick for a long time . . ." she began, but Rosie pulled away so she could look at Felicia's eyes. "*Was?* Felicia, he's dead, isn't he?" she said, her voice breaking as she tried not to cry.

Felicia nodded. "There's something else," she said cautiously, wondering just how to tell Rosie how and why Uncle Gresham was in the ice house, safely, she hoped, under the ice and sawdust.

"I thought there was something more. Things around here this morning weren't exactly what I would call normal, Felicia. Lord Kingston was more than a little curious, and I really didn't know what to say." She sat down, still trying not to cry. "Uncle Gresham," she said in a choked voice, and put her hands over her face. "Felicia, I'm—we're—going to miss him so much." She gave up and started to cry.

"I know, Rosie, I know." Felicia leaned down and held her, patting her shoulder and making soothing noises.

Finally, the tears were finished, and Rosie dried her eyes. "Did he know? Was he in pain? At the end, I mean."

"Yes, he knew, and no, he wasn't in too much pain. Ridley was there, giving him laudanum drops. Uncle Gresham did make one request, though, Rosemary, and you must swear not to tell anyone about it."

Rosemary was miffed. "Of course I won't tell. Do you think I would commit such a fox paw?"

"That's a *faux pas*, and I don't think a social error is in the same class as what would happen if this got out." She looked straight at Rosie. "Everything depends on keeping this a secret."

"Don't be so dramatic, Felicia," Aunt Soledad said. "Lord Kingston must never know. It doesn't matter about anyone else."

"Someone else could tell Kingston," Felicia pointed out. "Kingston was questioning Dr. Quigley last night, so I'm quite sure it's just a matter of time until he'll get around to asking everyone near." She shook her head.

"No, it's got to be known to as few as possible. I know Adam told the men, but that was necessary."

Rosemary looked up unexpectedly and managed a watery smile. "It doesn't appear that I'm ever to know anything, Felicia, if you keep agonizing so. What is it?"

As carefully as possible, Felicia told her, emphasizing that this was Uncle Gresham's wish and that they had all promised him to do what he asked of them. Felicia pointed out that, while Adam knew and was doing everything he could, Cavendish did not know. "So," she concluded, "you can see why secrecy is important. Adam tells me that what we're doing is probably a criminal offense, but even if we didn't go to jail, Kingston would dismiss the lot of us."

"And engage someone else to finish Uncle Gresham's work. That person would get all the recognition that should go to Uncle Gresham," Rosemary said slowly.

"Exactly." Felicia leaned back in a chair and closed her eyes. "We must be on guard every moment, Rosie, and even at that, things will happen that we can't control."

Rosie looked at her ruefully. "Like me saying I loved ices and practically inviting us over for some. I could kick myself. Do you suppose they'll find Uncle Gresham when they go up there?"

"I hope not." Early as it was, Felicia's voice was weary. "Adam said he and Connaught went back up there and did a thorough job of hiding Uncle Gresham."

There was silence in the room, broken only by the sound of the clock ticking. Finally, Aunt Soledad spoke. "How much longer, Felicia? I'm not sure I was cut out for the role of a conspirator."

"Certainly you are," Felicia said briskly, standing. "It'll be weeks yet. The only thing I'm really worried about is the performance Mr. What?—the Great Scot—will be giving. That may be our weak link. What if someone comes to see Uncle Gresham?"

"We'll simply have to intercept everything and everyone," Rosie said. She smiled at Felicia. "Do you know, Felicia, I think that if Uncle Gresham were here, he'd thoroughly enjoy this."

Felicia shook her head. "Well, he isn't, and I can't say that I'm enjoying it very much, but now it's up to us. We must do as Adam says and keep Kingston occupied as much as possible. That's going to be very difficult."

"Why so?" Aunt Soledad frowned.

"Aunt Soledad," Felicia explained patiently, "Kingston is quite accustomed to the society and wit of the ton. I'm quite sure he'll find our company more than a little insipid."

Rosie looked at her shrewdly. "I don't think that for a moment, Felicia. I saw the way he looked at you this morning. Perhaps Lord Kingston is one of those who is rather tired of the jaded life of London society. I thought he was quite taken with you. You are quite pretty, you know."

"Blondes are in fashion, Rosie, not brunettes. Also may I point out that you are probably the only person in the world who thinks I'm pretty, and you don't count because you're my sister."

"Bosh," Aunt Soledad snorted. "You are pretty or could be if you'd ever get your nose away from Gresham's drawings and all those lists he forever had you making. Look at yourself: that dowdy gown, your hair slapped up in combs. I doubt that you even

135

brushed it this morning."

Felicia put her hand to her hair where her comb was slipping again. "I didn't," she sighed. "I really didn't have time."

Rosie and Aunt Soledad looked at each other. "We don't really have time to send for a proper dresser or maid," Rosie said to Aunt Soledad, "so I suppose it's up to us. Felicia, you're going to look stunning this evening."

"You? Rosie, you? Whatever do you know about hair and fashion? I thought your forte was chasing down paths after the dogs and falling into mill ponds."

Rosie stood up, and was eye to eye with Felicia. "You would mention that, Felicia. Well, I want you to know that I've changed. While I was in London with Mama, the only thing I could do to pass the time was sit around and look at her pattern books or go shopping. She usually sent Margaret to accompany me—you remember Margaret, Mama's dresser. While I still don't care for London very much, Felicia, I have decided it has some things to offer. I also decided it was time for me to act my age and behave as becomes a young lady, a fact you don't seem to have noticed yet."

"I noticed, Rosie," Felicia said with a grin, "especially when you arrived completely unchaperoned. Tell me, did this sudden about-face have anything to do with Cavendish Temple?"

To Felicia's surprise, Rosie blushed furiously. "Cavendish and I are simply friends," she said when she was able to speak. "After all, he *did* save my life when I fell in the mill pond and broke my arm. I certainly owe him a debt of gratitude."

"Of course," Felicia noted dryly, "don't we all." She

looked at Rosie and giggled. "Do you know what I really thought last night? I thought your acting like such a grand lady was a part of your disguise when you were coming down from London. I thought you were playing the young lady of fashion to impress inn-keepers on the way."

"I'm hurt, Felicia," Rosie said in a injured tone. "After all I went through learning how to look haughty. I even learned to use curl papers."

Felicia broke out laughing. "I'm sure the two are connected."

"What?" Rosemary looked offended.

"Looking haughty and curl papers." Felicia was still laughing.

Rosie attempted to look haughty. "I'll have you know that curl papers are the very devil to use properly. They keep falling out." She glanced over at Aunt Soledad. "Are you ready to go upstairs and look at Felicia's wardrobe while I get the scissors after her hair? Lord Kingston isn't going to know her when she walks through the door."

"Absolutely not," Felicia said firmly. "I don't have time to waste on such frivolities. I need to go see Adam and discover what Kingston said to him. I also simply *must . . ."* She stopped as Rosemary took one arm, Aunt Soledad the other, and they propelled her toward the door, out of the study, and up the stairs. "Adam may have something important to tell me," she protested.

"Felicia, this is important." Rosie paused on the steps and lowered her voice to a whisper. "Don't you want to impress Lord Kingston? Aren't you supposed to keep him occupied?"

"It'll never happen," Felicia said, resigned, "but just to satisfy you, I submit. If I don't, I'm sure I'll never hear the end of it."

"Never," Rosie said with a giggle.

By midafternoon, Felicia was in such a state that she simply had to find out how Adam had gotten along with Kingston. Rosie had cut her hair all around the front of her face, washed it, and put it up in curl papers, so she couldn't go out until it dried. Aunt Soledad was insistent that she stand still while her dress was altered and pinned on her. She had finally sent Adam a note but, afraid it would be intercepted or read by someone else, she wrote only that she had forgotten to tell him something Uncle Gresham had wanted him to do and asked him to stop by at his earliest opportunity. To her amazement, while she was still wandering around in her curl papers, with pins and threads hanging from her dress, he and Cavendish came knocking on the door.

"This is all your fault," she said to Rosie as Rosie prevented her from tearing the curl papers from her hair. "I can't go talk to him while I look like this."

"Why not?" Rosie refastened a paper. "After all, you're not trying to impress him at all, and I'm sure he's seen women in curl papers before."

"Rosie, what are you saying!" Felicia was scandalized. "I'm sure Major Temple has never . . . has . . ." She stopped. She realized she really didn't know very much about Adam Temple. Perhaps he had a mistress somewhere. Didn't most men in the Army? She felt herself blush.

"The man has sisters," Rosemary said. "After all, Cavendish is his *nephew.* I would imagine both of them have seen ladies getting ready for an evening. Some men even use curl papers." She dropped her voice to a whisper. "I heard from a reliable source that even Byron puts his hair up in curl papers every night."

"I," Felicia pointed out, trying to see what she would look like with a shawl over her head, "am not Lord Byron. Besides, I'm quite sure Byron would never appear like this in front of his wife, much less someone who's come to call." She tossed the shawl aside. "Whatever will I do?"

"Put on a bonnet?"

Felicia shook her head. "I can't go downstairs wearing a bonnet. That would look ridiculous. The curl papers must go. Take them out."

Rosie stood firm. "Your hair's all wet. If I take them out, your hair will be straight and fall right into your eyes. How are you going to impress Kingston if you have to look through a hank of hair dangling down all over your face?"

"How do I impress Major Temple with papers sticking up all over my head?" Felicia took one last, desperate glance in the mirror. "All right, but you come down with me and help me explain that this is all your fault." She grimaced. "I can't believe I'm meeting a guest while I have my hair all done up in papers. Come on."

Adam glanced up at her in surprise as she came in the room. "Don't say a word," she warned him. "Rosie seems to think that I need to look like a London pattern card tonight when we go to the Priory. I've been cut, pushed, and pummeled all day to that end."

"She's going to impress Kingston," Rosemary said confidently.

Adam grinned. "I would have to say that this sight

139

has made quite an impression on me."

Felicia glared at him. "I warned you, Adam."

He laughed. "All right. It isn't that I've never seen women looking like this before." Felicia glanced at him. Did he, she wondered again, have a mistress?

Aunt Soledad wandered in just as Rosie asked Cavendish if he would like to stroll in the garden with her. Aunt Soledad looked quickly from Adam and Felicia to Rosie and Cavendish. Torn, but quickly deciding which needed chaperonage worse, she followed Rosie and Cavendish out the door, giving Felicia a stern warning glance over her shoulder as she left.

"I do believe," Adam said idly as he watched them leave, "that the two of you are going to send your poor aunt into nervous fits. Is your sister going to stay awhile?"

Felicia looked at him sharply. "Why do you ask? Are you worried about Cavendish?"

Adam grinned at her. "Of course not. I merely wondered because every person here manages to complicate this . . . this bumblebath we're in a little more. Actually," he said, reflecting, "I think Rosemary might be quite good for Cavendish. He's really quite shy around females."

"My sister," Felicia snapped, "is not in the business of helping young men overcome shyness. You make her sound like . . . like . . . like something other than a well-bred young lady."

"I'm sorry, I didn't mean it that way." He grinned at her again. "You know, it's devilish hard to look at you seriously when you have all those papers bobbing around every time you move your head."

"And I suppose every male looks perfect all the

time." Felicia snapped. "I'm sorry. I'm as embarrassed as you are about this."

"Oh, I assure you that I'm not embarrassed at all. It makes you—how shall I say it—less perfect."

"Such compliments," she said dryly. "I may lose my head completely."

Adam laughed aloud, a full, rich laugh that was infectious. Felicia found herself laughing along with him. "Such a set-down," he finally said. "I admit I've never been adroit with the perfect *bon mot*. Still, I hope you know what I meant and didn't take offense."

"No, but I would hope we could forget my appearance and get to the matter at hand."

"Fine." Adam moved and readjusted his leg. Felicia felt a touch of remorse as an expression of pain and fatigue crossed his face. "What is the matter at hand?"

"Do you want some tea?" She reached for the bell, but Adam shook his head. "I didn't mean for you to rush right over here when I wrote you. I merely wanted to find out how your morning went with Kingston."

"All right. I don't think he suspects anything at all." He looked at her and smiled. "I thought perhaps you were upset at the thought of someone going into the ice house. That's why I came over so soon—I wanted to reassure you that I don't think there's much of a possibility that your uncle will be found."

"But there *is* a possibility?"

"There's always a possibility." He leaned toward her and put his hands on his knees. "But I don't think it's a probability. With this warm weather, other than the ice house, I don't think we have another choice except to bury him somewhere, and I know you don't want to do that."

"No, I want to bury him at home." Felicia closed her eyes briefly. "Adam, I'll do what I can to keep Kingston occupied, but I warn you that I'm certainly no accomplished flirt, so I don't expect too much from that quarter. Is there a possibility of speeding up the work on the Abbott's House?"

"No. That is, we could hurry everything, but it wouldn't be a job Captain Fortune would be proud of. I'm trying to do everything as he would have done it."

"Thank you," she said softly, looking at him. "Nothing you could do would please me more." She reached for the bell and rang. "Now, I'm going to ply you with tea and cakes and make you sit right here for at least an hour, Adam Temple. If I don't, I think you may fall over from fatigue."

"How did you know?" He leaned back and closed his eyes. "I thought I was doing a good job of hiding that."

"Don't forget," she said with a laugh, "I've been watching Uncle Gresham for years, and by now, I'm quite adept at spotting fatigue. Why don't you rest until tea gets here?"

To her surprise, he did. He kept his eyes closed, and in a few moments, he was asleep. Felicia motioned to the servant who brought the tea tray to be quiet, and she let Adam sleep for the better part of an hour until Rosie, Cavendish, and Aunt Soledad returned. At that point, they decided cold tea was not to be endured and sent for fresh tea, lemonade, and a cold collation. Felicia put her hand to her hair, and discovered that her curls were finally dry, but by now, what did it matter?

After she was dressed that evening, Felicia had to admit that Aunt Soledad and Rosemary had worked

142

wonders with her. She had a touch of rouge that heightened her dark good looks, her hair framed her face in front in soft curls and was caught up in the back in ringlets, and her dress was unbelievably becoming and fit her figure perfectly. Kingston had sent a carriage for them, and when Felicia got out of the carriage and swept into the front door, he looked at her in surprise, his eyebrows lifting. He held her hand for a moment and kissed it lightly, eliciting a noise from Aunt Soledad which only Rosie and Felicia interpreted as another "oh dear."

"You're looking quite charming, Miss Fortune," Kingston said. Felicia had to own that he was, as well, looking quite elegant. He was dressed in a very dark blue coat, his cravat was snowy, and his waistcoat was a light blue, embroidered with flowers of dark blue. It suited him very well, and the coat molded to his shoulders perfectly. It was easy to see why he had a reputation for breaking hearts in London—and elsewhere.

The evening was an unqualified success. The only time anything unexpected happened was when a small boy ran across the floor and grabbed Kingston by the knees. "Don't want to go to bed!" he wailed. He was followed by a harried-looking young man who stopped abruptly at the door. "Oh, I do apologize, Lord Kingston. He got away from me and I couldn't catch him."

"Quite all right, Williams," Kingston said, picking up the little boy and tossing him up in the air, then catching him. "In case you haven't guessed," he said with a smile at Rosie and Felicia, "this is my nephew, Simon, and his tutor, Solon Williams." He handed the

143

boy to the tutor. "To bed, you scamp."

"Do I have to?" Simon stared hard at Kingston, and Felicia was struck at how much alike the two of them looked.

Before Kingston could reply, Rosie stepped over to Simon. "Would you go to bed if I tell you a story? That's what Felicia always did for me. I know some good stories."

"You don't have to do that, Miss Fortune," Kingston said. "I'm sure Williams will put him right to bed."

"We're going right up," Solon Williams said, looking with interest at Rosie.

Rosie took no notice of his admiring glance. She was looking at Simon. "Simon, the very next time I'm here, I promise I'll tell you a story. My sister taught me some really good stories."

"Ghost stories?" he asked with interest.

Rosie nodded. "Really scary ones. Maybe you could come visit us and we'll tell stories. We'll even get Felicia to tell one to you. She knows the scariest ghost stories ever."

Simon looked at Felicia with respect and Felicia smiled back at him. "I had no idea you had so many talents, Miss Fortune," Kingston said as Williams carried Simon out of the room. "A good teller of ghost stories is a valuable addition to any gathering."

"I'm afraid Rosemary has exaggerated my talents," Felicia said, resting her spoon in her blackberry ice. "However, I do hope you know that we would welcome you and Simon at any time you want to stop by the Misery."

"Thank you for that invitation." He looked at her, a strange, speculative look that Felicia couldn't interpret. "The two of us may develop a fondness for ghost stories to occupy our time."

She smiled at him and spooned up the last of her blackberry ice to keep from telling him that she fervently hoped something—ghost stories or *anything*—would keep him occupied for a long, long time.

Chapter 10

The next weeks went by rapidly for Felicia. Lord Kingston either came by every day or had something planned for her, Aunt Soledad, and Rosemary. Sometimes it was a carriage ride, sometimes a picnic, sometimes an outing with Simon in tow, sometimes a visit to some ruins or scenic spot, or sometimes just a trip to the Priory for dinner. He was unfailingly charming, smiling at just the right time, and always ready with the perfect remark.

During this time, Felicia and Adam had "Uncle Gresham" return to the Misery for a night. He was there only long enough for the servants to see him and know he was on the premises. He found it necessary to return to London the next morning. Felicia was full of Uncle Gresham's regrets at missing Lord Kingston yet again.

As for Kingston, Aunt Soledad thought the man was kindness and goodness personified and Felicia had to keep reminding her that Kingston might have an ulterior motive in being kind to them. Worse, this might be only an act on Kingston's part—he might suspect what they were up to and be trying to lull them into revealing something. He was, as Felicia pointed out, constantly asking about Uncle Gresham. "Only natural that he should," Aunt Soledad always replied.

Since Felicia couldn't talk to Aunt Soledad about Kingston, she tried Rosemary. Rosie listened politely to Felicia's fears, allowed as how Felicia was probably imagining things, and thought Kingston was quite nice. Rosie preferred to discuss Cavendish Temple. *That* was blossoming into what Adam had called a full-blown case of calf love. Felicia could only hope that Rosie wouldn't be hurt. Young as he was, Cavendish already had the looks to be a ladies' man. The only thing that kept Felicia from being frantic about that situation was that Adam kept a tight rein on Cavendish, making sure the boy was with him as much as possible.

There was that, and then there was also worrying herself sick about what might have happened to Ridley in London since no one had heard anything at all from him since he had left.

There was that, and then there was also worrying herself sick about her own feelings for Kingston.

Felicia looked at herself in the mirror as she thought about Kingston once again. "Don't be foolish," she said to her reflection. "Lord Kingston could have any woman in London he wants. There's no reason at all that he should pay attention to a country miss who doesn't even know how to flirt and play the games of the marriage mart. He doesn't want you. He couldn't want you. The only reasons he's even paying any attention to you is because there's no one else here in

the country and he's curious about Uncle Gresham."
Her reflection stared back at her with no answer.
Felicia turned away and bit her lip as she worried. Was
this the beginnings of falling in love? She had never
been in love before and wondered if what she felt for
Kingston was love. She liked being with him and he
made her laugh and forget her problems. She had
to remind herself constantly of her own advice to
Aunt Soledad and remember to watch what she did
and said.

During those weeks, she saw Adam very few times.
He sent Connaught over with several bills and requests
and she had duly taken care of them. He came to see her
to arrange the visit by "Uncle Gresham," and he
stopped by to tell her she was doing an excellent job of
keeping Kingston occupied. He also saw her out
walking once or twice and paused for a few minutes,
telling her the work was progressing wonderfully well.
Felicia thought he looked tired and he'd lost some
weight. As he left each time, she noticed he seemed to
be in some pain from his leg, but he said nothing about
it, and glossed over Felicia's questions about his health.
His main concern, aside from the progress of the
Abbott's House, was Lord Kingston.

Kingston. There was that name again. "You're a
fool, a silly, romantic fool," she said to herself with a
sigh. It was impossible—all she would get out of falling
in love with someone like Kingston was heartbreak. He
wouldn't want a nobody like Felicia Fortune. She
needed to stay away from him, but she couldn't—it was
up to her to keep him away from Adam and the
Abbott's House. Tonight, he had invited her and Rosie
to supper at the Priory and she had to go. Even if she

knew she shouldn't see him again, he simply had to be kept from going to London and inquiring about Gresham Fortune. Wearily, Felicia thought about the dozens of questions Kingston had slipped into conversations, questions about Uncle Gresham's health, questions about Uncle Gresham's whereabouts, questions about Uncle Gresham's time of return. The problem was that, as Captain Fortune's employer, his questions were valid ones.

The one question Felicia wanted answered right now was where was Ridley? Adam had said Ridley was going to look for MacDonald down by the docks. That was a rough section and maybe something had happened to Ridley. He might even be dead, and what would happen then? Felicia bit her bottom lip. Being a conspirator was making her a complete wreck and only one thing would help: she needed to talk to Adam again. He'd know what to do.

Aunt Soledad had outdone herself in remodeling another of Felicia's gowns, a pink and white striped muslin, trimming it with cherry ribbon and some white lace. It became her wonderfully, and Rosie put some matching ribbons and two small white feathers in her dark hair. "Very fetching," Rosie said, standing back to admire her handiwork. "Even better than Margaret does with Mama. You're well on the way to becoming a beauty, Felicia."

"Quit trying to flatter me, Rosemary Fortune. It won't work." She sat Rosie down and dressed her hair in return.

"Quit frowning, Felicia, you'll get wrinkles."

"I can't help it. I just *know* something's going to go wrong," Felicia groaned.

"It probably will," Rosemary said almost cheerfully, "but I'm sure we'll manage. First of all, you've got to stop worrying about Ridley," Rosie said, shaking her head as Felicia pulled a strand of hair. "Cavendish says Ridley's an old Army man, and they can handle any situation."

Felicia stopped. "Cavendish! Rosie, you didn't tell him! I distinctly told you not to say a single word."

"Cavendish won't tell, Felicia. I thought he had a right to know. After all, his uncle is involved, and besides, Cavendish is frightfully intelligent. He might be able to help us." She looked at Felicia defiantly. "You're always off with Kingston somewhere and I have to have *someone* to talk to."

Felicia came around and stood in front of her. "Rosie, you haven't been meeting Cavendish somewhere, have you? Your reputation will be in shreds. Tell me you haven't. Aunt Soledad would die. Mama and Papa would die. *I* would die."

"How could you, Felicia? Don't you trust me?"

"Answer my question, Rosie."

"Questions. You asked more than one." Rosie looked hurt. "How could I meet Cavendish anywhere? Adam keeps him almost on leading strings. Besides, I have better conduct than that, Felicia. I've only been able to talk to Cavendish two or three times: twice he and Major Temple came by here while you were gone but we didn't have much of an opportunity to talk." Rosie grimaced. "Major Temple is as bad as Aunt Soledad."

"And the other time?"

"Oh, that." Rosie looked at her and smiled. "The other day when you went with Kingston to the village to buy ribbons, Aunt Soledad and I took a short walk, wound up over at the Abbott's House to see how it was going, and just happened to meet Major Temple and Cavendish there."

"'Just *happened.*' Poor Aunt Soledad," Felicia murmured. "She's putty in your hands."

Rosie ignored her. "As I said, it just happened. Major Temple showed Aunt Soledad around, and Cavendish and I had a few minutes to talk. He suspected something havey-cavey was going on and so I told him all about it. I thought Major Temple might have told him, but he hadn't. If I were Major Temple, I would have."

"And did."

"He won't tell, really he won't. Cavendish isn't that sort, and he might be able to help." Rosie jumped up. "Quit frowning, Felicia, we've got a whole evening in front of us, and you look wonderful." She paused and looked at Felicia. "The other day, you were talking a great deal about Kingston and I wasn't paying much attention. I'm sorry." She bit her lower lip, much as Felicia did when she was thinking about something. "Felicia, you and Lord Kingston . . ." She stopped, then smiled. "It's getting late, so perhaps we can talk about this later. Right now, I'm glad I'm going along to the Priory. I promised Simon you'd tell him another ghost story."

"Oh, *I* would?" Felicia said with a laugh.

Rosemary looked prim. "Yes. I've noticed your attention to Simon impresses Kingston greatly. That's why I've been throwing Simon your way as much as possible."

"That Simon's a little scamp and I enjoy him, but I

151

wondered why you were always sending him to climb all over me. I thought it was simply because you wished to be in the company of Mr. Williams."

"Felicia!" Rosemary was scandalized. Felicia laughed as she left her and went to get their shawls.

Kingston had sent his carriage for them, and when they arrived at the Priory, they were surprised to find that they weren't the only supper guests. Two other couples were there: Sir Oliver Pangburn and his wife, Mary, neither of whom Felicia had ever seen; and Colonel Maurice Dedlock and his wife, Lottie, close friends of Rosie and Felicia's parents. Worse, the Dedlocks were on very good terms with Uncle Gresham.

"Kingston here tells me that Gresham's in London," Colonel Dedlock boomed as soon as the introductions were all over. Colonel Dedlock had been an Army man who had been in the thick of things and cannonfire had damaged his hearing. "Strange, I says to Lottie, that he hasn't come by to see us if he's been in London for some days. Gresham and I go way back to our salad days. I can't believe he'd forget his old friends that way."

"He had to see about some materials for this building project, and I think that took some time. Then his health worsened somewhat." Felicia hoped she looked normal. There was a silence and she felt forced to say something else. "Ridley—you remember his man, Ridley, don't you? Ridley is, of course, with him, and we had a note from Ridley saying that Uncle Gresham wasn't seeing anyone right now." She took a deep breath. At least, the last part was certainly the truth, as far as it went.

"Well, when will he be back?" Colonel Dedlock

asked loudly. "I'd like to see him and talk over some old times."

"I'm not sure," Felicia yelled back. "Ridley didn't say."

"I thought," said Colonel Dedlock, "I'd stay around a few days. Kingston here suggested that we stay awhile here at the Priory with him. Said it might make Gresham feel better. Besides, I'd like to talk to him—haven't seen Gresham in an age."

"I don't . . ." Felicia started to say, then stopped. What was the use. "Fine," she yelled to Colonel Dedlock, who turned to look at his wife, who had been tugging on his arm for some time. Felicia took the opportunity to make her escape, and wandered over to where Kingston was talking with Sir Oliver Pangburn.

"I've heard of your father," Sir Oliver said, looking at her through a rather large quizzing glass. "Doing rather well in government, isn't he? I dabble in government and have a good many friends scattered in various branches, although I've never had the opportunity to make your father's acquaintance. I'd like to meet him sometime."

"I'm sure he'd be happy to meet you," Felicia said politely.

"Sir Oliver's working with the magistrates in London," Kingston informed her. "He's been something of a liaison between the Bow Street Runners and some members of government who are trying to make London a safer place. As anyone who's ever walked the streets in London knows, there's crime everywhere and most people, myself among them, are quite tired of not being able to go out without risking life and limb."

"Or at least life and pocketbook," Sir Oliver noted. "Pickpockets, petty thieves. I tell you, it ain't safe anywhere, but we're going to change all that. Criminals are going to get their just desserts. Most of us won't rest until lawbreakers are hunted off the face of the earth." Sir Oliver pinned Felicia with a beaming stare and she felt her heart fall right down into her cherry-colored shoes. This was all she needed: one of Uncle Gresham's old Army friends as well as a man intimately acquainted with the Bow Street Runners. She felt faint.

To her dismay, Kingston noticed her pallor. "Perhaps we'd better change the subject, Sir Oliver," he suggested. "This talk of crime seems to have distressed Miss Fortune." He put a hand on Felicia's arm and began chatting about the state of grouse shooting, then followed that by a sparkling story concerning an acquaintance who had filed his teeth to points and assumed the identity of a coachman to win a bet. Felicia was glad for the respite.

Felicia managed to get next to Rosemary as they went in to dinner. "Be careful what you say," she murmured into Rosie's ear. "Pangburn's connected to the Bow Street Runners." She laughed a little, hoping to convince everyone else that Rosie's look of horrified surprise was something of a joke between them. Then she turned her attention to what Kingston was saying to her.

Dinner was interminable with Colonel Dedlock droning on and on about his Army experiences and Sir Oliver countering with his vast knowledge of the workings of government and other assorted thieves. Felicia couldn't imagine why Kingston would invite two such bores to be guests in his house.

It was finally over and they all adjourned to the drawing room for cards. Solon Williams came down to join the group, but Felicia thought privately that he had come down just to see Rosie. He sat beside her and told both Rosie and Felicia that Simon was asleep, but that he had a slight fever. Dr. Quigley had been by and prescribed laudanum drops. Mr. Williams noted that the doctor and Kingston had been closeted for some time, so he hoped Simon wasn't worse than he appeared. Felicia glanced at Rosie and they both had the same thought: Dr. Quigley and Kingston hadn't been discussing Simon—Kingston had been probing to find out more about Gresham Fortune. Felicia smiled brightly at Williams as she reminded herself to stay calm.

Staying calm wasn't particularly easy as Colonel Dedlock began discussing the dinner and praising Kingston's chef, remembering the last time Kingston had had a large dinner party. "Had a beautiful ice sculpture there," the colonel bellowed to Sir Oliver. "The best thing I've ever seen done like that. A swan, it was, looked like it was ready to take flight."

"Lovely," Lottie Dedlock agreed, her eyes closed with the memory. She turned to Kingston. "Lord Kingston, you simply must have another dinner party and have an ice sculpture for Sir Oliver to see."

"I'd be delighted," Kingston said as both Rosie and Felicia looked at each other. "Why don't we do something next week? By that time, you'll be bored with the dull life of the country, and I'm sure the chef would love to delight you."

"Splendid," Colonel Dedlock said. "Always love a good dinner." Mrs. Dedlock looked reflective. "An ice castle," she finally announced. "That would be perfect in this warm weather. There would be towers and turrets and whatever." She paused and looked at Kingston. "It would have to be large. Would you be able to get a piece of ice that large at this season?"

Kingston nodded. "I'm sure we have plenty. What would you say to Friday evening next? Could you spare your company with me here at the Priory that long?"

Mrs. Dedlock was flattered beyond reason and nodded in happy agreement. It was settled. Felicia and Rosie glanced once at each other in alarm but realized there was nothing they could do. For the rest of the evening, they spent all their time smiling mechanically and trying to sham their way through Colonel Dedlock's and Sir Oliver's interminably boring discussions. Finally, distracted beyond words, Felicia protested a headache and made her excuses. To her surprise, the party broke up immediately.

Kingston decided to drive them back to the Misery himself. On the short drive back to the house, he was at his most charming, telling story after story until both Felicia and Rosie were laughing. "There," he said as they came in sight of the house, "I knew I'd make you feel better." He reached over and touched Felicia's hand.

At the house, rather than simply escort them to the door, he stepped inside with them. "Are you all right now? You looked so distracted and pale at the Priory that I was concerned about you." he asked Felicia, looking at her in the candlelight.

She nodded. "I'm much better, and thank you for cheering me up. I've been worried about Uncle

Gresham lately and I'm afraid I'm not at my best in company."

"You're always charming," Kingston said, glancing around. "Are you feeling up to talking with me for a moment? If not, I'll come back tomorrow, but there are some things I'd like to say to you now, if it's at all possible."

"Of course." Felicia smiled at him. "Would you like me to ring for tea or refreshments?" She supposed he wished to talk about the Abbott's House and led the way down the hall toward the study. She came to a stop and caught her breath as she saw Ridley's coat tossed over a bench in the hall. A coat she recognized as Adam's was there, too, as well as a hat, gloves, and a cane she didn't recognize. That must belong to the man Ridley had brought back to impersonate Uncle Gresham. What if they were in the study? Could the Great Scot—MacDonald—carry this off in front of Kingston without any practice? She paused and Kingston looked at her quizzically. There was nothing she could do except throw open the door to the study and step inside.

Glancing around quickly, she didn't see anything. The room was dark, with only the remains of one candle still sitting on the desk, guttering in its holder. She went over to the desk and started to light a branch from the flickering flame. She had lit only two candles when Kingston put out a hand to stop her. "Enough," he said, a strange tone to his voice. Felicia blew out the guttering candle and looked at him in the halo of the two candles. All the rest of the room was in darkness.

Her nerves were singing. He must know more than anyone supposed. Had his men found Uncle Gresham's

157

body, had any one of a dozen things happened to let him know what was happening? Standing behind the desk, she took a deep breath and smiled at Kingston. "What did you wish to ask, Lord Kingston?"

"I think I could talk to you better if that desk weren't between us," he said with a smile she couldn't decipher. He held out his hand to her, and when she took it, he led her around the desk to stand beside him. For a long moment, he looked down at her.

"You're quite beautiful, Felicia," he said at length, "and quite unlike anyone I've ever met before."

"Thank you," she stammered, unsure where he was heading.

"See, that's just what I mean," he said with a smile. "If I had said that to any girl in London, she'd be simpering and smiling coyly, or perhaps giving me a flirtatious reply. You're different—at last I've found a woman I can talk to. Do you know what that means to me, Felicia?"

She couldn't think. "No." She couldn't think of anything else to say, and Kingston took advantage of her confusion to take both her hands and pull her closer to him. "It means a great deal to me, Felicia," he whispered. "You're beginning to mean a great deal to me." With that, he pulled her close to him and kissed her, softly. One part of Felicia's mind was registering complete amazement, another was noting that, along with his many other talents, Kingston was quite accomplished at kissing.

Felicia was breathless when he released her. She stepped back and looked at him, unaware how beautiful she looked in the candlelight, her eyes enormous. "Lord Kingston," she stammered, not knowing what to say.

He laughed softly and touched her lips with the tips of his fingers. "Don't be so formal with me, Felicia. I wish you'd call me Charles." He paused and smiled. "Did I frighten you? I didn't mean to."

Felicia took a deep breath, more from relief that he didn't want to know anything about Uncle Gresham than from the kiss. "I'm sorry, my lord . . ."

"Charles," he prompted.

"Charles." She closed her eyes and thought about how she felt. Was he toying with her affections or was he as attracted to her as she was to him? She didn't know. "I'm sorry," she stammered. "This was unexpected."

He chuckled. "I might say the same thing for myself, Felicia. I certainly didn't expect to discover that you were so enchanting and I don't want to frighten or rush you." He stepped toward her. "Perhaps I should leave now. Remember we planned a picnic tomorrow, so I'll be by." He took her hand again and Felicia knew he was going to kiss her again. Common sense told her to move, to say something to him, but instead she stepped forward to him and let him kiss her again. This time, all she could think of was how wonderful it was to be next to him, how wonderful his touch was. It ended and he stepped back as she leaned against the desk edge. She had to either lean or fall down, and fervently hoped he wouldn't notice how he had affected her. He simply smiled at her again, touched her under the chin, and said, "Good night. I'll see myself out. Until tomorrow."

The door closed softly behind him before Felicia would allow herself to take a breath. Then she took a deep gulp of air and breathed it out in a long sigh.

"I trust that's a true love sigh instead of one of those I'm-really-glad-that's-over sighs." The voice, quite amused, came from the darkness.

"Adam!" She was furious. "How long have you been there? What do you mean, spying on me in the darkness?"

He walked into the circle of light and took a candle from the branch. "Do you mind if I light these?" He didn't wait for an answer, but began lighting the rest of the candles on the branch. "I'm really not in the mood for dusky shadows and romance." He stepped back and replaced the candle. The several candles lit up most of the room and he pulled up a chair near her. "Do sit down, Felicia. You look a little dazed."

"Dazed? I'll have you know, Adam Temple, that you're rude and totally lacking in manners. No gentleman would sit in a dark room and spy like that. What kind of man are you?"

He rubbed his head with his fingers. "Right now, a tired one. Since I got involved with this family, a man who's skirting the edges of the law and taking chances." He looked up at her. "Is there anything else you want to know?"

Felicia glared at him, but his expression didn't change except to become more fatigued. "Do sit down, Felicia," he said wearily. "It's too much trouble to look up to talk to you." He waited until she sat in the chair opposite him. "I don't care what arrangements you and Kingston have, so don't worry. I certainly don't intend to tell the world that he finds you enchanting, et cetera."

To his and Felicia's amazement, she stared at him for a long minute, then burst into tears.

"Good heavens, girl," he said, producing a handkerchief, "don't go to pieces on me now. You've been as strong as granite through this whole thing, and I'm—all of us are—depending on you to stay that way. I'm sorry if I offended you. I told you I was rude and irascible at times. I apologize."

Felicia mopped at her eyes. "You didn't offend me." She paused. "Well, yes, you did, but I suppose that was to be expected."

He threw back his head and laughed. "Felicia," he said at length, "no wonder Kingston's besotted. You're a nine-days wonder." He stopped laughing and looked at her. "You look better now, and I'll even let you keep the handkerchief. I do apologize for being in here during a private moment, but I was waiting for you. Ridley's come back from London and brought MacDonald, and I wanted to talk to you about it."

Felicia reached for his fingers on the chair arm. "Adam, it doesn't matter—you being in here, I mean. I wanted to talk to you right away anyway, and it concerns Ridley and MacDonald as well. Adam, there's something else."

In as few words as possible, she told him of Kingston's houseguests. Adam leaned back against his chair and closed his eyes. "It's going to be tricky as hell to produce MacDonald for Kingston to see and then try to hide him whenever Colonel Dedlock's around. I know Dedlock from my days in the Army, and he's like a dog with a bone—he never lets go if he's on to something. A good trait for the Army, but bad news for us." He rubbed his eyes with his fingertips. "As for Pangburn, I've never heard of him, but anyone associated with the Runners is someone I'd rather avoid right now."

"It gets worse," Felicia said, looking at the fatigue stamped on his face. "Adam, you look exhausted. There's no one in the kitchen, but if you want to, we'll go in there and I'll fix a pot of tea." He raised his eyebrows at that, and she laughed. "Be a skeptic, but I assure you that I can make a tolerable cup."

"Is it private?" He looked around. "Whenever you have servants, the very walls hear everything."

Felicia nodded. "Mrs. Sprague goes home after supper, and then comes back early in the morning. Since we went to the Priory tonight, she left early, so I'm sure there's no one there. Everyone else seems to have gone to bed."

He smiled at her, the lines around his mouth emphasizing his fatigue and pain. "Tea would be wonderful."

They took the candles with them, and Adam chunked up the coals in the kitchen fire. In a very few minutes, Felicia had a kettle of water on and had hunted up some cakes Mrs. Sprague had left in the warming oven. They sat at the table, the teapot between them.

Adam took a long swallow. "I needed that," he said. "Sometimes between seeing to the work on the Abbott's House and worrying about this other, I feel I'm torn in ten directions."

"I know." Felicia smiled at him. "I appreciate it so much, Adam. I really can't tell you what it means to me. I know Uncle Gresham would, too."

He returned her smile briefly took another swallow of his tea. It was hot, strong, and sweet, just what he needed. "You said there was something else to add to

162

the litany. Let's hear it."

Felicia told him about the dinner planned at the Priory for Friday and Kingston's promise to have his chef carve a large ice castle for decoration. "From the way they were talking, Adam," she concluded, "it'll take a large chunk of ice."

Adam rubbed his eyes. "They'll try to get old ice for that, too, since it doesn't taste as good and they probably wouldn't want to use it for anything else. That's where we hid Captain's Fortune's body . . ." he glanced up at her face and was surprised to see the shock registered on it. "I'm sorry, Felicia, I didn't think."

"It's all right," she whispered, swallowing. "I need to say it to myself to make it real. It's still hard for me to say that he's dead." She paused. "Go on."

He looked at her a moment, meeting her eyes, then continued. "He's as close to the bottom of the pit as we could get, in the sawdust and old ice."

"What will we do?" Felicia asked in a small voice.

Adam closed his eyes. "Friday, you said? That gives us some time, not much, but some." He drained his teacup and poured himself some more, looked questioningly at Felicia, then filled her cup. They drank in silence for a few minutes. Finally, Adam shook his head. "Felicia, I can't think. I wanted to talk to you about Billy MacDonald and this impersonation, which is going to be tricky at best, and then this comes up. My mind seems to have turned to mush."

Felicia put her hand on his arm. "You're tired, Adam. Why don't you go home and go to bed? Tomorrow will be time enough to talk."

"Will Kingston be here tomorrow? I thought I heard

him say he would."

Felicia nodded. "Yes, but not until almost noon. Why don't you come over for breakfast, and we'll all . . ." She stopped. "That won't work—we couldn't talk or Mrs. Sprague would know, wouldn't she?"

"Probably—servants always know everything." He paused. "Let's plan to meet somewhere private and try to think this thing through tomorrow. I can't think now. The way I'm feeling now, I'm not sure I'm effective enough to remember the way to my bed."

"I think you'll manage to get there," Felicia said with a laugh, standing up. "Where shall we meet then? The inn?"

Adam stood. "No, Quigley always parks himself by the door. He's another we're going to have to dodge." He thought a moment. "This would really be the best place. Why not just in Captain Fortune's room? It wouldn't look unusual for us to go visit him, even as early as breakfast. He could be resting after the trip and have a huge tray sent up. We could all eat breakfast up there while we talk." He stood and stacked his cup and spoon.

"Fine." Felicia smiled at him and gave him a little push. "Now you go on. For that matter, why don't you stay the night here? We have room."

"Thank you, but I'd better leave. I'll need to get up early and see Connaught before I come here." He paused and looked down at her in the candlelight, then licked his lips as though he would speak. Abruptly he turned away. "Good night, Felicia. I'll see myself out."

Alone in the kitchen, Felicia cleared the table and put the leftover cakes back in the warming oven. Then she sat down with the last cup of tea and tried to think

164

about the events of the evening—both Kingston and Adam.

Her mind had evidently done the same thing Adam had said his had done—it seemed to have turned to mush. After a futile time of her mind whirling from this to that with nothing solved, she finished her tea and went to bed.

Chapter 11

Felicia had remembered to write a note to Ridley and push it under his door before she went to sleep, so he knew to keep Billy MacDonald hidden in Uncle Gresham's room until Adam got there. To Felicia's surprise, she got a good night's sleep. When she went to bed, she thought she would be spending the whole night worrying about Kingston. Lately, her feelings for him had been even more confusing and intense—a sure cause for worry. She blew out her candle, settled back to worry, and didn't wake up until a knock on her door roused her.

She opened the door, thinking Aunt Soledad or Rosie was there to wake her. To her amazement, Adam was standing there. Before he could stop himself, he looked at her, his glance going from top to bottom. She was standing there in her nightgown, her hair all down and curling around her face. He smiled at her, his eyes crinkling in the corners. "I'm sorry to wake you. Here I thought the ever-efficient Felicia Fortune would have been up for hours, but I find you to be a complete slugabed."

"No doubt you've been up since before daylight," Felicia said, glancing up and down the hall to see if anyone was around and had seen him. "You'd better get out of the hall or Aunt Soledad will have an attack." She opened her door wider, but he stepped back.

"I don't think anyone, most especially Aunt Soledad, would countenance me waiting in your room waiting while you're getting dressed." He gave her a mischievous glance, then laughed. "Tempting as the prospect may be, I'm going on to Captain Fortune's room. Ridley's already in there and he's sent downstairs for breakfast. I don't know how he manages to eat so much."

"And still be as thin as a rod." Felicia shook her head. "Has he recovered from his London trip?"

"I don't think he'll ever recover from any of this." Adam stopped as he heard a sound. "Ridley again, I think. He pointed out your door to me, but now I'd better disappear. Come on in whenever you're dressed." He grinned at her. "I promise your reputation will stay intact."

"I never had the slightest doubt of it," she retorted, closing the door in his face. She could hear him chuckle as he went across the hall to Uncle Gresham's room.

It didn't take Felicia long to dress. Determined to at least look like a lady, she did take a few pains with her hair, making sure it at least was framing her face properly. She also put on a pink striped dress that Aunt Soledad had just reworked, making the bodice cut straight across with a trim of beading and ribbons. "There," she said to herself with satisfaction, surveying her reflection in the glass, "only fifteen minutes and at

167

least I look human."

The door to Uncle Gresham's room opened as soon as she knocked softly on it. Inside, Mrs. Sprague had already sent up a huge breakfast and Ridley and another man were well into it. Adam made the introductions, and Billy MacDonald came over and took Felicia's hand. "Charmed," he said, making a most elegant bow. Whatever she had expected, Billy MacDonald wasn't it. She had expected someone slightly seedy, someone who associated with thieves and riffraff and looked it. Billy MacDonald would have been at home in any drawing room she had ever been in, and would have actually looked better than about half the people who belonged there. He had an air of confidence about him that bespoke good breeding. For the first time, she was convinced that they could carry off the impersonation if only they had a little luck.

Adam drew up a chair for Felicia and sat down with a cup of tea. He handed Felicia a cup, and she noticed that Ridley had his own cup, but Billy MacDonald was drinking an amber liquid from a glass. Surely the man wasn't imbibing at this hour! If he was, what would he be like by evening? She realized Adam was speaking to her. "What?" She gave him a distracted look.

"I said I spoke to Connaught this morning and told him what we're up against. He's become—um—somewhat friendly with a girl who works in the kitchen at the Priory. He's going to have her find out exactly when they plan to get the ice for the ice sculpture. It'll probably be very early on Friday. That means we can move Captain Fortune on Thursday night."

"Damned rum mess," Billy MacDonald offered,

downing some more of his liquid breakfast before he attacked the food on the tray. He was thin enough to pass for Uncle Gresham, in spite of what seemed a good appetite. "Still," he said with a laugh, "I have to own that it'll be a hell of a coup if we can pull this one over all the gentry around." He laughed aloud, a laugh that wasn't at all like Uncle Gresham's.

"Do you think you can be Uncle Gresham?" Felicia asked. Her optimism faded as he talked, and it looked hopeless to her. Uncle Gresham *never* spoke like this man, laughed like this man, or even acted remotely like this man.

Billy MacDonald waved his fork at her. "Easy as pie," he said. "Most of acting is *appearing* to be something or someone. All we have to do is convince everyone else that I'm Gresham Fortune." He paused. "God rest his soul." He glanced at Adam. "By the way, what are you going to do with the captain when you move him? It's damned devilish hot right now, you know."

Felicia paled and Ridley waved his fork toward Billy. "Watch what you say," Ridley growled, "or you'll be back on those stinking docks or even someplace hotter."

"Might as well talk plain," Billy said, not at all perturbed. "Plain talk's easily understood, and we can't afford confusion."

"You're quite right, Mr. MacDonald," Felicia said, looking around and forcing herself to be steady. "Now, gentlemen, what do we do next?"

They sorted through dozens of options, looked at different sides of several plans, and finally settled on what seemed the best. "Remember, though," Adam

169

reminded them, "that we're going to wind up dancing to whatever the piper plays. As Robbie Burns pointed out, 'the best-laid schemes o' mice an' men gang aft a-gley.' No matter what happens, we're just going to have to take our cues from each other and play out the story the best we can."

"Right now, I think the best thing is for Charles—Lord Kingston—to meet Uncle Gresham," Felicia said, "and the best place would be right here."

"All right. You can take care of that this afternoon. Just make sure Dedlock isn't with him. It probably won't matter if Sir Oliver's around. He didn't know your uncle." Adam stood to leave.

"Wait a minute." The sound was a croak and Adam and Felicia turned to see a very pale Billy MacDonald. "Sir Oliver, did you say? Sir Oliver Pangburn?"

Felicia nodded, then paled. "Oh my goodness, you haven't had a run-in with Sir Oliver or the Bow Street Runners, have you?"

Billy recovered his aplomb somewhat. "Let me just say that in certain areas, we are all on rather intimate terms."

"In other words, Sir Oliver has had you before a magistrate before and would recognize you immediately." Adam grimaced.

"Something like that," Billy admitted.

Felicia sat back down in her chair. "Now what do we do?" She looked up at Adam.

"We do just what we planned," he snapped, running his fingers through his hair. "We have to do something, and this is the best thing we've come up with. Billy, whatever you do, dodge Sir Oliver, even if you have to hide somewhere. We'll work it out somehow."

"The best-laid plans . . ." Felicia murmured. "You're right, Adam. Let's just get on with this. How much longer until the Abbott's House is finished?"

"With luck, we could have everything except the most minor details completed in two weeks or so, maybe even ten days if we really push it. At any rate, if we can carry this off for a few more days, it would be pointless for Kingston to get someone else to finish it. We could even announce that Gresham Fortune died at that point. For all practical purposes, the work would be complete."

Felicia gave him what she hoped was an encouraging smile. "Let's do it then." She turned to MacDonald and Ridley. "Ridley, keep coaching Mr. MacDonald how to act like Uncle Gresham. Lord Kingston will be here at midday and we'll introduce him to 'Uncle Gresham' then. I'm sure Char—Lord Kingston will come alone, so it'll be a good time."

"I'll pull one of the men from the job to shadow Billy and make sure that Sir Oliver or Quigley or someone of that ilk isn't around. I hate to do it because I need to use every man I have, but I think it's necessary," Adam said, frowning. "Better to lose a man's time than have Billy walk into a trap he can't talk himself out of."

"Don't pull off anyone," Felicia said. "Get Cavendish to do it. That way, you won't lose a workman."

He looked at her, puzzled. "Would that be wise? Cavendish doesn't know. I promise I haven't said a word to him."

"No, but Rosie has," Felicia said dryly. "If you give him a job, it may keep him from doing something on his own. I think both Cavendish and Rosie feel they should be involved."

"That's all we need," Adam muttered, then took a deep breath. "All right, since the damage is done, I'll send him over to stay with Billy, but you'll have to make sure it's all right with Aunt Soledad. I don't want to incur her wrath for putting Cavendish in the same square mile as Rosemary."

Felicia laughed. "I'll take care of those two, don't worry."

Adam turned as he left. *"Don't worry? I think I've heard those words before, haven't I?"* He grinned as he pulled the door shut behind him.

Downstairs, Felicia went to the study and talked to both Aunt Soledad and Rosie. Rosie was delighted that Cavendish was going to have something to do, while Aunt Soledad was almost distraught at the thought of having Cavendish nearby all the time.

"That's the problem," Felicia told her. "We're not supposed to know Cavendish is around. He's going to be staying out of sight. He's just around to warn Mr. MacDonald if anyone's around who might recognize him. In that case, Mr. MacDonald will disappear for a little while. We go on as usual."

"Shreds, I'm telling you, shreds. Your parents trust me so, and here I am letting the both of you send your reputations right into shreds," Aunt Soledad moaned, her cap slipping. She gave up and took it off. "They'll turn me out, and rightly so."

"Don't be ridiculous," Felicia said briskly. "You know we'd never do anything to cause you pain, Aunt Soledad. Now, here's our plan for the day: Lord Kingston will be here shortly and he's going to finally get to meet Uncle Gresham—Mr. MacDonald, that is. Ridley's coaching Mr. MacDonald on how to act, and we've all got to pretend that this is our beloved Uncle Gresham."

"A strange man?" croaked Aunt Soledad. "Felicia, I can't—"

"Yes, you can. Remember what we all promised Uncle Gresham, and this is a part of that promise." She looked sternly at Aunt Soledad. "Everything depends on how we act, remember that."

The clock chimed and Rosemary glanced at it. "You'd better get ready, Felicia. You want to look your best and provide as much of a distraction as you can."

It was Felicia's turn to be shocked. "Good heavens, Rosie, you make me sound like some . . . some *lightskirt*. Watch what you say. I assure you Charles . . . Lord Kingston is above reproach." She glanced from Aunt Soledad to Rosemary. "Just so you don't worry Aunt Soledad by tracking around looking for Cavendish, I think you should accompany Kingston and me on our picnic." She grinned and pulled Rosie's hair. "That way, you could do the chaperoning yourself."

Rosie replied, "I really don't—"

"Yes, do that, dear," Aunt Soledad interrupted her. "I really don't think I'm up to a picnic today. Actually"—she pushed her hair back on her head and it all fell back into her eyes—"I'm not sure I'm up to anything. Oh dear, Felicia, I don't think I'm going to live through this."

"Of course you are." Felicia stood, one eye on the clock. "Come on, Rosie, you've been elected. Kingston will be here in less than an hour."

"And he'll meet the man pretending to be Gresham." Aunt Soledad sighed. "It all bodes ill, Felicia, I tell you it does. There's a curse on this house, I just know it."

"Nonsense," Felicia retorted, pulling her to her feet. "Come along and help us get dressed."

Less than an hour later, Felicia and Rosie were both ready, Cavendish had stopped by and said he was going to post himself out of sight along the road, and Ridley had outfitted Billy MacDonald in Uncle Gresham's clothes. MacDonald, who had told Felicia not to worry about a thing—he hadn't earned his nickname of "the Great Scot" by accident—looked quite confident in his role. To Felicia's surprise, he *did* look remarkably like Uncle Gresham now. From a distance, no one would know. Even Rosie remarked on it. "Perhaps," Felicia said to her as they watched the Great Scot settle down at Uncle Gresham's desk, "we'd better put around that Uncle Gresham's very good at foot races. That way, Mr. MacDonald could run away without anyone commenting on it other than remarking how fleet of foot he was."

"Don't be cynical, Felicia." Rosie walked to the window and glanced out, then rushed back to Felicia. "Cavendish just signaled that Kingston's on his way, alone."

"Signaled? Good heavens, Rosie, have the two of you devised a system?"

Rosie just looked at her innocently. "Of course we have. We need to have some kind of way to know."

"What if it's dark? Lanterns?" Felicia asked with a giggle as they heard Kingston's rig pull up outside. Quickly Rosie sat down and picked up a piece of embroidery while Felicia pulled a chair up beside Uncle Gresham's desk so it would appear she and Uncle Gresham were going over accounts. Ridley dashed into the room and sat in the corner where he could watch

174

the Great Scot, ready to prompt him or step into the breach if necessary. Ridley had his handkerchief ready and it looked as if he had already been mopping at his neck. Billy MacDonald smiled around at all of them. "Relax, mates," he said expansively. "This cove will be an easy one, mark my words."

They looked wildly at each other, then settled down. There they were, a happy family group doing their everyday things, when Kingston was announced.

Billy MacDonald looked up as though he had been interrupted then smiled and stood. He and Kingston surveyed each other for a moment, then Felicia stood and did the introductions.

"I'm delighted to meet you. At last." Kingston put the slightest emphasis on the last two words.

"I regret that between my illness and trips to London, we've missed each other in passing," "Uncle Gresham" said, sitting back down. "I've been looking forward to seeing you. Major Temple tells me that you've visited our project regularly. We're close to the end now, and how do you like it?"

Kingston nodded and sat. "Excellent. The design is perfect, and so far, I'd have to say so is the workmanship. You've done an excellent job." He looked at MacDonald. "Since my mother is particularly fond of plastered ceilings, I wanted to ask you about the plaster. I noticed the scratch coat was about a quarter of an inch, as was the floating coat. What next?" He didn't take his eyes from Billy MacDonald's face.

Felicia looked at MacDonald and was amazed to see that he was smiling. "I'm delighted you're so knowledgeable about building," MacDonald said. "As for the plaster, the scratch coat had extra cement in it, and

175

we wanted to also have an excellent floating coat. Major Temple and I plan to discuss the final coat and the molding with the plasterer soon, probably today. Would you like to join us?"

Felicia's heart started beating again. She realized that MacDonald had said absolutely nothing about technicalities, but then perhaps it was enough to cozen Kingston. Kingston glanced at her. "I wish I could, but I've promised my afternoon to your niece. However, I would like to sit in on some of your conferences with Major Temple and the workers. This last work—the finish work—is extremely important."

"Excellent. We would welcome your contributions. After all, we all want this house to be perfect for your mother. By the by, how is she?" Billy MacDonald leaned back in Uncle Gresham's chair and turned slightly sideways, the way Uncle Gresham always did, trying to make the stump of his arm more comfortable.

"She's doing quite well," Kingston answered absently. "I got a letter from her a few days ago, and she thinks she's going to return sooner than expected."

Felicia froze to her chair and didn't trust herself to speak. Billy MacDonald didn't turn a hair and Felicia could understand how he had been able to make his way among the ton. The man had nerves of brass. "That's wonderful to hear. I hope I'll be able to see her before I leave. We're old acquaintances."

"I know." Kingston looked at him carefully again.

MacDonald leaned forward, his elbow on the desk. "I need to know when she's returning, however. I want to get as much of the Abbott's House completed as possible. Temple and I believe we might have it almost ready in, say, two or three weeks. Will she be returning

176

before then?"

"Possibly." Kingston glanced at him again and Felicia knew, simply *knew,* that the viscount suspected something. She gave Rosie a warning glance.

Rosie jumped up and ran over to MacDonald, putting her arms around him. "Uncle Gresham, I know you too well. You'll prose on all day about this old building if we let you. As we told you, Felicia and I are going on a picnic with Lord Kingston. Why don't you come with us, and you and Lord Kingston can talk to your heart's content?" Felicia stared at her, trying to keep the shock from registering on her face.

Billy MacDonald kissed Rosie on the cheek. "I'd love to, my dear, but as I said, Major Temple and I have a meeting with the plasterer. The three of you go on and have a good afternoon."

Felicia and Kingston stood up, as did MacDonald. Kingston held out a hand before he thought, reddened as he remembered the empty sleeve, then nodded. "I'm delighted to meet you," he said to cover his embarrassment. Felicia grabbed Rosie and stood between the men. "We're ready to go," she said to Kingston, laughing to hide her nervousness. "I know you're surprised to have females ready so you don't have to wait for an eternity."

"As I've said, you're always surprising me," Kingston said, smiling down at her. He looked back at MacDonald. "I hope we may talk further, perhaps supper tonight at the Priory?"

"Much as I'd enjoy your invitation and, I'm sure, your supper company," MacDonald said, "I've promised my evening to Major Temple. We need to discuss what's been done while I've been ill and, of course,

177

what still needs to be done." He smiled broadly at Kingston. "Of course, you're welcome to come over here at any time and talk with me or Major Temple, or both."

"I might do that." Kingston walked with Felicia and Rosie to the door, then turned. "By the way, I have some houseguests you might remember: Colonel Dedlock and Sir Oliver Pangburn." He stared right at MacDonald's face.

Felicia's knees turned to water, but Billy MacDonald never blinked an eyelash. "Colonel Dedlock I know well, of course, but I can't recall ever meeting a Sir Oliver Pangburn." The Great Scot frowned as he pretended to concentrate on the names. "Is my memory failing me, or is he someone I should know?" He turned to Felicia. "Enlighten me, my dear, before I encounter this Sir Oliver and make a social fool of myself."

"I'm really not sure." Felicia risked a glance at Kingston. "He told me he had never met Father, but he was connected with several people in government."

"He's something of a liaison between the Home Office and the Bow Street Runners," Kingston said shortly.

"Wonderful," MacDonald said. "That's someone we've needed for a very long time. I almost dread going to London these days because of all the cutpurses and pickpockets around. I applaud Sir Oliver's efforts." He turned, apparently unconcerned, and picked up a sheaf of papers. "I certainly am looking forward to meeting Sir Oliver," he said, pretending to read the papers, and of course, I hope I can spend a good long time with Colonel Dedlock." He looked up and met Kingston's eyes without blinking and smiled. "It'll be good to talk over old times with another Army man. Perhaps you can spare Colonel Dedlock long enough for us to have him over for supper one night very soon."

Felicia almost felt Kingston relax. "I'm sure he'd be delighted to come over. He's planning on being here for another week. Perhaps Miss Fortune has told you that I'm planning a small dinner on Friday next. I hope I might expect you to join us, and please extend my invitation to Major Temple if I don't see him before then."

The Great Scot smiled broadly again. "I'd be delighted to join you, Lord Kingston, and I feel I may speak for Major Temple as well. I'm sure he'd be delighted to be there. I think he's also acquainted with Colonel Dedlock, so that will give all of us an opportunity to reminisce about our Army days." He glanced significantly at the door. "I don't mean to rush you, but since I've been away, I do need to get to all these details. I hope you'll excuse me." He walked toward the door, still holding the sheaf of papers, and left them, calling for Ridley as he went out into the hall.

Felicia held on to the back of a chair, hoping Kingston wouldn't notice that she was gripping it for support rather than merely looking languid. She tried not to take a deep breath. Instead, she turned to Rosie. "Are we all set to leave, then?" She turned and slipped her arm through Kingston's. "I can't tell you how I've been looking forward to this, Lord Kingston."

"Charles," he prompted with a smile. "I don't know what I'm going to have to do, Felicia, to get you to remember to call me by my Christian name."

She smiled back at him. "Charles. There. I'm always afraid of scandalizing Aunt Soledad beyond words, so

179

I prefer a safer style." She laughed again and began walking toward the door. "I must say, Charles, that dinner parties and balls are all very well, but nothing can compare to eating a picnic out in the open air." Felicia realized she was chattering, but at this point, it didn't matter. All she wanted to do was get Kingston away from the Misery.

He smiled down at her indulgently. "My dear Miss Fortune, I wasn't aware you were such a devotee of the great outdoors," he said with a lazy smile. "However, before we head out into the open air, perhaps you'd like to get your shawl—I do believe fog may roll in shortly."

"A picnic in the fog," Rosie said. "What fun."

"One of my favorite things," Kingston said, an undertone of laughter in his voice. "Shall we go, ladies?"

Chapter 12

The picnic was indeed eaten in the fog. Actually it was so damp that they all decided to sit in the carriage and eat. Felicia picked at her food, but Rosie ate heartily. "Isn't this fun?" Rosie asked, looking out at the swirling white fog surrounding them. "it's almost like being wrapped in cotton wool."

"At least Uncle Gresham and the men can still work," Felicia said, nibbling at the edge of a raspberry tart. "They're really trying to have everything ready when your mother returns." She looked at Kingston. "Didn't you say she might be back shortly?"

Kingston nodded. "My sister will probably come with her. I'm not sure if that will be good or bad for Simon. He's much calmer lately."

"That's because someone's been paying attention to him," Felicia said before she thought. She looked up to meet Kingston's startled gaze. "I'm sorry. I didn't mean to be critical. Rosie and I both care very much for Simon. He's just a little boy who wants to be around people and wants attention. That's why he's rambunctious."

"True," Rosie agreed, looking at her fingers and wondering if it would be overly gauche if she licked the raspberry from them. "I used to be that way myself. Felicia and I have parents who are evidently much like Simon's parents."

"And what does that mean?" Kingston asked, lifting an eyebrow. "I realize my brother-in-law is seldom home, and that my sister is heavily involved in society, but I can assure you that they love Simon dearly."

"Oh, Rosie didn't mean that," Felicia said hastily. "It's just that our parents have always been similarly involved—Papa with government, Mama with society. Rosie and I have discussed this before and concluded that children need to have attention though. We were fortunate that Uncle Gresham has been there for us. That's why both of us have been trying to pay attention to Simon."

He chuckled. "I've wondered why you volunteered for such an assignment."

"We enjoy being around him," Felicia answered with a smile.

"All the time?" His eyes crinkled with laughter. "I saw the three of you rushing across the meadow the other day. It looked as if Simon was leading you a merry chase. Did you ever catch him?"

Felicia laughed as she remembered the run after Simon as he darted through the grass and flowers on the hill. "Yes, although he did manage to beat us to the top of the hill. That was his objective, I think. He likes to stand up there, look out over the Priory, and think he's on top of the world."

Kingston nodded. "The hill where the ice house is dug. I've noticed him there several times. It is a pretty spot and gives a wonderful view of the Priory."

"Simon says it's his special spot," Rosie said with a laugh. "He says the ice house is really a deep cave that might go all the way to China and that he's going to explore it someday. Uh." She grunted as Felicia gave her a well-placed, but unobtrusive, kick on the ankle.

"We might as well go back," Felicia said quickly, leaning over and looking out the carriage window, trying to find some way to change the subject. "I don't think the fog is going to lift."

Kingston nodded. "I think it's here to stay." He leaned over next to Felicia as he looked outside. She turned her face and met his gaze. His face was very close to hers, only inches away, and he was looking at her most peculiarly. She was again struck by how handsome he was, how very fine his eyes were, and how nice he smelled—a whiff of soap mixed with a touch of tobacco. She couldn't keep herself from remembering how it had been when he had kissed her, how very *nice* it had felt. Worse, her lips tingled as she now had the incredible longing for him to do it again.

Blushing furiously at her thoughts, she made herself look again into the fog, but not before he smiled briefly at her, almost as though he knew what she was thinking. He put his fingers over hers, then glanced out at the fog. "I was planning on taking a little stroll, but I suppose that isn't too practical in this weather." She made the mistake of looking at him again, and he looked right into her eyes. "I had some things I felt we should discuss."

Felicia gulped and sat straight up, snatching back

183

her hand as though his fingers were burning her. Did he know something? Had he stumbled on to the real identity of Billy MacDonald? Even worse, with all the attention he was giving to Simon's frequent trips to the hill that hid the ice house, had something been discovered? Keep calm, she reminded herself—remember to do exactly what Adam would do in a situation like this. Keep calm.

She tried to make her gaze level and smiled at Kingston. "Oh, I'm sure you had things to discuss with Uncle Gresham. Is there something I should pass on to him when we return? I'd be delighted to, although I'm sure everything's fine."

Rosie was staring curiously from one of them to the other. Kingston glanced over at her, then back to Felicia, and shook his head. "No, what I wished to discuss was with you and was something of a more personal nature."

There was an uncomfortable silence as Felicia wondered what to say next. She couldn't think of anything, so said nothing. Rosie characteristically jumped into the breach. "Lord Kingston, I really hate to ask you, but could we go back to the Misery soon? This fog is simply seeping into my bones and I'm uncomfortable beyond words. I wouldn't want to catch the ague."

Felicia didn't dare look at Kingston. The very idea of *anything* making Rosie uncomfortable was preposterous. Surely he had to know it was just an excuse. When she risked a glance, Kingston was signaling to the driver. "Of course," he said, "I should have noted earlier that it's getting cold and damp in here. Do you need a rug?"

"Oh no." Rosie leaned down to shut the lid on the picnic basket, helping herself to the last raspberry tart before she did. "I'm fine right now, it's just that I'm sure I'm *going* to get cold. I thought we should leave before that happens. Felicia seldom gets cold, and forgets to inquire about me."

Felicia glared at her. Rosie was doing it up entirely too much. Rosie caught her glance and smiled mischievously. The minx was torturing her on purpose, Felicia was sure. Trying to distract Kingston, she turned to him and started him talking about his last trip to London. "I'm finding much of London a bore lately," he said, finishing up all the latest on-dits. "It's time I stayed more at the Priory. Creswicke's been after me to learn the workings of the estate, and I need to take some of the burden from him. London pales after a while—the same people, the same balls, the same wagers. The locale or the interiors may change, but basically everything else is the same." The carriage came to a halt and he stuck his head out the window. "We seem to be back at the Misery. If anything, the fog's getting worse."

He saw them to the door and Felicia was about to ask him inside when Rosie swept between them, declaring that she was so fatigued that she simply must rest. Kingston, always with impeccable manners, bade them goodbye at the door, pausing only to ask Felicia if he might call on her later. "I would prefer to come visit you this evening, but I think Lottie Dedlock is going to read some of her poetry to the assembled company."

"All the more reason to visit here," Felicia said with a smile.

He shook his head. "True. I really can't say that I'm

185

looking forward to it. May I come and see you tomorrow afternoon?"

"I'd like that very much," Felicia said as Rosie all but snatched her inside the house. As soon as the door was safely shut and the carriage rolling away, Felicia turned to her sister. "And just what was that display of poor manners all about, Rosemary Fortune? First you *insist* on dragging in mention of the ice house, then you all but drive Kingston away. *Fatigue?* You've never been fatigued in your life. Whatever has gotten into you?"

Rosie glanced around to see if anyone was listening, then dashed off to the study, motioning for Felicia to follow.

Felicia closed the study door behind her. "Will you stop acting like a character in some novel. One would think the very devil is pursuing you."

"No, he's after you," Rosie said, flopping down in the nearest chair.

Before she could stop herself, Felicia looked over her shoulder, then caught herself and marched around to sit behind the desk. She always felt more in charge when she was sitting there. "Don't be silly. We're all in this thing together."

"I mean Kingston," Rosie said. "Felicia, you're going to have to discourage him. 'A discussion of a private nature,' the man said. That can only mean one thing."

"*Discourage* him! Up to this point, it's been that I should do everything I could to *encourage* him to spend time with the two of us. If I discourage his company, he'll be right over at the Abbott's House or else at the inn hunting up that disreputable Quigley. At least we're managing to keep him occupied."

"Well, I'm not sure it's *we* whose company he fancies. Actually, Felicia, I for one think you should get rid of the man right now," Rosie said, going over to where a small fire had been laid and probing at it with the poker. "Personally, if it's marriage you're after, I think you should marry Adam."

Felicia stood up and put both hands on the desk in front of her. *"Marry!* Rosie, have you lost your mind? I have no intentions of marrying anyone. Not to mention the fact that I don't think there's anyone out there who has any intentions of offering for me."

"Kingston's going to," Rosie said matter-of-factly, putting up the poker and turning to look at Felicia.

"That's ridiculous!"

Rosie shook her head. "No, it isn't. Felicia, you simply can't see it. Kingston's intrigued because you don't act like all the London flirts he's accustomed to. He's been bitten by the marriage bug anyway. Didn't you hear all that talk about taking over the estates and staying in the country more?"

"That doesn't signify at all."

"Yes, it does." Rosie sat down on the sofa and motioned for Felicia to sit beside her. "Think about it, Felicia. Kingston's thinking of marrying and settling down at the Priory. He's, what, about five and twenty now, just the right age to be in the market for a wife, and you're right here."

Felicia sat down beside her and sighed deeply. "All right, Rosie, I do admit I've noticed his attentions seem more marked."

"More than marked."

"All right, all right. I didn't want to admit it at all, but I think you may be right."

187

"May be? I *am* right." Rosie looked hard at Felicia. "The big question is what are you going to do about it? Personally, I don't think you and Kingston will suit after, say, five or ten years or so. Major Temple would be much better for you."

"Adam Temple?" Felicia looked at her skeptically. "The fact that Major Temple is Cavendish's uncle wouldn't have anything to do with your choice, would it?"

Rosie blushed furiously. "Of course not, Felicia. I would never put my own interests above yours, and besides, I'm really not that crass. I'm only thinking of your welfare."

"The thing that would best help my welfare would be for this whole thing to be over and for us to be back home, with Uncle Gresham safely nestled in the cemetery next to Grandfather and Grandmother." She put her hands over her face. "Rosie, I'm so tired of this. When I promised Uncle Gresham to do this, I never dreamed it would become so complicated."

"Actually it's kind of fun," Rosie said with a giggle. "All we have to do is keep from getting caught."

Felicia looked at her wearily. "The getting caught is what's worrying me." She stopped and thought as they sat there together in silence. Finally, she spoke, more thinking out loud than talking. "Rosie, I don't mean to sound mercenary, but I would never have an opportunity like this again, not in a million years."

"To have someone like Kingston offer for you, you mean. You're right, you wouldn't."

Felicia grinned at her. "That's what I like about you, Rosie. I can always count on you to give me the most flattering opinion." Rosie made a face at her, and

Felicia continued. "Also, if Kingston does offer for me and I accept, then it's going to be even more difficult to carry this thing off. If we're discovered, then what?"

"A high stickler like Kingston wouldn't dare embarrass his fiancée," Rose said promptly.

"I suppose that's true. Or if he thought everyone knew about it, he could simply ask me to call the whole thing off." There was another silence. "Rosie, I don't know if I love him or not. Now I know that's not a requirement for marriage, but I'd always hoped to have a love match."

Rosie squeezed her hand. "I know."

"Kingston's polite, correct . . ."

"Rich," Rosie added.

To Rosie's surprise, Felicia started laughing hysterically. "Trust you to get to the heart of the matter," Felicia said when she could finally stop laughing long enough to speak.

"Well, it is true," Rosie said crossly. "You can't call a walnut a tennis ball."

Felicia shook her head. "Walnuts and tennis balls—I hope Cavendish acquires the knack of deciphering your English," she said, but continued before Rosie protest. "His wealth and position are the whole point, I suppose, Rosie. It would be wonderful for you if I married the heir to the Earl of Creswicke. Think of the balls, the parties, the doors that would be opened for you. Think of the advantage Papa would have. I know he's well connected in government, but it's nothing like the connections Creswicke has. Just think of it."

There was a one-minute silence. "All right, I've thought about it," Rosie said, "and I don't think any of that signifies much. I don't need balls or parties since I already know that I intend to marry Cavendish some-day . . ."

"What! You haven't . . ."

"No, silly," Rosie said with a giggle. "I assure you that Cavendish has no inkling of his fate, but you know how we both are once we set our minds to something. I think perhaps in three or four more years . . . but back to you."

Felicia stood and started for the door. "Rosie, I'm not going to worry about it now. I'm not going to think about Kingston at all, not in that way, at any rate. If he does offer for me, *then* I'll worry about what to do. Right now, I've got other things to worry about: Friday's supper at the Priory, that dratted ice sculpture, getting the Abbott's House completed . . ."

"How about adding defeating Napoleon, reconcil-ing Prinny and Princess Caroline, and re-annexing the colonies while you're at it," Rosie said, getting up to follow her. "You'll probably do as much good worrying about those things."

Felicia frowned at her, then stopped and laughed. "Rosie, you're a goose." She looked at Rosie fondly and gave her a hug. "I'm glad you're here," she said, smiling. "You're an incorrigible ape, but I'm glad you're my sister and I love you." She let her go, turned, and picked up her shawl.

"I love you too, but now that you've buttered me up, what are you going to do?" Rosie asked, watching her.

"I'm going to talk to Adam." Felicia tossed her shawl around her.

"Walk to the Abbott's House in this fog? Are you out of your mind?"

"Yes," Felicia said with a laugh. "Tell Aunt Soledad

where I am, will you?"

Rosie grabbed her pelisse from the chair. "Tell her yourself—I'm going with you."

By the time they reached the Abbott's House, both Felicia and Rosie were covered with a fine, white coating of mist. The door was shut and they knocked and were admitted by a workman. The inside of the house was hot, there were fires in the fireplaces, and the men were busily working. Felicia was amazed at the amount of work that had been done since she had last visited the house. She said as much to Connaught, and he laughed. "Not more work, missy, not that at all. It's just that it's all finally coming together. A building's like that: for a long time it seems as if everything's being done at cross-purposes and nothing makes much sense. One man does this, another does that. Then somehow, everybody just keeps working in his own way, and then in just a day or two, everything seems to mesh."

"It's looking beautiful," Felicia said, looking at a lovely ceiling that was adorned with plaster trim.

"That's your Uncle Gresham's doing," Connaught said gruffly. "He knew what he wanted and knew how to get the right effect. Not that Major Temple can't do as well," he added hastily.

"I know he can," Felicia said as Adam came through a double doorway toward them. He had taken off his coat in the hot house, and evidently had been working near one of the fireplaces. His skin was flushed and there was a fine sheen of sweat on his skin that caused his shirt to cling damply to his torso. He smiled broadly at them. "How does it look now?" he asked. "Let me show you around."

Felicia took off her shawl. "Why the fires? Aren't

191

you about to roast?"

"Not really. We were in the process of papering and painting and trying to dry all this plaster, and there was no way to do it in this weather." They paused in front of a fireplace that was burning scrap wood. "Now all I have to do is lose my mind worrying about whether or not smoke is going to get all over everything." He laughed as he checked the draft of the flue.

"You two are just alike," Rosie said with disgust. "Always worry, worry, worry. Uncle Gresham was the same way."

"*Someone* in this family has to worry—you're certainly not going to," Felicia said archly, following Adam as he led them from room to room.

Everything was, as Connaught had said, coming together. Some of the rooms looked far from complete, but Adam pointed out that the only things lacking to finish them were the plaster, paint, and paper. All the remodeling work was completed, and just as Uncle Gresham had envisioned, the house was a jewel, both inside and out.

After they finished touring the rooms, Adam led them to a small octagonal room and motioned for them to sit on a window bench while he checked the fireplace. There were only embers in this fireplace and the room was very comfortable. "This will be the room where the countess can come to read or do her embroidery," Adam said.

"I remember it from the plans," Felicia answered, getting up and walking around. "It's going to be just beautiful. What kind of paper are we using?"

Adam glanced around the room. "I don't know. Captain Fortune had listed a stripe, but I wasn't sure."

He paused. "It doesn't seem to fit exactly right."

"A stripe! Heavens, no." Felicia made another turn around the room. "This room is for resting. We need something peaceful—painted wallpaper with a scene." She stood and looked at the wall. "Yes, that's it. Painted wallpaper with peaceful scenes on it. Shepherds and sheep, country scenes." She looked all around the octagon. "And cream paint instead of pure white. That will be more restful." She nodded in satisfaction.

Rosie leaned over to Adam. "What did I tell you—Uncle Gresham lives."

They laughed as Felicia blushed and came over to sit between them. "Go on and laugh, you know I'm right about this."

"Actually you are," Adam said. "I hadn't thought of painted scenes, but it'll be just perfect."

Felicia took a deep breath and smiled back at him. "I know we're all counting the days until this is completed, but in a way I hate to see it over and done. I love this: all the smells of building—the wood shavings, the scent of the plaster, the paint." She turned to Rosie and frowned. "And don't you dare say 'Uncle Gresham lives' again."

"I don't need to," Rosie said with a laugh. "You two talk paint and paper for a while. I'm going to look around a little more."

Adam glanced at her. "Cavendish isn't here right now. He's with Billy MacDonald."

"I knew that," Rosie said, lifting her eyebrows as she swept out of the room and into the din of saws and hammers beyond.

Adam shook his head slowly and laughed. "I don't think the world would ever be the same if Rosie and

Cavendish got together. They're both incorrigible."

"True." Felicia leaned back against the wall and they sat there in silence for a moment. "Adam, is this what you're going to do for the rest of your life? Build houses, I mean."

He glanced at her and nodded. "Yes. I had hoped to work with Captain Fortune for a few years until I learned everything he had to teach me. I studied for a while in Italy before I went into the Army, and I like to think I've got a good feel for building."

"I think you have. You've done a wonderful job with this building. I know the original ideas weren't yours, but I know Uncle Gresham would be more than proud of the way you've executed them."

He smiled briefly, then averted his eyes. "Thank you." He paused for just a second. "Felicia, speaking of Captain Fortune, there's something I wanted to discuss with you."

"Yes, Adam?"

He hesitated for only a moment. "Felicia, I've been thinking that it may be the time to go ahead and declare that Captain Fortune has died." He moved so he could look directly into her eyes. "Hear me out before you say anything, please." She nodded at him and he continued. "I know that Ridley feels that anything justifies the end here. Also, we've all agreed that Captain Fortune would say that we should do whatever we have to in order to accomplish our purpose. That's the way we're trained in the Army." He stopped, groping for words. Felicia thought for a moment that he had finished speaking, but realized he had more to say. He smiled ruefully at her. "Felicia, there's just no way to say this except straightforwardly, so please don't be offended."

"I'd never be offended by what you said to me, Adam," she said, touching his arm briefly. "I know you have my—our—best interests at heart."

"That's why I've . . ." He stopped, then started again. "We both cared for Captain Fortune, and want to do whatever he asked of us. I think we've done that, and now the building is almost complete. I really don't think Kingston will call in anyone else to finish it if we declare that Captain Fortune has taken ill and gone to Devon to die. After a suitable illness, say two or three weeks, we could announce that he had died. In the meantime, I could finish up here." He gave Felicia a troubled look. "It isn't that I'm trying to take over the building for myself, or to make any kind of name for myself. It's just the thought of Captain Fortune being frozen on a slab in the ice house, and of us having to go get him and stash him somewhere until everyone's out of the ice house, then having to put him back. Felicia, I respected the man too much to be doing that."

"Dignity," Felicia said, looking into his eyes.

"What?"

"Dignity is what you're talking about, isn't it?" He nodded and she went on. "It's bothered me too, Adam. I can't countenance the thought of Uncle Gresham's body being moved around like a—a sack of potatoes." She paused, then looked at him with a question in her eyes. "Do you really think Kingston will let you finish the house?"

He nodded. "I can't say for sure, of course, since I don't know what he'll think or do, but it seems reasonable. I know Kingston wouldn't get anyone who wasn't first class and I don't think anyone reputable would come in here with everything almost complete. After all, from here on out, it's mostly a matter of paint, plaster, and paper. I think we're safe."

"On that head, anyway," Felicia said wistfully.

He smiled ruefully back at her. "Perhaps. Now about Captain Fortune . . ."

"I agree with you, Adam, but I don't think we have time to do anything until after the supper party on Friday when Lottie Dedlock gets her ice sculpture. They'll be expecting Uncle Gresham there, and that would be a good time to tell them he's ill again. Then we could have Ridley take him to Devon the next week." She grimaced. "That means that you and Connaught will have to take Uncle Gresham out of the ice house on Thursday and put him back in on Friday."

"All right," he said quietly, "but I'm going to have Connaught go ahead and build a coffin. We can put him in that, and then use it to take him to Devon. The captain deserves that much respect."

He was sitting with his hands on his knees and Felicia reached over and touched the back of his hand. "Thank you, Adam. I know I seem to be always saying that, but I want you to know how heartfelt it is. Uncle Gresham knew what he was asking of you and he had enough confidence to know you'd do it. I know he thanks you, and so do Rosie and I."

He looked at her and smiled, a smile that touched his eyes. Felicia was surprised to see the depths in his eyes, and the warmth that was in them. The thought crossed her mind that she would always remember this moment: the warmth and concern in Adam's eyes, the faint smell of fresh wood shavings that clung to his clothing, the sound of the hammers and saws in the background. The only thing missing was his touch.

With a start, she realized what she was thinking and jerked her gaze away from him, blushing furiously. To cover her confusion, she jumped to her feet. "It's decided then," she said, looking at the opposite wall. "I'll tell Ridley what we're going to do, and . . ." A thought hit her and she turned to face him. "Adam, whatever will we do with Billy MacDonald?"

"I'll take care of it," he said, standing next to her. Once again Felicia was aware of his presence. She suddenly felt she would melt in the heat. "Fine," she said shortly, moving away from him and toward the door. She could breathe better there. She forced herself to turn and look at him as he stood there, a puzzled look on his face. Before he could say anything, she called for Rosie. "We've really got to get back to the Misery," she said quickly, gathering up Rosie and hustling her out the door. It was a rude leave-taking, she knew, but she simply *had* to get out of there. She was halfway home before she could breathe normally or listen to Rosie's chatter.

Chapter 13

As soon as Felicia opened the door to the Misery and walked inside, she heard voices in the drawing room. She glanced at Rosie in warning, shook the mist from her shawl, and gave it to a servant. Ridley was standing on the stairs and glanced toward the partially closed door.

"Sir Oliver, Colonel Dedlock, and their wives," he whispered hoarsely. "Evidently your aunt met them in the village the other day and invited them over."

"She didn't mention anything of the sort to me," Felicia whispered back. "Surely she wouldn't deliberately ask them here when Mr. MacDonald's trying his best to dodge the lot of them."

Ridley nodded affirmatively. "She did. As soon as I saw them I went on the search for Billy but I can't find him anywhere. The best I can figure is that he's slipped out to the tavern for a nip. He was saying as how he could use a pint or two and he'd be undetected in the fog."

"I suppose he's also going to be undetected while he's in the tavern swilling down ale," Felicia said in disgust. "Ridley, you've got to go get him and hide him until we can get rid of Sir Oliver and Colonel Dedlock. Adam and I have decided it's time to kill off Uncle Gresham."

"But he's already dead," Ridley said, a puzzled frown on his face. "Isn't that what we've been trying to hide?"

"Of course it is, Ridley," Felicia whispered impatiently, one eye on the drawing room door. "I mean it's time for us to end this. We'll talk about it later. Right now, you go find Mr. MacDonald and Rosie and I will go in there and see if Aunt Soledad has done any damage." She started for the drawing room, then looked over her shoulder to see Ridley still staring at her. "Hurry, Ridley! We don't have any time to waste." She paused and walked back to Ridley. "If Mac-Donald's drinking, he may get in his cups and say something he shouldn't. You know Dr. Quigley is always around there drinking and God knows he's absolutely dying to discover something. Go on, Ridley, hurry!"

She watched Ridley scurry down the hall toward the back then followed Rosie into the drawing room. Colonel Dedlock and his Lottie were sitting close to the fireplace, while Sir Oliver was pacing the floor while his wife was placidly sipping tea. "We've just got to rid the country of such scum and droppings," Sir Oliver was saying, crashing his fist onto the mantel. "Our country demands it, I tell you."

"Of course, dear," his wife said with a bright smile. "Do stop prosing on. Sit down and have a macaroon. They're quite good." She turned to Aunt Soledad.

"Your own recipe?"

Aunt Soledad nodded and looked up at Rosie and Felicia with unmasked relief. "Here you are, dears. Sit and have some tea and macaroons with us."

Sir Oliver was not to be overlooked, especially now that he had a larger audience. He began again. "A civilized country simply cannot be overrun with criminals. I was talking to Bobby Peel the last time I was in London, and we agreed that it was time something was done. Government must take a strong hand with wrongdoers." He looked hard at Felicia, his black eyebrows drawing together. "Don't you agree, Miss Fortune? Get rid of 'em all! All these criminals should be sent off to Australia. Or hanged." He crashed his fist down again for emphasis.

Felicia felt herself go pale. "That's a rather final ending, don't you think?"

Sir Oliver jumped toward her and stood towering over her while she tried to hold her teacup steady. "Final," he snorted. "Of course it is. That's the best thing to do—get rid of 'em once and for all. If we keep them around, you can mark my words, criminals breed criminals."

"What's that you say?" Colonel Dedlock asked, putting his hand behind his ear. "Who's critical? Don't tell me Gresham's being fussy again. He always was too much of a perfectionist. Far too critical for his own good, I always said so, didn't I, Lottie?"

Mrs. Dedlock nodded in agreement. "Of course you did, dear." She turned to Felicia. "And where is dear Gresham?" she asked. "We were so hoping to see him."

"He had to go out," Felicia said quickly, "and I'm so

worried about him. This fog simply couldn't be good for him, you know. He's been so ill, but he will not listen. He worries so about getting the earl's house finished in time. It's to be a surprise for the countess." Felicia realized she was chattering, but she couldn't help herself. All she could think of was being chained up and sent to Australia.

"He'll be sick again if he doesn't watch out," Rosie said, giving Felicia a glance. "His lungs are weak."

"True," Felicia said. "Have you been to see the work he's done on the Abbott's House?" It wasn't much of a change in subject, but it was better than letting Sir Oliver get back to crime and transportation. Deprived of his favorite topic of conversation, Sir Oliver cut short their visit in just a few minutes, saying he needed to get back and write some letters. He peered out the window as they stood in the hall saying their good-byes. "Damned fog," he growled. "Just about like walking through water."

"Did I ever tell you about the time Gresham and I were fighting and got trapped behind the lines?" Colonel Dedlock asked Sir Oliver as Felicia shut the door behind them. She couldn't hear Sir Oliver's answer, but it was clear that Colonel Dedlock wasn't to be denied telling his story. Felicia took a deep breath and leaned against the door.

"We seem to have survived another episode," she said to Aunt Soledad and Rosie, "but only barely."

At that moment, there was a sound of a commotion outside and they could hear Sir Oliver yelling. Felicia jerked open the door and the three of them ran out into the yard. The fog was so thick they couldn't see anyone, but it was easy to follow the voices. Then they saw them: there with the fog swirling around them was Sir Oliver with his hand on Billy MacDonald's shoulder. "You blackguard! You rogue!" Sir Oliver was roaring. "What are you doing in a respectable neighborhood? Swine like you are fit only to grace the worst of the docks and the stews in London!" Felicia thought the Great Scot might break free and run, but as she got closer, she saw the contented smile on his face. Instead of running from Sir Oliver, Billy MacDonald proceeded to put his arm around Sir Oliver's shoulder and begin singing that ubiquitous old drinking song "To Anacreon in Heaven" in a very fine baritone.

"Oh, my stars," Mrs. Dedlock said, as Billy warbled some not-so-genteel lines.

"Shut that up!" Sir Oliver roared. The Great Scot looked up at him and smiled blissfully. He was, Felicia realized, quite drunk. "As you say, my dear man," Billy MacDonald said in his best urbane accents. His accent, if anything, was improved by his inebriation.

"Why are you here, MacDonald?" Sir Oliver demanded, removing Billy's arm from around his shoulders. "I know you're up to some mischief. He glanced at Aunt Soledad, who was cowering at the fringe of the group, then back to the Great Scot. "You're not here to prey on helpless females, are you?"

Billy MacDonald stepped backward. "Really!" he said in miffed tones. "I happen to be on a very important mission."

It was time for immediate action. Felicia looked at Aunt Soledad. "Rosie!" she screamed. "Aunt Soledad's going to faint! Catch her!" Aunt Soledad stared as Felicia ran right into her and knocked her down. Felicia knocked the breath right out of her, and Aunt Soledad went down with a garbled "Oooffff!"

"Help, someone, help us!" Felicia said, tugging at Sir Oliver's sleeve. "Pick her up and carry her inside." Aunt Soledad tried to move, but Felicia put both hands on her shoulders, trying to push Aunt Soledad back down on the ground without anyone noticing. In desperation, she put her knee on Aunt Soledad's stomach and peered right into her face. "Be still," she hissed under her breath. "Uuuugggggh," was the only reply Aunt Soledad could manage, but she blinked her eyes. Felicia moved her knee.

"Hurry, please. She'll catch her death out here in this mist. Hurry, Sir Oliver!"

As Sir Oliver reached down for Aunt Soledad, Felicia stood and tried to motion for Billy MacDonald to disappear into the mist. He just stood there, a beatific smile on his face, humming another tavern song. Felicia heard a twig snap in the mist behind her, then there was a crackling sound in the woods just as Sir Oliver hoisted Aunt Soledad up. "Get the door, Dedlock," Sir Oliver shouted, "I can't stand here holding this female all day."

"What's that? What'd he say?" Colonel Dedlock asked, his hand behind his ear as his wife pushed him toward the door. Aunt Soledad had finally figured out what Felicia was trying to do and she moaned piteously.

"Do hurry," Felicia urged as Rosie tried to shove Billy MacDonald out of the way. Just then Cavendish appeared out of the mist and grabbed Billy's arm, pulling him away into the fog. Sir Oliver saw Cavendish, but he was helpless to intervene since he was standing there holding Aunt Soledad, who was moaning loudly by this time. "Stop there, you young scamp!" Sir Oliver yelled as Aunt Soledad cried out, "Oh, the pain! Oh dear!"

Sir Oliver looked down at Aunt Soledad as though he'd like to throw her on the ground while Cavendish pulled Billy MacDonald, still singing, away from the group and into the mist. "Stop! I tell you, stop!" Sir Oliver roared. "You'll not get away from me this time, MacDonald. I'll see that you hang and your young friend swings with you." He glared at Colonel Dedlock, who was standing on the step staring at him. "Will you open that damned door!"

Colonel Dedlock opened the door, but Rosie stepped in front of Sir Oliver before he could get inside. Rosie was as pale as the white swirls of fog. "Hang him! You couldn't do that. He hasn't done anything." She stopped long enough to glance at Aunt Soledad, who was still in Sir Oliver's arms, moaning loudly. "Do stop that a minute, Aunt Soledad. I mean to have an answer from Sir Oliver."

He glared at her. "Oh, you do, missy. Well, I'll give you an answer. Yes, I mean to hang that scoundrel and I'll hang anyone who gets in my way of doing it. I don't know what's going on here, but I mean to find out."

Rosie started to speak again, but Felicia intervened, pushing her inside. "Don't mind Rosie," she said to Sir Oliver. "She's upset about Aunt Soledad and not at all accustomed to seeing criminals up close." She led them toward the drawing room. "Just bring Aunt Soledad right in here and I'll ring for her vinaigrette." She gave Rosie a sharp nudge in the side to hush her and they all trooped into the drawing room behind Sir Oliver. Inside, Sir Oliver unceremoniously dumped Aunt Soledad on the sofa and turned to them to take his leave. "I'm sending to London for some runners right now to apprehend that scoundrel and his accomplice," he told them. "Don't you ladies be dismayed a whit. I'll have someone here to clap them in jail before you know it. Just you rest easily and don't go far from the house until I tell you to. I assure you that the likes of Billy MacDonald won't bother you—that is, unless you care to come watch him stretch the hemp."

Felicia put her hand on Rosie's arm to quiet her. "No, thank you, Sir Oliver, and I want to tell you how safe it makes us feel to know you're doing all you can. I only ask that you keep us posted as to how your . . . your investigation is progressing. I know we'll all sleep better knowing you're taking a personal interest in this."

Sir Oliver preened. "Never fear, Miss Fortune." With that, he motioned imperiously to his wife and they went out the door, followed by Colonel Dedlock and his wife, Colonel Dedlock pulling at the corner of his wife's shawl, asking over and over, "What's that? What's he on his high horse about now?" Felicia didn't dare breathe until they heard the door shut behind them.

Rosie rounded on her instantly. "How could you be kind to him? That odious man! Did you hear him: he's going to *hang* Cavendish. And Billy MacDonald as well!" Rosie's anger dissolved into tears.

Aunt Soledad sat up. "It's this house," she said, waving her vinaigrette under her nose. "I told you it would lead to no good."

There was a noise behind them and Felicia whirled as the door opened. Cavendish slipped in, shoving the Great Scot into the room in front of him. Billy MacDonald was still humming under his breath. He saw them and bowed low, smiling at them. "Good evening, ladies."

"Cavendish, why on earth did you bring him back here?" Felicia asked, kicking the door shut, then propping up one side of the Great Scot so he wouldn't fall on his face. Cavendish held up the other side.

"It seemed to be the safest place right now," Cavendish said. "We've got to get him out of here. Not out of the house—out of the country. Where's Ridley?"

"I sent him to find Mr. MacDonald." Felicia helped Cavendish put Billy MacDonald into a chair, where he smiled at them, hummed a few more bars, let his head drop against the side of the chair, and promptly went to sleep.

Rosie came up to stand with Cavendish. "Sir Oliver said he'll see you hang," she said bluntly.

Cavendish looked at her, then laughed out loud. "Good heavens," Aunt Soledad observed, sitting back down with her vinaigrette, "Cavendish, you recall Dick Turpin laughed his way to the gallows. I'm afraid this—this—I'm afraid we've led you into a life of crime." She waved her vinaigrette under her nose again. "It's this house. I know it."

Felicia sat down and put her hands over her face, struggling to keep from getting hysterical. "Cavendish, do you suppose it's safe for you to get out and bring Adam here? If it isn't, I'll go get him."

"In this fog, it's safe for anyone to be out there, although I think my reputation might suffer less than yours if I went wandering out." He grinned at her, then walked over to the window and looked out. "However, I do think perhaps we'd better draw the drapes. I don't think Sir Oliver would peep into windows, but with a man like that, anything's possible." He pulled the draperies while Rosie lit some candles. "There. Do I understand that you want me to bring Uncle Adam back here so we can get rid of the Great Scot?"

"Something like that," Felicia admitted. "I hadn't thought of it as getting rid of him, but we do need to see that he escapes from Sir Oliver and the Bow Street Runners, and the sooner the better. Adam and I had already discussed some of this earlier."

"Cavendish, you're not going out in this weather without a coat," Rosie said firmly. "You can wear Uncle Gresham's coat. It's beginning to rain hard now, and you'll catch your death if you're not careful. Don't you dare leave until I get back with the coat." Rosie slipped out the door silently, looking up and down the hall.

"Is she always like this?" Cavendish asked with a grin that was very much like Adam's.

"Always," Felicia said. "And sometimes she's worse."

After Cavendish had gone, the three of them sat in the drawing room watching Billy MacDonald sleep. They had thought about putting him to bed, but decided it was too risky. Mrs. Sprague was about, and it simply would not do for her to see or hear of them having to drag "Uncle Gresham" up the stairs and him passed-out-drunk in the late afternoon. It was better to sit and watch him, and make sure no one came into the drawing room. Ridley returned after an hour or so, completely drenched. He knocked on the drawing room door and Rosie let him inside. He was dripping water from his clothes and his hair was plastered in long strands to his skull. He was shaking from the wet and cold. "Look at that!" he exclaimed through chattering teeth as he saw Billy MacDonald slumbering like a babe. "I'm freezing to death and skulking around the tavern while that devil's whelp is here sleeping." He sneezed and sat down, water puddling at his feet. Aunt Soledad, with an amazing presence of mind, handed him a glass of brandy.

Ridley had gone upstairs to change when Cavendish returned with Adam. "I was afraid this might happen," he said. "From what Cavendish tells me, we don't have time to waste. We can keep Billy here for a while, but he'll get out again and Sir Oliver will find him." Ridley came back in the door as Adam was speaking.

"Aye, that he will," Ridley said with disgust. "Billy's going to have his pint—and more—no matter what."

Adam regarded Billy and Ridley for a moment. "Ridley, we—Felicia and I—decided it was time to call an end to all this charade." He gave Ridley an almost verbatim rendering of the conversation he and Felicia had had earlier. "Felicia doesn't want to announce Captain Fortune's death until after the Friday supper at the Priory, but by that time, you could be on your way to Devon with the body. I've had Connaught make a coffin."

Ridley released a deep breath. "That's the best news I've heard. It just don't seem too right—the captain down there all froze, although I know he'd agree to it if that's what it took to get that house done."

"What about Billy?" Cavendish asked.

Adam looked at Cavendish, sizing him up. "Could you and someone else take him to Edinburgh? I feel responsible for him since we brought him here from London, but I don't want to take him back there. Sir Oliver and the Runners will be looking for him there."

"Edinburgh? Of course I can." Cavendish looked extremely confident. And, thought Felicia, extremely young. Adam must have thought the same thing as he reflected a minute more. "I'd send Connaught with you, but I can't spare him. I could send Bentley with you—he's a good man." He looked straight at Cavendish. "You'll have to leave as soon as possible. Go get Bentley and then take what money you need from my box. You know where it is."

"Right now?" Felicia asked. "Mr. MacDonald can't travel."

"Right now," Adam said decisively. "As for as travel, he's better off drunk than he is sober. By the time he's sober, he's going to have a headache and not want to move." He looked at Cavendish, who was already putting on Uncle Gresham's coat again and going out the door. "Be back as soon as you can."

Adam turned to Ridley. "Can you make arrangements to travel to Devon as soon as Connaught and I can remove Captain Fortune from the ice house?"

209

Ridley nodded. "Tomorrow night soon enough?" Adam nodded in confirmation and Ridley leaned back against his chair. "I can't tell you how glad I am that this is over."

"It isn't over yet," Aunt Soledad said. "This house may well exact revenge."

Felicia rolled her eyes upward. "Do hush, Aunt Soledad."

By the time Cavendish returned with Bentley, the other five had their plans in place for moving Uncle Gresham. Cavendish and Bentley were on horseback and had brought a horse for the Great Scot. "I thought about a carriage, but we'll travel faster on horseback," Cavendish explained as he and Adam shoved Billy up into the saddle. The mist had lifted and the sky was clearing. "The moon's coming out, and it'll be easy to travel tonight. We need to put some distance between us and Sir Oliver."

"I'm not sure Billy knows how to ride," Ridley said dubiously, looking at the Great Scot wobbling and weaving in the saddle.

"He does now," Adam said shortly. "Be on your way, Cavendish, and be careful." Adam nodded to Bentley, who nodded in return and lifted his coat to reveal a pistol in his waistband. "Godspeed." He slapped the rump of MacDonald's horse and the three of them went down the road, Cavendish leading MacDonald's horse with Billy swaying from side to side. "They're going to have to tie him to the saddle," Felicia said with a giggle that had more than a touch of hysteria in it.

Adam laughed in return and put his arm around her shoulder as they watched them go out of sight. Felicia moved closer to him in the damp night. It felt so comfortable to be next to him, so *right* that she didn't want him ever to move. He glanced down at her, realized his arm was around her, and moved away. "I'd better be leaving," he said formally. "I'll be in touch tomorrow. Be ready Ridley."

Felicia stood in the doorway and watched him walk away, his leg dragging slightly. He stopped once and reached down to rub it, then walked on, limping. "Rainy weather," Ridley said behind her. "Old bullet wounds always hurt in rainy weather." He paused. "That Major Temple's a good 'un." Felicia had to agree.

Chapter 14

For the first time in weeks, Felicia slept soundly that night, sleeping late into the next morning. The day was beautiful and sunny when she got up, the leaves and flowers gleaming in the sun, rainwashed from the day before. She looked out the window toward the Abbott's House, feeling as if a weight had been lifted from her shoulders. At last it was almost over. In just a few days they could announce to everyone that Uncle Gresham had died and he could be buried in Devon with all due respect. The Abbott's House would be his monument, and it was a jewel that would be remarked on for years to come. Felicia smiled.

She was still smiling as she went downstairs to eat breakfast. Rosie came into the breakfast room while Felicia was sitting there, sipping her chocolate. "You're looking like the cat that ate the cream," Rosie remarked, sitting down across from her.

"Just relief, I think." Felicia stirred her chocolate and added a litle more of her special ingredient—sugar in which she had stuck a vanilla bean. "Rosie, I'm

212

looking forward to getting back home and things being normal again."

"Have you considered what 'home' and 'normal' are going to be from now on?" Rosie asked. "I have, and frankly, it's bothering me. I didn't think you'd had time to reflect on it."

Felicia stopped a second to reflect, then looked at Rosie as the thought sunk in. "Oh good God! With Uncle Gresham gone, we'll have to go to London to live with Papa and Mama. There'll be balls and visits and . . . Rosie, you know that Mama will try to get me married off right away."

Rosie nodded. "Probably both of us. We're going to have to have a plan."

"I can't," Felicia said, gulping the rest of her chocolate. "Only one plan at a time for me, if you please. I'll worry about Mama and Papa after we get back to Devon."

"*I* have a plan," Rosie said. She leaned across the table. "You're going to have to get married, and then I can live with you until Cavendish is ready to find a wife. Then I'll get married to him."

Felicia lifted an eyebrow. "Oh, and I suppose you've decided that I'm to marry into Cavendish's family so you can be right there."

"It would be helpful, but if you want to marry Kingston, that's all right too. By the way—"

Felicia interrupted her. "I don't know why you keep insisting that Kingston is planning to offer for me. I know he seems somewhat interested"—she paused to fight down a blush—"but that's a long way from offering for someone."

"Quit being modest, Felicia. I thought we were

213

agreed that he would offer, if not now, shortly." Rosie paused and looked at her sharply. "What will you do when he offers?"

Felicia bit her lower lip as she thought. "I don't know, Rosie. He's handsome beyond measure, wealthy, witty, all the things I've ever wanted in a husband and more. It would be to my advantage to marry him. Looking at it in that light, I'd have to say yes."

"It would certainly solve our problems." Rosie laid a note in front of Felicia. "As I was going to tell you, by the way, this came from Kingston this morning. I haven't opened it, but maybe it's important." She grinned. "I point out that I haven't opened it, but it was certainly a temptation."

Felicia quickly opened the note and scanned it. "It's nothing, Rosie. He's merely confirming that he plans to come over this afternoon." She refolded the note and tossed it down. "I imagine that what he has in mind is seeing Uncle Gresham and finding out how the house is going. Adam told me Char—Kingston was over there yesterday and looked over everything carefully. He was asking Adam about expenses and landscaping."

Rosie sighed. "I knew it would be today. Another blow to romance."

Felicia laughed as she got up. "No such thing, Rosie, everybody knows that."

"Even Cavendish," Rosie said morosely as she stood. "Are you going over to the Abbott's House?"

"Yes," Felicia said with a nod, "I wanted to talk to Adam about the paint and wallpaper in the main bedroom. I looked at Uncle Gresham's notes, and saw that he wants green in there. Green won't do at all— blue, I thought."

214

"It never ends," Rosie said, rolling her eyes toward the ceiling.

Felicia and Rosie walked over to the Abbott's House and paused when it came into view. The outside was finished except for the landscaping, and it was standing beautiful and rain-shined in the morning sun. "I wish Uncle Gresham could see it," Rosie murmured.

"I think perhaps he can," Felicia told her. "His spirit is here anyway. Everyone will remember Uncle Gresham because of this house."

Inside, they discovered that Adam had gone to talk with the landscapers, leaving Connaught in charge. He took them around, and Felicia quizzed him about the bedroom paint and paper. He told her that Adam had ordered the paper she had suggested for the small octagonal room. "A very nice scene with shepherds, he said it was," Connaught said. "I hadn't thought of it, but it'll be just right. A woman's touch, I said to Major Temple, that's just what was needed in there."

Recognizing the compliment from a man who seldom complimented, Felicia thanked him. "I mean it, Miss Fortune," Connaught said. "There's not many who'd understand buildings and what's needed." He looked at her for a moment. "You're much like Captain Fortune, you know. Working for a woman is often . . . difficult"—he stumbled over the words—"but working with you has been a pleasure."

"Thank you, Mr. Connaught." Felicia took his speech in the spirit in which it was offered. "Perhaps women are often not given the opportunity to work with building. I enjoy it, and I want to thank you for everything you've done." She glanced around and changed the subject. "It's almost completed, isn't it?"

215

He nodded. "A few more days, the major says. A week and a half, a fortnight at most, I'd say. What's left is mostly small detail work. Most of the crew can leave by Friday or Saturday."

Felicia looked up at him. "You'll be staying, won't you?"

He spoke with perfect understanding. "Yes, Major Temple and I will see *everything* through to the end."

Felicia thanked him again, then told him that Kingston was coming to discuss some things with her during the afternoon, and that he might stop by the Abbott's House afterward. "Any time," was Connaught's reply. "We're ready at any time."

Rosie glanced back over her shoulder at the house as they walked back toward the Misery. "I'd love a house like that. It's so beautiful, inside and out."

"Perhaps you'll have one someday," Felicia said.

"More likely it'll be yours."

Felicia laughed. "Get that bee out of your bonnet, Rosie. I've thought about that in the cold light of morning, and decided that's not likely to happen, at least not in this lifetime."

Kingston arrived promptly at three o'clock and Felicia welcomed him into the study, where she was finishing a tabulation of the costs of the Abbott's House. She had thought he might like to see that.

"You're looking lovely today," he said rather formally, looking appreciatively at her green and white striped muslin. Felicia noted that Kingston himself was looking particularly fine this afternoon. He was dressed in a coat of a very dark gray, almost a black, and had on pearl-colored pantaloons and a waistcoat of pearl and dark gray stripes. *Elegant* was the word that came to her mind.

They sat and she brought out the papers she had been tabulating. "I thought you might want to see these," she said, moving beside him so she could point to various things as she mentioned them. He sat quietly while she talked, occasionally asking about something. "I was there yesterday and noted everything was almost complete," he said when she had finished talking.

Felicia nodded. "I spoke to Connaught this morning when I was over there, and he assured me that most of the men would be let go Friday or Saturday. The rest of the work is detail work that will need only a few men."

"So you and your family will be returning to Devon."

"Yes." Felicia smiled at him. "I know Aunt Soledad will be glad to get out of this house before it gobbles her. She thinks it's got an evil presence."

Kingston raised an eyebrow. "The Misericorde? It was named after a refectory, I think, and the owner was fond of giving dinners. He died from overeating, if I recall correctly, but there are no ghosts or stories associated with this that I know of. Now if your aunt wants ghosts, the Priory is supposed to have its resident ghost—a monk who walks the halls at Christmas."

"Of all times for a ghost to be wandering," Felicia said with a laugh. "I'll pass on what you've said about the Misery to Aunt Soledad. She's been blaming everything that's happened around here on the house. I told her houses aren't responsible for anything."

"Has something happened around here?" Kingston looked at her in surprise and Felicia quickly caught herself. Every time she felt comfortable with him, she managed to say something she shouldn't.

Kingston didn't seem to note her lack of answer. "Houses are responsible for some things," he said, looking at her with a smile. "For instance, if it hadn't been for the work on the Abbott's House, I would never have stopped by to see your uncle and met you. You would never have come to the Misery to stay, and I wouldn't have come to know what an interesting, intriguing person you are." Felicia didn't know how to reply to him, so she smiled at him and said nothing. He stood and walked to the window, then looked back at her, his hands in his pockets. "I suppose I should have gone to London to speak to your father before I said anything to you, but two things stopped me: first, I felt you were a person who wished to speak for yourself, and second, I didn't want to wait that long."

Felicia felt her heart stop beating as she looked up at him striding across the room toward her. He sat back down beside her and took her hand in his. "Felicia, you must know how attracted I've become to you. I've never met anyone quite like you—an independent sort of woman, a woman who can manage things and yet still be charming and feminine."

Attracted. No word of caring, of love. "I feel much the same way about you, my lord," she said, looking at his hand holding hers rather than into his eyes. "I find you quite—quite charming."

He laughed aloud. "Oh, Felicia, you're priceless. *Charming.* I doubt anyone in London would agree with you, or anyone in the world for that matter, except perhaps my mother." He stopped and looked at her seriously, his eyes capturing hers. "You know what I'm going to ask you, Felicia, and I want you to know that I

218

don't do this lightly. I've never asked a woman to be my wife before."

"And you're asking me?" The question sounded inane to Felicia, but it was all she could think of to say at the moment.

He laughed and tucked a stray wisp of hair behind her ear. "Yes, my dear, I'm asking you. I know I'm not doing a very good job of this, although I assure you I've rehearsed this in my head for days. Somehow, when I get around you, I never quite get my wits together."

"My lord," she began, but he put a finger to her lips.

"Charles, remember?" He smiled at her. "First, let me say some things before you answer me, Felicia." She nodded and he went on. "I'm sure you've heard a good many things about me, especially my reputation in London. Unfortunately, too many of those things are true, but I realize that I can't live my life being a rakehell. I want you to know that if you agree to marry me, I intend to settle down and be something of a model husband and father. Would you like to live in the Abbott's House in the beginning?"

"My lord, I mean Charles," Felicia said firmly, "there might be misgivings. There is, for example, the matter of my birth. I'm sure there's no reason your family could object, but I'm also sure they had set their sights for you a bit higher."

He laughed again. "No other woman in the kingdom would think such a thing, much less say it to me. Felicia, you're more than a match for me." He put a finger under her chin and looked at her. "Felicia, my parents will be happy with my choice, whoever she is. They've never been concerned with position or wealth . . ."

219

"Perhaps because they've always had it," Felicia said with a smile. "Others will talk."

"I've never cared about others, Felicia. Now, my dear, are you going to let me do this properly?" He stood and pulled her to her feet, facing him. "Felicia Fortune, will you do me the honor of being my wife?" His eyes searched her face.

She bit her lower lip as she looked at him. "This is very unexpected, Charles. Please, do you mind giving me a day or two? I need to think about this and . . . and there's Uncle Gresham."

He kissed her lightly on the forehead. "All right, my dear. I know this is sudden, but I've always been one to know what I want and then to get it. Right now, I know that you and I will suit, and I sincerely want you to marry me." He looked at her, a question in his eyes. "Could you let me know by Sunday? I had hoped to be able to announce our engagement at the dinner on Friday night, but Sunday will do as well."

"Yes, I could tell you by Sunday."

"You look so solemn," he said, running his fingers along her chin. "Smile for me, Felicia. There, that's better." She reached up and entwined her fingers with his and smiled at him. "Felicia, this is going to be perfect for both of us. I know it." Before she could say anything, he had bent his head to hers and kissed her. He kissed her softly at first, then a little harder. She was aware that he wanted her, but she was more conscious of her own feelings. Before, when he had kissed her, she had felt strange emotions, but it was nothing compared to this. As he kissed her, she became aware of a need, a slow warmth spreading up through her body. She put her arms around his neck and was aware of him kissing her throat and the murmured sound of her name as he touched her ear. He moved slightly, but she didn't loosen her arms from his neck. "Don't stop," she whispered, and he kissed her again.

This time he stepped back, looking at the enormous darkness of her eyes. There was a strange look on his face and he was breathing heavily. "Felicia," he said hoarsely, taking another step back. He took a deep breath, and in just a moment, he seemed back to normal, and smiled at her. "My dear, I had no idea."

"No idea about what?"

He laughed as he touched her cheek and slightly swollen lips. "That you were such a minx. Felicia, you are a woman worthy to be Countess of Creswicke." He moved away from her toward the door. "I'd love to stay with you all afternoon, but frankly, I don't trust myself around you. I'll be anxiously waiting for Sunday." He paused at the door. "By the way, I promised Simon I'd ask if you would join us at the ice house tomorrow. It seems he's told everyone there are ghosts in there, and he's anxious to see them. We're going to get some ice out so I'm taking him up there with me so he can see firsthand that there's nothing in there."

"It's almost a shame to disappoint him," Felicia said with a laugh. "He told me about the ice house ghost, too. I think he's made it very real in his imagination. It has, so he tells me, a long white beard and icicles hanging from its hair. I don't think he's too sure about the gender."

Kingston laughed. "You've been very good for him, both you and Rosemary. You'll be a wonderful mother."

Felicia blushed and tried to change the subject. "I

think taking Simon up there will be good for him. I'm glad you're spending some time with him."

"Will you join us? I've been assured that the weather should be sunny, so we can have a picnic afterwards. I think Simon would like that, too." He smiled at her. "I know I would."

"I'd like that very much too, Charles."

"Good. Until tomorrow, then." He smiled at her and turned to leave. Just as he was ready to shut the door behind him, he looked at her and blew her a kiss. "One to think on, my dear," he said with a grin as he shut the door.

Felicia collapsed on the sofa. "Countess of Creswicke," she murmured. "Rosie's right—it would solve all our problems." Then she started to cry for absolutely no reason at all and, worse, couldn't seem to stop.

There was a knock at the study door and she dabbed at her eyes quickly. Had Charles come back for something? "Just a moment," she called, dashing to the mirror over the mantel to see if she truly looked as horrible as she felt. She did.

Wiping at her eyes only made them redder and her nose was beginning to drip. Where was Ridley with his handkerchief when one needed him? She hastily bent over and wiped at her face with the hem of her petticoat and dashed behind the desk where the room was a little darker. Maybe Charles couldn't see she had been crying. She settled herself as the knock came discreetly again. "Come in." Her voice sounded a trifle squeaky.

Instead of Charles walking through the study door, Adam sauntered in. "I've been skulking in the woods like some criminal," he said with a grin. "I saw Kingston in here and thought I'd better wait until he was gone."

Felicia stood. Her knees were weak, whether from relief or something else she couldn't say. "What's wrong? What on earth are you doing here, Adam?"

"Nothing's wrong that I know of." He walked toward her. "Connaught said you'd been over this morning and said Kingston was coming to see you. I thought I'd better stop by and see if there was a problem."

"No, there's no problem. None at all." She walked around the desk to stand in front of it. That was a mistake. Adam glanced at her face, then reached over and placed his fingers under her chin, tilting her face up so he could see it in the light. "You've been crying," he said softly. "What is it, Felicia?"

"Nothing, nothing at all." Then, to her chagrin, she began to cry again.

"Oh, my goodness." Adam put his arms around her and drew her to him. She burrowed her face in his shoulder, sagged against him, and cried. "Go ahead and cry," he said, holding her close and patting her on the back. "It'll make you feel better." Finally she stopped, taking in air in big gulps and wiping at her eyes with her fingers. Adam produced a handkerchief, which she took gratefully.

"Now," he said, "do you want to tell me what's the matter, or do I have to find out for myself?"

"Nothing's the matter. That is, it's Charles— Kingston," she said, sitting down on the sofa.

He sat beside her, rigid. "What did he do? He didn't . . . do I need to go call him out?" His fists were

223

clenched and there was a white line around his mouth.

"No, no, nothing like that." Felicia mopped at her face again. "Adam, he . . . he offered for me. He asked me to marry him."

Adam very carefully straightened out his fingers before he answered. "That should be a cause for joy instead of tears, Felicia," he finally said. "Any other girl would already be planning her trousseau. I understand Kingston's quite a matrimonial catch."

"I know, I know," she said tearfully. "I also know I should be overjoyed. Besides, it would solve all sorts of things for us: Rosie would have all the best connections, Papa would be able to expand his sphere of influence in government, Aunt Soledad would be taken care of, and most importantly, Rosie and I wouldn't have to worry about going to London to live with Mama and Papa. They dearly love us, I know, but they really don't want us."

"Of course they want you."

Felicia searched for the right word. "Of course they *want* us, it's just that they don't really. Like them not really knowing where Rosie went when she came here." She paused. "Accepting his offer would really be the best thing I could do."

"I agree." Adam's voice was light and he leaned back against the sofa, placing his hands carefully on his knees. "From a purely practical standpoint, Felicia, I don't believe you can turn him down."

"I know." She looked at Adam. "But I'd always hoped for a love match—no, not really a *love* match, but at least someone I cared deeply for. I know that doesn't signify."

"No," Adam agreed. "You and Kingston would

224

probably rub along quite well. After all, he'd be in London a great deal of the time, and you do like it here." He paused. "You said accepting the offer *would* be the best thing. You didn't accept him immediately?"

She shook her head. "No, I asked if I could think about it for a short while. I'm to give him an answer on Sunday." She looked at Adam. "I just couldn't say yes with all this . . . this deception going on about Uncle Gresham. I thought Sunday would be all right—things will have been resolved by then."

Adam nodded. "True, you can say yes then with a clear conscience." He sat up and changed the subject. "We're well on the way to being finished with the house. Things have gone even better than I'd hoped. Partly, I think, to Captain Fortune's plans and to your excellent organization."

"Thank you, Adam." She felt herself blush. "That's one of the nicest things anyone has ever said to me. I love doing it—all the lists and the figures and watching everything fall into place." She giggled. "Rosie says I've inherited that from Uncle Gresham."

"I'd have to agree." Adam stood up. He looked down at her for a moment, a smile on his face. "I've enjoyed it as well." He turned away from her. "If you don't need me, I'm going now. Connaught and I have a night's work cut out for us."

Felicia stood beside him. "Adam, be careful."

He smiled again. "As always. Don't worry, Felicia, I'll take care of everything." He strolled to the door and opened it. "I'll see you tomorrow and, Felicia, congratulations." He closed the door behind him. Felicia sat back down and put her hands over her face. Logically, she had to accept Charles—she knew it, Rosie knew it,

225

Adam knew it. Then why did she feel it would be such a mistake?

Felicia heard nothing of Adam that night. She paced the floor of the study while Rosie sat and read and Aunt Soledad occupied herself with embroidery. Once she even went to get her cloak to see if Adam and Connaught were getting Uncle Gresham from the ice house. Rosie forced her to sit down. "You'd only be in the way," Rosie advised her, but that didn't make things any easier. She went on to bed, but couldn't sleep. She thought about Uncle Gresham, about what Adam and Connaught were doing, but most of all, she thought about the one thing she hadn't been able to discuss with Rosie and Aunt Soledad: Charles's offer and the answer she would give him on Sunday.

Friday morning was clear and sunny. Felicia woke up groggy from not enough sleep and it took her a while to force herself to get out of bed and go downstairs. "Perfect day," Rosie said, looking into the breakfast room as Felicia got herself a cup of chocolate.

"Uuuhh." Felicia drank half her chocolate at one gulp, then sat down and stared into the cup.

"A wonderful day for a picnic," Rosie said, sitting down across from her. "Kingston sent a note by that they're going to get the ice out about eleven this morning, and then we'll picnic. I'm invited, too." Rosie gave her a critical look. "I think I'm supposed to keep Simon from interrupting the long conversation Kingston plans to have with you."

"He already had that conversation with me," Felicia retorted, "Yesterday. I told him I'd tell him on Sunday."

Rosie made a face. "And you didn't tell me. Felicia, I'm shocked and disappointed in you."

"I was worried about Adam and Connaught."

"Of course, and I'm sure you get so many offers that another one really didn't register with you."

Felicia glared at her sister. "Rosie, sarcasm doesn't become you. I merely didn't want to say anything in front of Aunt Soledad. You know how she is."

Rosie nodded. "She'd be planning your bridal gown right now, wouldn't she?" Rosie leaned forward. "What are you going to tell him on Sunday? I suppose you'll have to marry him—he's too much of a catch to lose, even though I still think you and Major Temple would suit."

"Adam told me that I should say yes."

Rosie was surprised. "You told Adam about it and he said *that?* Well, mercy. I thought . . . never mind. Adam actually told you that you should accept Kingston's offer?"

Felicia nodded. "Yes. There are all sorts of logical reasons to accept." She finished her chocolate. "I'm going to tell Charles yes on Sunday, Rosie. I'd tell him now except I want to wait until all this is over with Uncle Gresham. By Sunday or Monday, we can announce his death."

"Accept on Sunday, Uncle Gresham 'dies' on Monday, then you'll be in black gloves for a year." Rosie looked intently at Felicia. "Did you plan that? Do you think Kingston will wait for a year?"

"I don't know if he will or not and, no, I didn't plan that. Things just worked out that way. Weddings take months anyway." Felicia pushed her chair back. "We've got to get ready to meet Charles and Simon.

Have you heard anything from Adam?"

"No, but Connaught sent word that everything was taken care of."

Felicia let out a long breath and Rosie got up and hugged her. "Come on, Felicia, let's go have a picnic, and I promise we're going to have a good time." Felicia looked at her sister and laughed. "Rosie, you don't know how good it is to know this is almost over. We've done it—Adam says the house is closer to completion than we'd thought—and we've gotten away with it." Felicia smiled and left. Rosie could hear her skipping up the stairs, singing. It was the first time in a long time Felicia had been that happy. Maybe, Rosie thought, Felicia was really in love with Kingston after all. She had thought something else, but who ever knew what Felicia was thinking? She picked up a leftover muffin to nibble and went upstairs to change.

Chapter 15

The day was sunny and gloriously warm as they all walked up the ice house hill. Rosie held Simon's hand as they walked in front, while Kingston and Felicia walked behind, talking quietly. At the ice house, the workmen were already there and had opened the heavy outer door and propped it with a stick. Simon dashed ahead, dancing around in excitement and peering through the men's legs into the blackness of the ice pit. "I want to go inside," he announced to Kingston. "Felicia says no ghosts are in there."

"She told you that, did she?" Kingston laughed as Simon ran over to stand in front of Felicia. "If she did, that must be right."

"Then I can go in there, can't I?" Simon looked from Felicia to Kingston. "Nothing can hurt me in there."

"It's dark and you might fall," Felicia said.

"You don't want to get in the men's way either," Kingston said. "Perhaps a little bit later. Right now, why don't you look for butterflies?"

Simon and Rosie walked around looking for butterflies and Simon began picking some wildflowers. Kingston led Felicia up to the very top of the hill where they could look around. He stood close to her. "Look around, Felicia, all of this is part of the Priory. It's beautiful, isn't it?"

"Yes," she agreed, and it truly was. The fields were mowed, the tenant houses in good repair, the roads cleared. "It's a good place to raise children," Kingston said, a laugh in his voice.

"I can look at Simon and see that." She pointed to where Simon was frisking in and out by the heavy door, calling into the ice house to hear the echo of his voice, then darting back out again. Rosie was trying in vain to catch him. He eluded her and ran up to Felicia, hiding behind her skirts and offering her the limp wild flowers. "All right, you rascal," she said to him with a laugh, "any more of this and you're not going to get dessert."

He stood still and looked up at her with big eyes. "You wouldn't!"

"Yes, I would," she said firmly. "I'll tell you what. I'll let you go inside the ice house as long as you go in with one of the workmen. And as long as you behave."

"And I can have dessert?"

"Yes. That's a promise." She bent down and whispered, "I think we've got apricot tart."

Simon licked his lips. "All right. Promise." Felicia laughed as she and Kingston led him back down the hill and turned him over to a workman so he could go into the ice house. The workmen had lit the interior with torches and were hauling up big chunks of ice and loading it on a wagon. "Rosie and I will help lay out the picnic if you'll wait for Simon," she told Kingston.

Kingston reached over and touched her fingers. "You're very good with children. I like that."

Felicia drew back her hand, but laughed as she did. "Rosie's kept me in training."

"What a fudge!" Rosie exclaimed. "If you only knew how difficult it's been for me to keep Felicia in line." They looked at each other and laughed, then went to help lay out the picnic. Felicia was careful to place Simon's apricot tart on a napkin just for him.

He came running over to them, Kingston following behind. "You wouldn't believe it, Felicia! It's cold in there, and the edges where the torches aren't is all dark. Are you sure there are no ghosts in there?"

"Positive. Are you ready to eat?"

He shook his head. "No. I want to go back inside. One of the workmen was saying that someone had been in there and the sawdust was all disturbed. I bet it's a ghost, don't you? Could you be wrong?"

Felicia felt her stomach plummet to her feet. Had Connaught and Adam left any signs? What, exactly, had the workman seen? She tried to keep calm. "No ghosts, Simon, and you don't need to go back in there. Look at you—you're all covered with sawdust now." She dusted off his hair. "I promised you this after you'd eaten, but you can't have it until then." She placed the tart at the edge of his plate.

"Not now?" he asked, rubbing the edge of the tart with a rather dirty finger. Felicia took his hands and rubbed at them.

"Not until you've eaten." She handed Kingston a plate. "You might as well give up, Simon," he said cheerfully. "I don't think Miss Fortune is going to allow it. And as for ghosts—she's never wrong about

231

those things, you know."

Simon thought about this for a moment, then looke[d] at his uncle. "Well, maybe not most of the time, but sh[e] *could* be wrong about the ghost. I *know* there's one [in] there."

They all laughed at him as they sat down to ea[t.] Afterward, the wagon pulled away and the workme[n] shut the door, tossing aside the stick used to prop it. ["I] suppose I'm going to have to get a lock for that door[,"] Kingston said, "if Simon is right and the workme[n] found that someone had been in there."

"It was probably nothing," Felicia said quickly. "Ar[e] we ready to leave?" They left a footman packing up th[e] remains of the picnic and walked back down to th[e] Priory. There, Kingston sent Simon up for his na[p] while he ordered a carriage so he could take Rosie an[d] Felicia home. At the door of the Misery, he detaine[d] Felicia a moment. "I'll come for you early tonight f[or] the dinner party. I know Colonel Dedlock is lookin[g] forward to talking to your uncle."

Felicia froze, even though she had been expecting h[is] comment. "I don't know if Uncle Gresham is going t[o] be able to attend or not. He really isn't feeling well. W[e] thought he was on the mend, but he seems to have fe[lt] much worse lately."

Kingston lifted an eyebrow. "I certainly hope he'll b[e] there. I've invited several people from around, an[d] they're all looking forward to talking with him. Try t[o] persuade him, if you can."

"Oh, I will! I know he wouldn't want to miss talkin[g] to Colonel Dedlock unless he simply couldn't manag[e] it."

Kingston smiled. "Aside from that, everyone want[s]

to congratulate him on his work on the Abbott's House. It's the talk of the architectural world, or so I'm led to believe."

"Is it really?" Felicia's eyes glowed with pleasure. "My lord, nothing you could say would give him more pleasure."

"Charles," he corrected, "and I'd be delighted to tell him—just as soon as I see him." There was a dry note to Kingston's voice.

"I'll do what I can to have him there," Felicia said, averting her eyes. "Until tonight, my . . . Charles."

Kingston bent and brushed her forehead with a quick kiss. "I'm counting the hours," he said with a smile.

Felicia shut the door behind her. "Rosie, we're all going to Hades in a handbasket for lying. I can't do this anymore."

"Cheer up. After Sunday or Monday, you won't have to."

"And not a minute too soon."

Felicia and Rosie were almost ready when they heard someone banging on the door. It was one of the footmen from the Priory, and Felicia at first thought he had come to take them to the supper party, but that was not the case. She came running back up the stairs, a stricken look on her face. "Simon's missing," she told Rosie, "and Charles wondered if we knew anything of his whereabouts. The supper party is, of course, postponed."

"Missing!" Rosie's complexion turned ashen. "Surely he can't have gone far. He's probably at the stables or

233

he's just gone to sleep behind a chair. I did that once, if you recall."

"I hope so. The footman said that Simon had been put down for his nap, and when the tutor checked on him late this afternoon, he discovered that Simon wasn't in his bed."

Rosie sat down on the edge of her bed. "Do you think we should go over there to offer our support, or would we simply get in the way?"

Felicia reached for her shawl. "We'll probably get in the way, but I'm going anyway. I'm just going to stay there long enough to tell Charles that I'll do whatever I can."

"Wait for me," Rosie said, grabbing her shawl and following Felicia out the door.

The Priory was brilliantly lit, candles at every window. Out in the fields, Felicia and Rosie could see servants carrying torches walking in a line, searching. Kingston met them at the door, his face haggard. "We aren't going to stay," Felicia told him, "and we don't intend to get in the way. We just wanted to come tell you that we're here if you need us. We both love Simon."

"Thank you," he said hoarsely. "We've looked in all the usual places." He paused and put his hands over his face. "Someone suggested dragging the pond, but I can't bring myself to a step that drastic just yet."

"I'm sure Simon is around," Felicia said. "He's a very little boy, and if he didn't get his nap, he may be sleeping somewhere."

"That's what I'm hoping." Kingston left them to meet a man at the door who had searched the stables yet another time and had found nothing. The housekeeper came in, reporting that a second search of the house had revealed nothing, except that Simon's coat and boots were missing.

"Could he have run away to his mother?" Rosie asked. "I don't know why he would want to since he's so happy here, but it could be a possibility."

"I agree, it isn't likely, but at this point, I'll try anything." Kingston called a servant and gave instructions for the road to London to be searched thoroughly. He sat in a chair, his fists clenching and unclenching. "I don't dare leave, but how I'd like to be out doing something," he said. "Waiting here is the hardest part."

"I understand," Felicia said with what she hoped was an encouraging smile, "but it's necessary for someone to be here and know everything that's going on." She turned to Rosie as a thought struck her, then turned back to Kingston. "You don't suppose he would try to come to the Misery for something, do you?"

"He could be anywhere," Kingston said miserably, "but it is a likely possibility that he'd come to you. He cares very much for both of you. Is anyone at the Misery?"

Felicia nodded. "Aunt Soledad."

"And Uncle Gresham," Rosie added quickly.

"Yes." Felicia glanced at Rosie. "Perhaps Rosie and I should go back to the Misery in case Simon tries to come there." She looked around, her gaze settling on Kingston. "I hate to leave you, Charles. Will you be all right?"

He nodded. "I want you here with me, of course, but if Simon comes to the Misery, he won't want to come in if only your aunt and uncle are there. I think it a good possibility that he may come to see you, Felicia. You

235

are one of his favorite people." A ghost of a smile crossed his face.

"We'll go back there and wait," she said. "You'll keep us posted if anything happens here?" She couldn't bear to think of what might happen.

He nodded, and turned his attention to another searcher who came in the door. Felicia motioned to Rosie and the two of them slipped out and headed for the Misery. Out in the fields they could hear the searchers calling Simon's name over and over. There was no answer.

Back at the Misery, Rosie and Felicia searched the house and grounds, just in case. "I don't know what else to do," Rosie said, collapsing in a chair. "He's so little, and there are so many places. . . . Felicia, I really fear the worst has happened."

"So do I." Felicia paced the study floor, picking up first one thing and then putting it back down, then picking up something else.

"It's this house," Aunt Soledad said. "I knew something bad was going to happen."

Felicia gritted her teeth to keep from yelling at Aunt Soledad. "There must be *something* we can do," she said, walking to the window. "Has anyone told Adam about this? We could get all the remaining workmen to help us search." She snatched up her shawl. "I'm going to go get Adam."

"You'll do no such thing," Aunt Soledad said, aghast. "It's bad enough that you've run off to the Priory, but you certainly can't go gallavanting around the country alone to see Major Temple. You'll have to send for him."

Felicia tossed her shawl down and bit her lip. She

knew Aunt Soledad was right, but that didn't make the waiting any easier. Like Charles, she wanted to do something, anything. All she could do was sit down and pen an urgent note to Adam requesting that he come to the Misery right away.

The ticking of the clock was the only thing to break the silence as they sat there, waiting, waiting. It seemed an eternity until Adam knocked at the door. He came inside, still in his work clothes, sweaty and tired. His foot was dragging slightly as he walked beside Felicia to the study.

Felicia and Rosie told him about Simon and he agreed with them that the workmen should join in the search. "We've got to do something," Felicia said urgently.

Adam ran his fingers through his hair. "You wait here. I'll go back and get the men and go to the Priory. Kingston would rather tell us where to search than have us go off on our own. Besides, the boy might have been found by now."

"I don't think so," Felicia said. "Charles said he would send us word immediately, and we haven't heard anything." She noted that Adam lifted an eyebrow at her use of Kingston's given name, but right now it didn't signify. "Adam, as soon as the workmen begin to search, please come back and tell us what's going on. I don't care what time of night it is, please come back. The worst part is not knowing."

He hesitated a moment. "All right. It may be up in the morning before I get back."

"We're going to stay up all night, if necessary," Felicia said, walking with him to the door. "Adam . . ." She ran out of words to say, but he seemed to know what she meant.

"We'll all do our best," he said with a smile and a touch on her hand. "I'll be back." With that, he was out into the night and Felicia could hear the sound of his walk, his foot dragging slightly on the walkway.

"I shouldn't have involved Adam," Felicia said to Aunt Soledad and Rosie. "Did you see how tired he was?"

"Yes," agreed Rosie, "but he's the kind of man who would prefer to be involved, no matter how tired he was."

"Yes, there are few men like Major Temple," Aunt Soledad said.

The waiting was horrible. There was nothing to do, nothing that either Felicia or Rosie wanted to do. Every sound at the window sent them running to see if it was Simon trying to get inside. They finally convinced Aunt Soledad to go to bed after she dozed off and fell off the sofa. They promised to wake her if there was any news.

The clock on the mantel had chimed three o'clock in the morning when they heard a knock on the door. Adam came inside, swaying with fatigue. He sat down, his face wan with disappointmet and weariness. "Nothing," he said. "We've found absolutely no trace of him anywhere. Kingston thinks the worst may have happened. He's making arrangements to drag the pond in the morning."

Rosie started to cry softly, but Felicia refused to think that anything bad could have happened to Simon. "What do you think?" she asked Adam. "Do you think the pond?"

"I don't know." Exhaustion dripped from his voice.

238

"Someone saw him pass by the marge of the pond, his coat slung over his shoulder. It was the last time he was seen." Adam glanced around. "Do you have any brandy in the house?" Felicia started to get up and get him some from the decanter, but he stopped her, getting up and pouring himself a glassful. He drank it slowly, thinking. "Did he play around the pond, or do you know?"

Felicia thought a moment. "Not very much that I know of. I think he went fishing once or twice with his tutor. His favorite place was always the hill where the ice house is."

"What?" Adam crossed the room and sat down in front of her.

"The ice house," Felicia repeated. "We were there just this morning and he got to look inside. He was excited beyond words because he thought there were ghosts in there."

"That door has nothing except a latch on it," Adam said.

"But it's a heavy door," Felicia said. "Much too heavy for a five-year-old boy to open," Rosie added in agreement.

Adam shook his head. "If he could raise the latch, he could open it. I'm going to look there. It's worth a try."

"I'm going with you," Felicia said. "I can't stand sitting here anymore. If I do, I'm going to lose my mind. Besides, you shouldn't be going into the ice house alone."

"Wait for me," Rosie said, tossing Felicia her shawl and donning her own. "Aunt Soledad would expect a chaperone to go along."

Adam looked at them and Felicia knew what he was

going to say. She answered before he could protest. "It's no use, Adam. I'm going. If you don't want me along, I'll go by myself."

He grinned at her, the first time Felicia had seen the fatigue lift from his expression. "By now, I know better than to argue with you. Let's go."

The top of the ice house hill looked like always in the moonlight. The door was firmly closed, and there were signs that searchers had been over the terrain already. Adam looked at the door. "The latch is still in place," he said. "Still, I think I'll go inside. It could have fallen into place if the door slammed shut."

"That isn't likely, is it?" Felicia asked. She had a feeling of dread.

"It certainly could have happened that way," Adam answered, lifting the latch. "I need a torch to light my way."

Felicia pointed to the remains of a torch that had been left from morning. "Will that be enough?"

Adam picked it up and struck a flint to it. In just a moment it was blazing and he went inside, looking for the stick which propped the door open. He found it lying in the tunnel leading down to the pit. "Simon!" he called into the darkness. He heard nothing. Felicia came in right behind him trying to see into the pitch blackness beyond the torch. "Simon, are you here?" she called out.

"Fff . . . Felicia." The sound was so low it sounded like the whimper of a puppy. "Sssh," Adam said in a whisper. "Call again."

"Simon, are you here? It's Felicia. Please answer me." She held her breath.

The sound came again. "Felicia, here." This time

there was no mistaking it. "Oh, Adam, he's alive," she gasped.

"Here, hold this, and whatever you do, don't drop it." Adam thrust the torch into her hand. "Try to light my way as much as possible." He reached the edge of the pit and she leaned over to illumine it. Adam reached for the rope and basket that went down into the pit. "Simon, I'm coming to get you," he called into the darkness. "Where are you?"

"Right here." The sound was impossible to locate in the echo of the cavern. "Tell me again, Simon," Adam called, searching. "I'm here and I'm cold," Simon said, his voice full of tears. Adam plunged into the blackness and Felicia could hear a scuffling sound as he went over the ice. "Have you found him?" she called. In vain she tried to light the far reaches of the cavern.

"I've got him," Adam said. "Give me as much light as you can." He came into view, cradling a very tiny Simon against him. He almost fell as they got near the basket, his injured foot catching on the edge of a block of ice. He stood, and Felicia could see it was an effort for him. He caught the edge of the basket and placed Simon in it. "Pull him up, Felicia." Simon cried and held out his arms for Adam. "Go with me," he pleaded. Adam looked up at Felicia in the torchlight. She pulled the light back a little so he could see her face. "Can you pull me up?" Adam asked. "It'll take some hard pulling."

"Rosie can help," she said. He nodded and she called for Rosie as Adam climbed into the basket and cradled Simon in his arms again. "We're ready," he called up.

Felicia propped the torch so both of her hands were free and she and Rosie pulled on the rope. Even though

241

it was a well-balanced block and tackle, it was still difficult for them to pull. She was terrified every moment that they would slip and Adam and Simon would go crashing back into the pit. Adam kept talking to them quietly, encouraging them, telling them that the basket was almost there, almost at the edge of the platform.

At last they were there. Simon had his arms around Adam and was clinging to him. Adam reached out with one hand and grabbed a post on the platform, then helped move the basket to the solid edge. He tried to hand Simon to Felicia, but the boy wouldn't let go. "It's all right," Adam said soothingly. "Felicia and I will be right here. We're going to take you home."

"Home," Simon whimpered, burrowing his face into Adam's shoulder. "I want my mother." Felicia put out a hand to touch him and was horrified. "Adam, he's freezing. We've got to hurry."

She and Rosie held the basket and helped Adam get out of it. As they inched down the small tunnel behind him, Felicia held the torch to light their way. At the entrance, she pushed the door shut behind them. The workmen had oiled it and now it swung easily on its hinges, closing with a heavy thud. The latch fell down into place without her having to touch it.

"At least we know how it happened," Adam said wearily as they started walking down toward the Priory. Felicia held what was left of the torch to help Adam find his footing in the dark. She noticed he was having a great deal of trouble walking.

"I'll carry him," she offered, as did Rosie. Simon reached out with one cold hand and patted her on the shoulder, but refused to be parted from Adam. By the time they reached the foot of the hill, Adam was breathing heavily, not, Felicia guessed, from the weight of his burden, but from the effort of trying to walk with the pain in his ankle.

The Priory was still brightly lit and they went up on the porch together, Adam having difficulty with the steps. Felicia smashed down the knocker, then tried the door herself without waiting. It opened and the four of them went inside. The housekeeper saw them and screamed. "Bless good Mary! They've found the wee one!" She reached out for Simon but he held on tightly to Adam's neck. Kingston came rushing out into the hall and paused to look at them. He went over to take Simon from Adam, but Simon kept his arms around Adam's neck. Finally, the little boy let go, and Kingston looked down at him with a sigh of relief. "Where was he?" he asked.

"In the ice house," Adam said briefly. Simon's tutor came running in and Kingston handed the boy to him. "He's freezing. Take care of him and I'll be up in a while."

Simon held out his arms, first to Kingston, then to Adam. Adam reached out and took the boy back. "He's still afraid," he said to Kingston. "I'll go with him and see to him until he feels better." He turned to Felicia. "Could you tell Lord Kingston how Simon came to be there?" She nodded. "About your getting back home . . . ?"

"I'll see to it," Kingston said. Adam nodded and went up the stairs, carrying Simon, who had once again fastened his arms around Adam's neck and burrowed his head into Adam's shoulder. Adam stumbled a time or two trying to climb the stairs. Felicia wanted nothing more than to run and help him, but she knew it would only embarrass him in front of the other men gathered around.

Kingston turned to a footman and gave him instructions to stop the search and call in all the men looking in the countryside. Then he motioned for Felicia and Rosie to go into the drawing room and offered them tea. Felicia accepted gratefully, and as she drank, she mentioned that perhaps someone should send some tea or coffee up to Adam. "My manners are somewhat ragtag tonight," Charles said with a grin as he dispatched a footman with a tray. "Now, tell me where Simon was and how you found him."

For the first time, Felicia realized how unusual it must look for the four of them to come dragging in at almost five o'clock in the morning. She looked at Rosie, and they began to giggle, partly from fatigue, partly from hysteria. It took a moment before she could control herself long enough to tell Charles what had happened. When she finished, he frowned. "Yes, they oiled those hinges this morning—yesterday morning—before we got the ice out. I'll have a lock put on that door today so this will never happen to anyone else." He glanced up the stairs. "He was so small— and so cold. I had Dr. Quigley here at the ready, just in case, and I suppose he's looking after Simon by now." He leaned back in his chair and rubbed his eyes. "I don't think I've ever faced anything like this in my life."

Rosie yawned and couldn't quite cover it up. "None of us have, and none of us ever want to again," she said fuzzily, leaning her head against the back of the chair. Felicia's own eyes felt as if they had grit in them.

"Rosie," she said, "I don't know about you, but I've got to get back to the Misery and go to bed."

Charles leaped to his feet. "I apologize." He called for the carriage and soon both Felicia and Rosie were back home. They woke Aunt Soledad, told her the good news, then went to bed.

Chapter 16

Felicia fell asleep on top of her bed just as the morning was breaking. She slept until noon and was still sleepy when she woke up. Still, there was no going back to sleep then—she was worried about Simon and Adam. Over toast and tea, she and Rosie decided first to go to the Priory and check on Simon, then stop back by the Abbott's House to see if Adam was all right.

Felicia was deep in thought as they walked in the midday sun. "He was barely walking, Rosie," Felicia said with a worried frown. "I knew he was in agony but he just kept on, with never one word of complaint. He shouldn't punish himself by walking on that bad ankle as much as he does. He's probably hurt himself."

"He might have," Rosie answered. "I don't think he'd be the type to give in to an infirmity."

"That's true." Felicia paused and turned to Rosie. "Do you know what thought struck me last night, Rosie? When Kingston—Charles—was saying he'd never been through anything like that, I thought that

Adam had seen terrible scenes in the war. He'd seen people hurt and killed, yet he was able to go on and do what he had to do."

"Like Uncle Gresham." They came into view of the Priory. "Are you going to say anything about Uncle Gresham today, Felicia?"

"Not unless someone asks me about him, and if someone does, all I intend to say is that he's very ill again. You do the same. Frankly, Rosie, I'm just not up to anything else today. I don't mean to put things off, but . . ."

Rosie laughed and clasped her hand. "I understand perfectly and agree. I didn't think I could muster up any more emotion at all."

At the Priory, they found that Kingston was away, but they were allowed to go upstairs to see Simon. He was in bed, but had recovered enough to think that he had had a glorious adventure. "Uncle Charles says I was very bad to go into the ice house," he told them, "but I just had to see for myself if there were ghosts. I had to . . . to *explore*."

"I told you there were no ghosts," Felicia said, hugging him.

"But there were, Felicia. There were all sorts of noises, and I got awful afraid." He paused and swallowed hard. "It wasn't so bad until the door slammed shut and I couldn't get out. I thought everybody would just forget about me. Mama does that sometimes, but I'm always at home when that happens."

Felicia gave him a kiss. "Simon, I promise that you're not going to be forgotten. Dr. Quigley tells me that you've got a little cold from your adventure and have to stay in bed for a few days." Simon nodded and she went on. "As soon as you're better, we'll have another picnic if you want."

"I'd like that." Simon patted her hand and they stayed for a while longer, Simon making each of them tell him a story before they left. They promised to come back as soon as they could.

As they went out the door, they met Kingston riding up. He looked very fine, sitting tall on a magnificent chestnut. He swung easily off the horse, handed the reins to a groom, and walked toward them, taking long, easy strides. "I admit it, Felicia," Rosie murmured, "he's the best catch in the whole marriage market."

"Hush," Felicia muttered through her smile as Kingston came towards them.

"Leaving so soon?" he asked, falling into step beside Felicia.

"We need to get to the Abbott's House. Do you want to go along with us?"

He smiled down at her. "I'd love to, but my man of business is coming in shortly. Have you been visiting Simon?"

Felicia nodded. "He's recovering quite nicely, we thought."

Kingston laughed. "Actually, he's probably recovering better than I am. It may take me a while to get over the thought of losing him."

"I know," Felicia said, smiling back at him. "I feel much the same way." She glanced over to discover that Rosie had wandered toward the flower garden, away from them, leaving them alone.

Kingston leaned slightly down toward her. "I only

248

hope you've examined your other feelings, Felicia.
Tomorrow is Sunday, or do you wish to give me your
answer today?"

"I'd rather wait until tomorrow, my lo . . . Charles. I
know what I wish to say, but I want to discuss it with
Uncle Gresham first."

He took her hand. "Felicia, my dear, how you keep
me on tenterhooks! Could you give me a hint?"

She laughed. "You gave me until Sunday, Charles. I
refuse to say a word until then."

They walked over to where Rosie was standing.
"Would you feel better if I came by the Misery and
talked to Captain Fortune? I know I've breached the
proprieties by asking you directly."

Felicia shook her head. "He's still ill. That's why I
haven't discussed this with him." She looked at Rosie.
"We've really got to get on to the Abbott's House. I
wanted to go by in the brightest sunshine so I could
check the paint in the little breakfast parlor." Actually,
she hadn't planned to check anything, but she had to
get away from Charles and his questioning before she
said something she shouldn't. She always worried that
his questions asked more then she realized.

The activity at the Abbott's House was muted. Many
of the workers had gone, and only the finish workers
were left. Felicia asked if Adam had come in yet, and
Connaught pointed toward the back. Rosie wandered
off to see what had been done, exclaiming over the
paper in the dining room. Felicia made herself go
through the breakfast parlor to look at the paint—it
looked exactly as it had the previous day.

Satisfied she had salved her conscience, she went on
to the back of the house searching for Adam. She saw

him as she rounded the corner into the hall. He was sitting on a rough carpenter's bench with his back to her. He was slumped over, his bad leg straight out, and he was rubbing it gently as though it hurt a great deal. Felicia walked quietly up behind him and touched him on the shoulder. "Are you in pain, Adam?" she asked quietly, pulling up another bench and sitting across from him.

"It'll pass," he said briefly. "Have you been to the Priory to see about Simon?" She nodded and he went on. "How is he? He didn't want me to leave him, so I stayed until he went to sleep—about daylight. I hoped he wouldn't have any ill effects when he woke up."

"I think he's fine. He has a slight cold and Charles and Dr. Quigley are making him stay in bed a few days."

Adam laughed. "Punishment enough for Simon, I think."

They sat in companionable silence for a few minutes. "It's almost over, Adam," Felicia finally said.

He nodded. "Captain Fortune's reputation is made with this building. I'm glad." He looked at her and smiled. "I'm glad I had the opportunity to know you and Rosie. I hope we'll see each other in the future. That is," he added without looking at her, "if you're not too busy with your wedding plans and such."

"I'll never be too busy, Adam." There was another pause. "I'm going to tell Charles tomorrow that I'll marry him. On Monday, I'll have to tell him that Uncle Gresham has died. That means there will be no wedding until after a suitable mourning period."

"There could be. Something small, quiet, just the families. It's been done before."

Felicia looked at him in exasperation. "Are you trying to marry me off, Adam Temple? It certainly sounds that way."

He grinned. "Merely playing devil's advocate." He stood. "Pay no attention to me—you'll have to work those plans out in your own way. Come on." He held out a hand to her. "Let me show you around since it's almost finished." His hand was firm and warm on hers.

It was true. The house was beautiful. Everything Uncle Gresham had planned had materialized and Adam had made it happen. Felicia and Rosie paused at the doorway as they left. "Adam," Felicia began hesitantly, "I know you don't expect thanks, but I want you to know that we can never thank you enough."

"You already have," he said. "Now I've got to get back to work, if you ladies will excuse me. I expect Kingston over later and I want to check some details." He smiled at them and left. Felicia and Rosie turned back toward the Misery, walking silently, each one of them occupied with her own thoughts.

The evening was quiet as everyone sat in the study after supper. Aunt Soledad elected to go to bed early, claiming the excitement of the previous night had left her exhausted and her nerves in a total shambles. Rosie and Felicia stayed up awhile, Rosie reading while Felicia worked on the accounts for the building. It was coming in right on Adam's final projections, and they would make a tidy sum from it. Rosie went on to bed, and after a while of double-checking her rows of figures, Felicia did too.

Up in the night, she was awakened by a sound. Groggily she wondered what it was, then turned over to try to go back to sleep. The sound came again, the sound of hail on the roof, she first thought, but then, there wasn't enough of it and, besides, it wasn't raining. She burrowed her head back into her pillow and the hail came again. Groggily, she realized it couldn't be hail—it wasn't wintertime.

Sitting up in bed, she forced her mind to function as the sound came again, then got up. It sounded like something hitting the side of the house. She went to the window to see Adam standing below, throwing pebbles at her window. She opened the window and peered out. "Adam, is that you?"

"Ssshhh," he whispered, "I don't want to wake up anyone else. Come down and let me in. I need to talk to you."

"Has anything happened?" She couldn't hide the alarm in her voice.

"No, I just want to talk. I'll be at the back door so no one will see me. Come down there." He disappeared around the back corner of the building.

Felicia quickly put on her dressing gown, checked her hair in the mirror, and patted it straight. There wasn't time for anything else. She hurried downstairs and opened the kitchen door.

"I had no idea you were such a sound sleeper," Adam said with a grin as he came inside. "I've been tossing pebbles at that window for half an hour. I even had to go replenish my supply." He pulled a handful of pebbles from his pocket and put them on the table as he sat down.

"Would you like some chocolate?" Felicia asked, remembering their earlier time in the kitchen. Adam nodded and went outside to get the milk from the box in the spring while she poked up the fire. She sat down

252

next to him while the milk was heating. "What is it, Adam? Are you sure nothing's wrong?"

"I'm sure. Why is it that every time you see me, you expect me to bring news of some new catastrophe?"

She laughed softly and poured the chocolate in the cups, then sweetened it with the sugar that had the vanilla bean in it. "Because it always does. Every time. A catastrophe is either going to happen or has happened. I didn't think this time would be an exception, so I'm glad it is." She paused and sipped her chocolate. "What did you want to talk to me about?"

He ran his fingers through his hair. "Now that I'm here, it seems a fool's errand." He stopped and took a deep breath. "I have to do this, Felicia, no matter how much of a fool I make of myself. I can't let you go without at least letting you know." He stopped and took hand. She started to say something, but he stopped her. "Don't say anything just yet, Felicia, let me say what I have to say. God knows I've rehearsed it enough. If I don't get it all out at once, I probably won't say it."

She looked at him, her eyes big in the firelight. "All right, Adam, tell me."

"You're going to tell Kingston tomorrow that you'll marry him, and that's the logical thing for you to do, but dammit, Felicia, you won't have a marriage if you do. Don't misunderstand me, you'll be married to him, and you'll have one of those polite kinds of marriages, but you won't be truly happy."

She opened her mouth to protest, but he reminded her of her promise. "No, let me finish. This isn't the way I wanted to say it, but it's the best I can do right now." He looked into her eyes. "Felicia, I love you. I've loved

253

you since I first saw you and got to know you. I know I could never offer you any of the things Kingston can, but I can offer you a lifetime of love. That isn't much when you compare it to Kingston's lands and fortune, but maybe over a lifetime, it might mean something." He let go of her hand and stopped. "Oh, hell," he said in disgust.

"Are you proposing to me, Adam?" Felicia reached out and touched his hand.

"I'm trying to, but I'm not doing a very good job of it." He put his other hand over hers, capturing it. "Felicia, I know you can't accept me, but I had to make the effort. I just couldn't let you go off and marry Kingston without at least telling you how I feel. I'm going to be an architect and a builder, not a titled gentleman like Kingston. Believe me, I have no illusions about what's best for you."

"Why don't you let me decide what's best for me, Adam?" she said softly.

"Because I want you to have everything in the world, and I couldn't give it to you. You should marry Kingston and have all that he has to offer—it's the logical and practical thing for you to do."

She laughed. "Adam, since when have I ever been practical and logical?"

"You're always practical and logical," he said morosely. "You're the only woman I've ever seen who could think through a problem and come up with the right answer every time. Well," he said as he thought, "not *every* time, but most of the time. And look what you've done with the accounts." He stood up. "At any rate, that's all I had to say. I wanted to tell you how I felt. It was a foolish thing to do, but I had to."

She stood facing him and laughed. "You're right, Adam. If this is a proposal, you're not doing a very good job of it. Do you want to try again?" The firelight flickered on them, giving her skin a rosy glow. He reached for her and pulled her to him, then kissed her, softly at first, touching her lips lightly. "Don't play with me, Felicia," he said hoarsely. "I couldn't stand that."

"Propose to me, Adam," she whispered back, her fingers touching his cheek.

He put his hands on the sides of her face, pushing back her curls, and his face was close to hers. "Marry me, please, Felicia. I love you and I'll always love you. I'll spend my whole life trying to make you happy. Marry me."

"Yes, Adam."

He stepped back. "I can't give—"

"You can't give me anything except the kind of life I want," she said softly, taking a step to bring her close to him again. "Adam, I love you. I want to be with you. Always."

He looked down into her eyes for a moment, then to her surprise, he picked her up and turned in a circle, twirling her off the floor. "Felicia, I love you!" he said, kissing her as he put her back down. He kissed her again, softly at first, then thoroughly, until she was breathless. He stopped and touched her face with his fingers. "Marrying Kingston would still be the practical thing to do. If you marry me, the whole world will say it's folly."

"I'm sure they will," she murmured, then pulled his head down to hers and this time she kissed him. He looked at her and smiled. "Actually, who cares what they say," he said, sitting down and pulling her down on his lap, where he proceeded to kiss her quite thoroughly once again.

They were interrupted by a noise from the door. "I thought I heard . . ." Aunt Soledad began, but stopped, her eyes wide, as she saw them sitting there. "Oh dear, oh dear, *oh dear!* It's this house, it *must* be this house."